MW01596821

A Storm of Wings and Ruin

CASSANDRA REID

Copyright © 2024 by Cassandra Reid

All rights reserved.

No portion of this book may be reproduced in any form without written permission from the publisher or author, except as permitted by U.S. copyright law.

Contents

Chapter 1

*T*HEY CAME WITHOUT WARNING. *A dozen of the queen's most elite soldiers flooded into the small village nestled deep within the Prestile Forest, their torches illuminating the barren branches, casting eerie shadows into the homes and terrifying the residents. They stormed through homes, leaving nothing but destruction and despair in their wake. As they worked through the village, in a small cottage that brushed up against the tree line, a woman panicked as the chaos drew near. She could hear the screams, the sobs, and the pleas from the villagers to spare them and leave their children. The man in the house looked at the woman, pointed to the cradle, and motioned for her to flee. Distraught but understanding, she quickly picked up the infant and prepared to run. But before she could, the doors burst open and soldiers flooded the house, one of them taking the baby from the woman's arms.*

Sobs and pleas rang through the little cottage, but they fell on deaf ears as the woman gave the order to burn the house with a cold voice. There was a flicker and then a spark before the cabin burst into flames. The sound of the burning wood, the screams of terror from the people inside the cabin and around the village, and the cries of the children for their parents echoed through the woods as the heat from the numerous fires followed the soldiers out of the village.

The unbearable heat that followed her from the dream and the screams of terror woke Ari from her restless sleep. To escape the heat, she threw off her covers and ran to the balcony, hoping the cool fall air would take the sting from her skin. This was not the first time that dream had disturbed her sleep. She'd had the same dream over and over since she could remember, always waking as the heat followed the soldiers as they left the woods. The breeze cooled her, erasing the lingering heat from the dream, but it did little to erase the screams of terror from her mind. She rubbed her face and looked over the castle's grounds trying to clear her thoughts and push the screams from her mind. She stared blankly out over the gardens, which usually impressed her, even more so in the silver light of the waning moon. But tonight, they held no interest for her as she replayed the scene of death and destruction that haunted her dreams. A rustling below pulled her attention away from the fire in her mind and she looked down, only to see two figures making their way through the gardens, meandering aimlessly. They didn't move with purpose, so it didn't alarm her. All the same, her curiosity piqued, and she decided to change from the loose-fitting bed clothes into something that would let her move silently and unseen before she fluttered down to the gardens.

Unaware that someone else was now following him, Finn Ophir, crown prince of the Thenndin Faedom, wandered through the bushes and flowers, mind heavy with news he'd learned during a war council meeting earlier in the day. Behind him trailed his bodyguard, a man chosen for his honed instincts, ever alert for danger even behind the fortified walls of Tena Castle. He knew what thoughts weighed on the prince's mind and how much the boy's heart hurt for the people he couldn't help. They passed the lilies and the lilacs, eventually coming to a gazebo situated in the middle of the garden. It was Finn's place to come and think, to sit and let his mind clear, and occasionally work out a problem. He knew he would be unable to solve this problem, so he had come to clear his mind and say a prayer for those who had been lost.

As soon as the prince had gotten lost in his thoughts, his faithful friend and bodyguard doubled back toward the lilacs and stopped next to a particular clump of them that seemed more shimmery than normal. He chuckled and shook his head before sitting down on the ground, waiting for the shimmery speck to join him before speaking.

"It's a bit late for the queen's pet assassin to be out in the gardens, isn't it?" he asked as Ari came into focus and sat next to him.

"Why am I not surprised you spotted me?" she asked, shaking her golden wings, so they folded against her and disappeared. "It's a little late for the two of you to be out as well." He chuckled as she stretched out before crossing her legs in front of her.

"Because I know what to look for. And because I taught you those same tricks," he said, patting her knee. "It was far more visible than normal, though. What's troubling your mind?"

"Restless night," she said, looking over at the gazebo, not wanting to talk about the dream again. "For him as well?"

"Yes, though I doubt your restless night is the same as his. What's got you up so late, little one?"

"Same thing that's kept me up for the last twelve years or so, Master Danril," she said, looking back at him. Danril nodded and patted her knee again. "What's troubling him?" she asked, looking back at the prince. "He seems upset by something."

"The news from the north isn't good," he said. "The village of Trinda is completely lost. They've compared it to the attack on Reudena near the Prestile Forest some twenty-five years ago."

"But Reudena was burned to the ground," Ari said, thinking about the history lessons she'd gotten from the order after she arrived at the order once the orphanage had closed its doors for good.

"Yes. Though Trinda still stands, there were many casualties, and many people have fled. Our biggest producer of crops is no longer viable."

"It's on the northern border," she said, shivering slightly as the breeze blew, ruffling her loose hair. The chill it sent down her back was enough to make her wish she'd grabbed her sweater. "Why would our northern border be under attack? We're not on the best of terms with Pertina, but they wouldn't put that many civilians at risk."

"I don't know," Danril said. "But the war council was ready to send our soldiers against Pertina, believing them behind the raiders that forced Trinda's residents to flee."

"It won't be long before I'm on my way to Pertina then," Ari said with a sigh.

"Why do you say that?" Danril asked, looking at her curiously.

"The queen had her own council meeting, that yours truly got left out of, but I picked up some tidbits through the door."

"You glimmered and snuck in through the window again, didn't you?" She smirked and shrugged. "What tidbits?"

"I have no idea how she came by the information or if she's making wild accusations, but she believes both Stuttgad and Pertina are responsible."

"Well, they do have a history of being very outspoken against Queen Tatiana," Danril said slowly. "But I don't think they'd order attacks against civilians."

"Since when has she needed proof?" Ari asked with a hollow laugh. "How many people has she sent me to kill on less than a scrap of information?"

"I know, child. Calm yourself." Danril patted her shoulder. "If you have concerns, you should send them to Lord Simeon."

"Concerns? We're not supposed to have concerns, Master Danril," she said bitterly. "We serve at the whims and desires of the Thendin Faedom, me more so than others. My concern is how much blood of innocent Fae rests upon my hands, because of mere scraps of information, whether it be true or not?" She stared at her hands in the faint moonlight, staring at blood only she could see. "How many names in my ledger should've been allowed to continue their lives, see their families again?"

"Such is our lot child," Danril said quietly, "dwelling on it, thinking of the anger you feel will not serve you. That's why we're taught to repress our emotions, especially when it comes to our duties."

"Could've used a few lessons on dealing with them after the fact," she said.

"You clearly didn't pay attention during some of your classroom studies," he replied dryly. "Just because I deal with things a particular way doesn't mean you have to."

"Your way means I don't have to deal with people," she said as a rustling from the gazebo drew her attention away from the conversation. "Your ward is done brooding. I should go."

"Rest well, little one," he said as she faded out of view just as the prince joined him. "Feeling better, Your Highness?"

"Danril, you know not to address me in such a manner," Finn said wearily. "Though I'm not sure I feel better. What brought you over here?"

"We had some company on our walk tonight," he said.

"Pleasant company, or at least company that didn't pose a threat," Finn said as they started back toward the castle.

"I suppose you could consider it both," Danril replied, suppressing a smile at the idea of Ari hearing herself being referred to as pleasant company. "Though pleasant is a word I very much doubt she would ascribe to herself."

"She..." Finn looked over at Danril. "Lady Ari joined us?"

Finn's weary demeanor faded away as he thought about Ari and its place settled a kind of boyish wistfulness. Danril smiled faintly, knowing that for some strange reason, his student and eventually his partner and backup to more dangerous missions, was the only thing that could break the normally quiet boy's ice. Though Ari was more like a sister to him, even he knew that her looks turned heads. She was petite, with golden hair and eyes to match, a look that stood out among the dull browns and grays of the court.

"Yes, though I dare say she didn't intend to," he said gently. Finn's face fell a bit, causing Danril to sigh. Finn's fondness for Ari was still one sided after four years of her being part of the court at Tena Castle. Ari tended to keep most everyone at arm's length, himself included, to avoid anyone getting hurt. "You know ours is a dangerous profession, one where often we don't come back."

"I know," Finn said, head still in the clouds. "Doesn't stop me from hoping or dreaming about her, though."

"She's about as dense as that wall you're about to walk into," Danril said as he pulled Finn back onto the path. "And you know she's as deadly as the blades she carries."

"I'd expect nothing less from someone as sharp and keen as her," he said a little wistfully, as he stumbled on the path again. Danril rolled his eyes as he caught the prince and straightened him up.

"You should keep your head in the here and now, and your feet on the path," Danril said. Finn opened his mouth to retort but before he could, a servant came running up to them. She stopped in front of them and looked around. "My pardons, but have you seen Miss Ari?"

"She should've returned to her room by now," Danril said, knowing that the servant was carrying a summons. "If not there, perhaps the library."

"Thank you, Sir Danril," the young girl said before taking off again. Danril grimaced, both at what he knew she was carrying and at being called sir.

"What was that about?" Finn asked, looking at Danril curiously. "And what's with the expression?"

"Nothing good," Daril said, as they rounded another corner of the garden. "But it's nothing you should probably concern yourself with."

"I'm not an idiot, Danril," Finn said sulkily. "I know that's one of my mother's servants, and I know what Ari does. The only question is who does my mother want gone now?"

"I do not know, but I hope the moon and stars guide and protect that child." He looked up

"Mother would have you flogged for that," Finn said. "You know how she feels about the old ways."

"I am very well aware, Finnian," he said. "But it's your mother sending that girl out there to have her sanity slowly ebbed away at. Makes little sense to ask her to protect the child."

Finn shook his head and chuckled. "That child is nearly as old as I am, Danril. And if half the rumors are true, she's the deadliest assassin to ever come from the halls of the Blade."

"Second deadliest ever," Danril corrected, "though I gave it up for the queen's wishes to have someone watching over you," Danril said as they approached the castle. "But a summons this soon after the war council convened isn't good. Both councils," he added as they stepped out of the night air and into the castle.

"As usual, mother has more information than she's willing to share again. Does the war council know of her activities?" Finn asked. Danril laughed.

"If they did, do you think your sweet little Ari would have a place in the palace?" he asked. Finn stopped and stared in shock. "What, you think I hadn't noticed?"

"I wasn't aware anyone had," he grumbled, causing Danril to laugh again. "It's not funny Danril."

"Very little escapes my notice. Same with Ari, though the minutiae of human emotion past happiness and anger are lost on her. Why do you think your mother chose us?"

"How does she still manage to look so unbothered? How do you manage it, for that matter?"

"Cheap whiskey mostly," Danril said as they reached the prince's chambers. "The occasional whore, though I don't think Ari strays too far down the path of needing that much forgetting, most of the time. She's more adept at compartmentalizing than any trainee The Blade has ever seen."

"And what happens when that damn breaks?" Finn asked, his hand on the doorknob.

"Depends on the person Finnian," Danril said, his voice indicating the prince should drop the subject. Finn picked up the warning and nodded. "Try to get some sleep, Your Highness. You need your rest for whatever comes next." Finn's nose crinkled in disgust at being called *your highness* but in the castle he didn't dare correct him.

"More meetings I'd much rather sleep through," Finn said with a yawn. "Good night Danril." The door opened and closed, leaving the bodyguard in the hall, wondering how Ari's meeting was fairing with the queen. Danril headed off toward the kitchen where he knew he could pick up on the castle's gossip at any time of day,

The servant had indeed found Ari in the library, where she'd been trying to forget her troubled dreams in a tome. The late night summons, though unsurprising, were most unwelcome. She grumbled as she left the library and made her way toward the queen's chamber, wishing that this could've waited until the morning. She continued down the marble hall, her body moving of its own accord before she came to a stop at the door and knocked. When a soft, impersonal voice told her to enter, she did, coming to a stop in the middle of the room.

"Late for you to be out of bed, isn't it Ari?" the queen asked, looking up at her from the piles of papers that littered the table.

"That would depend on your definition of late, Your Majesty," Ari said calmly. "To some, this meeting could seem just as late as me not being in bed, doing what I wish."

"You do know you're only allowed to speak to me like that because I let you," Tatiana snapped. Ari just stared at her, unblinking, unfazed by the outburst. The queen took a deep breath and composed herself, returning to the matter at hand. "But that is of little matter. I require your other skills."

"I assumed so, otherwise there'd be little point to this supposedly clandestine meeting," Ari said dryly, deciding that there was little point in continuing the niceties.

"Why do I put up with your impertinence?" she said, getting up to stand in front of the assassin. There was little difference in their heights, which made the queen's plan to intimidate the girl seem foolish.

"Because no one else within Shadow and Blade will deal with your whims and fancies," she said, a tad harshly. "And if it wasn't for the arrangement you and Lord Simeon made, I wouldn't be putting up with them at all. Now what can I do for you, Queen Tatiana?" Ari stared the queen down, her honey eyes boring right into the queen's cold silver ones. Tatiana held the gaze for as long as she could, but something about Ari's unblinking stare caused her to look away first.

To regain some semblance of control and burn off the nervous energy, the queen began pacing the room while she laid out the situation. "Our primary hub for farming in the north has been lost to raiders. Those who survived the attacks in Trinda have fled to the neighboring towns. Raiders sponsored by both Pertina and Stuttgad ministers are behind the attacks." Tatiana tried to make the lie sound convincing to fool the shrewd assassin. It had been her elite palace guards that had coordinated the attack on Trinda, as well as several others, all so she could stir up discontent and hatred toward the other countries.

"Am I to hunt down these raiders?" Ari asked, keeping the boredom and irritation from her voice. This was quickly turning into something that could've waited until morning.

"Not until my spies ascertain if they're still in the area around Trinda," the queen replied. "No, I need you to eliminate the Stuttgadian minister who we suspect to be colluding with our northern neighbors to attack our northern borders."

Ari sighed. Political figures were such a pain to eliminate. "How many, Your Majesty?" she asked, putting her hands behind her back.

"Just the one. But I do want you to bring me back the name or names of who they were working with."

"Excuse me?" Ari looked at the queen with narrowed eyes. "My queen, I am not a spy. I do not gather intelligence. That would compromise me as an assassin. You wish to have them interrogated; you will need to ask Lord Simeon to send a Shadow with me."

"You think I want to send more people on an errand this sensitive? I trust you and nobody else to keep my activities quiet. I need you to get me those names, Ari."

"And I am compelled to tell you that by the decree set down by the founders of the Shadow and Blade,which were agreed to by your forefathers, I cannot comply. I do not gather information. I end lives."

A loud smack rang through the room as the queen struck Ari. The assassin stood there, simmering in anger as the spot where the queen had slapped her grew warmer by the second. She'd barely contained her rage when a second slap followed the first. A third would've followed, but Ari reached up and grabbed the queen's wrist.

"I wouldn't push me if I were you," Ari said thinly, dropping the queen's hand.

"How...how....how dare you," the queen sputtered as she took a step back. "You have no right to remind me of what that cockamamie order says or does. You have no right to touch me as you did. I am the queen! I demand respect."

"Respect must be earned, milady, not given so freely as you wish. If you want my respect, then you must show you respect the rules and laws of the order I serve."

"You do not belong to them any longer," she hissed.

"If you wish we could summon Master Danril to clarify but I distinctly recall Lord Simeon saying that should your orders ever clash with the rules of the Shadow, I was to follow their rules and should you punish me for following their rules, I would be removed from your service." Ari waited as the queen fumed and raged about her room. When a few moments passed and nothing the queen said was of any importance, Ari turned to go. "Send your spies if you must, but otherwise I will see to it that this man ceases to draw breath and nothing more."

"His name is on the paper on the drawing table," Tatiana said thinly. "Now go and don't come back until he is dead."

"As you wish, Your Majesty," Ari said, grabbing the note before leaving the room. As soon as the door shut, she heard things being thrown about the room. She shook her head and went to prepare to leave.

As she approached the rear gates of town where the stables were kept, a figure materialized beside her. They walked in silence until they reached the stables. In the low glow of the lamplight, Danril noticed the red mark on her cheek.

"She struck you," he said, turning her head to get a better look at the mark.

"She lashed out after I told her that the orders she gave me violated my oath to the Shadow and Blade."

"Ah, a reminder that we are not truly her playthings," he said as he put his palm to her cheek. The area grew warm for a brief moment before it faded, along with the sting. "There, it wouldn't do for you to run off to wherever with that noticeable mark."

"I would've dealt with it when I arrived," she said, but they both knew that there was no way she could've. "But thank you all the same." She mounted her horse and reached down for her pack. "Listen for orders of spies to be sent after me," she said in old Thenndin, a language long forgotten by many, except for those who'd sworn to serve Shadow and Blade. "The queen wants information my targets may have."

"But our laws forbid you from obtaining it from them," he replied in kind as he handed her the bag. "The queen knows this."

"Exactly. I told her I would carry out my duty as an assassin. Lord Simeon should be aware." She patted the horse and sat up straight. "The queen is an enigma I cannot crack, even after watching and studying her for four years."

"I'll go speak to Lord Simeon in the morning, see if there is anything that he can do to mitigate any wrath."

"Just make him aware of the situation," she said. "Further interference could put us in a very precarious position within the castle."

"Very well," he said, knowing she was right. "Ride safe and swiftly, little one, and return in one piece." Ari was just about to nudge her horse until he spoke. She paused and looked at him curiously.

"Is everything ok?" she asked. "You've never asked that of me before. Has your sabbatical made you go soft?"

"I could still do your job in half the time, little one," he said, knowing she was joking by the faint smile on her face. "But it's not for my sake that you should come back safely."

"Then who?" she asked, but he shook his head.

"Leave it at there is someone who would be sorely grief stricken should something happen to you," he said, not willing to divulge the prince's secret, but knowing if she thought about it, she could figure it out. "Now go while you still have the night." Ari nodded and nudged her horse forward and out of the stable, the horse's hoofs making no noise on the cobblestone path as she left the city. Danril watched as she faded from sight before he turned and headed through the city to speak with the lord and master to the order he and Ari had dedicated their lives to.

Chapter 2

Danril's parting words about returning safely for the sake of someone bothered Ari as she trotted through the fading moonlight toward her destination. There were precious few people that cared about her but not to the extent that they'd want her back well and in one piece. She was a Blade for the order, an assassin. Danger and risk were part of her life and those around her knew that, Danril especially, even though he was the closest thing she had to family. *So who could want me back safely?* she wondered as the moonlight gave way to sunrise. It certainly wasn't the queen. The castle staff had little interest in her. Many of the lords and nobles that frequented Tena Castle for the council meetings pretended she didn't exist. Eliminating all those left her with only one person, but that option seemed very farfetched.

A nearby nicker and snort from another horse brought her back to the road in front of her. She hadn't realized she was that close to Thiamult. A poor night's sleep and the fact that she couldn't work out who would be so upset if she didn't return had distracted her enough that she'd gotten right up to the edge of town, completely unaware of her surroundings. Grumbling, she headed straight for the inn, secured a room, a meal and then went and collapsed on the rickety bed, mind wandering back to where it had left off on the road. The only other person who could be that upset would be Tatiana's son, Finnian, but he had no reason to want her back, or did he? Her mind recalled the last time she'd run into him and Danril in the castle's library. His face, which had been downcast from some news he'd received, had suddenly brightened and she swore his smile stretched from ear to ear. *That wasn't because of me, was it?* she asked herself as she felt her eyes grow heavy. *It couldn't be possible, I'm nothing to anyone.* Her thoughts grew quiet as she fell into a heavy sleep.

The morning sun brought Danril to Lord Simeon Callwell's office, the lord and master of the Shadows and Blades. The conversation had been pleasant at first, just two old friends chatting and catching up. When Danril finally turned the conversation toward why he'd come, Simeon let out a deep sigh and rose to grab a decanter filled with whiskey and two glasses before he sat down, poured them a drink and slid a glass toward Danril.

"Why does she vex us so?" he asked, before taking a sip. "The rules and laws that govern us predate the Ophirs taking the throne. The first Ophir king had such reverence for our order that he carved it into the throne room's wall that our rules can never be superseded by any rule or law set forth by him or his successors. But like her father before her, Tatiana is hell bent on trying to undermine us."

"Ari herself told me that the queen demanded she get information from her target," Danril said quietly.

"And how do you know she was being truthful?" Simeon asked, raising a brow.

"One, she's never given me a reason not to trust her in the twelve years I've known her and two, she spoke in Old Thenndin, which meant she wanted only me to hear it."

"I see," Simeon said. "She had reason to fear a spy in the vicinity?"

"With the queen, anything is possible. She clearly had an issue with Ari telling her she would not, could not fulfill her request."

"That is unsurprising," Simeon said, rubbing his temple. "I trust Miss Penndra is ok?" Danril nodded. "Then she's not concerned about the queen interfering with the errand she's on."

"She wanted you to be aware. I would assume she'll probably handle anything else herself." Danril paused. "Though I wonder if the queen would come at us directly if Ari were to dispatch anyone sent to kill her."

"You know that if that happened, I would have to step in. You're acting awfully protective of her today Danril. Is your sabbatical making you soft to how we do things?"

"No Lord Simeon, but perhaps young love is." Simeon looked confused. "For some reason, Prince Finnian has developed an infatuation with her."

"Oh, that's rich," Simeon said with a chuckle. "Has Tatiana caught on to this?"

"No. If she knew, the crown wouldn't have an heir," Danril said. "Only you and I know. If Ari wasn't so dense, I'm sure she could figure it out. If it's not a basic emotion like happiness or anger, she wouldn't know it even if it bit her in the ass. It's the one thing I utterly failed at teaching her."

"You remember what she was like when she came to us," Simeon said, looking at the rays of sun that were now streaming through the window. "It's an accomplishment to have gotten her to recognize enough emotions to learn to read people around her."

"Now if only she'd quit pretending she doesn't have them," Danril said, staring at the empty glass on the desk.

"She learned that lesson a little too well," Simeon said in agreement. "But at this point, we can only hope she comes to realize these things on her own." Danril nodded, squeezing his tired eyes shut for a brief moment and then opened them again. "You should get some rest. I'll have a note sent to the prince in regards to your whereabouts."

"Thank you, Lord Simeon," Danril said through a yawn. "Give Tissa my best." Simeon nodded, and a page appeared to show Danril to his room.

As they left, Simeon leaned back in his chair and sighed. The order had continually butted heads with the stubborn queen, the first one in history to ascend to the throne without succeeding her husband's death. She had married for a time, long enough to produce an heir before her husband had died under mysterious circumstances. Rumors flew about the Faedom and the surrounding ones that she had him murdered to avoid giving up her claim to the throne, a rumor that wouldn't surprise him in the least if it were true, especially since the man passed shortly after his son was born. Shaking his head to clear the thoughts of rumor and fancy, Simeon reached for his pen and wrote a quick note to the prince before summoning a Cloak. He gave them explicit instructions on how and when to deliver the note before he handed it over and watched them disappear. A bell sounded somewhere, indicating time for the morning meal. Rising and stretching, Simeon got up and went to join the rest of the council for breakfast.

The bright midday sun woke Ari by sneaking through the smallest gap in the curtain and landing right in her eyes. She rolled on to her side, groaned and sat up, looking around as her fuzzy brain worked to piece together exactly where she was. It wasn't until she had made her way down to the inn's great room and dug into her meal that reality caught up with her. Ari had made it as far as Thiamult, a small hamlet that sat just before the Stuttgad border, which meant if she could get her tired ass moving, she could be across the border before long and in Stannard by sunset. She hauled herself out of the chair, her body stiff from the long ride and the shoddy inn mattress, and stretched before grabbing her pack and leaving the inn, coin for the meal on the table and pulled herself up on the horse and nudge her on so they could make Stannard before nightfall.

While she was trotting down the road, the prince was bored to tears dealing with the day-to-day affairs that his mother claimed she was too busy to deal with now. He had no desire to wear the crown, and even though he cared about people as a whole, what the merchants were doing for trade or whether or not the treasury had coin to fortify the border, held no interest for him. He let his thoughts drift off towards the garden, and the petite blonde assassin who frequented them when she was at the castle, and not off on some errand for his mother. Everything about her was enticing and captivating to him from the sense that she was something forbidden to him. From the round honey colored eyes that hid countless horrors behind them, always scanning for a threat, to the way her body was always poised to strike, to the way her golden hair shimmered in the sun even when she had it pulled back in a very tight braid. She'd been at the castle for four years, and in that time, he'd only ever seen her crack one smile. He wondered if he was wasting his time, pining after her, when there were much more suitable matches out there waiting for him. He was a prince after all, at some point he was expected to marry for an alliance of some kind, even if his mother didn't agree.

His thoughts continued to wander down this path, wondering if he could convince Ari to at least spend some time with him, or something, anything to avoid a political marriage, knowing that it would piss his mother off to know end for him to spend that much time with a commoner and maybe even get her to disown him, which would strip his rights to the crown. He allowed a faint smirk to cross his face as he thought about all the times he'd snuck out of the castle and mingled amongst the people, which if his mother knew about them, would definitely get him removed from the succession, not that he had hopes for the throne. Finn always looked forward to them because nobody knew who he was and

Danril often turned a blind eye to these twice monthly escapades, which he was thankful for since he often got bored in the castle because his mother rarely allowed him to go anywhere even within Thannid, which meant his illicit little jaunts were the best way to go release some pent up energy.

His thoughts turned to planning his next one as the Finance Minister finished preaching how broke the crown was again like he had every two days for the last month. Finn's head was somewhere in town rather than in the meeting room, which meant that he missed the Master of Coin asking him repeatedly if he understood what was going on. Finn finally pulled his head back to the meeting when the Master of Trade kicked him under the table. He blinked and looked up at the worried master just as he asked him again if he understood.

"Understand what, Master Thornbock? That you've been preaching the same things for the last four years?" Finn looked at him. "I understand wars are costly, but until Queen Tatiana is wholly satisfied that our people are not under threat from the surrounding Faedoms, we will continue to spend whatever is necessary for the war."

"But sire, we simply do not have the funds," the minister protested.

"Then take this matter to the queen," he said. "But I guarantee you she'll tell you to find the funds and make it happen, Master Thornbock." Finn rose and studied the shocked expressions on everyone's faces. Clearly, nobody expected the prince to snap. "Is there anything else of major importance to discuss?" They all shook their heads. "Good. Then I shall take my leave."

He left the meeting room and went to his chamber, and flopped on his bed, staring at the ornate ceiling above him. He used to appreciate the castle's beauty as a child, the carvings in the ceiling, the tapestries that were centuries old that hung on the walls, the majestically painted scenes depicting the old ways that graced the ceilings of the grand hall and the throne room, but now, they just felt like they were gilding the walls of the prison he found himself trapped in, held in place by his mother's desire to rule her Faedom as she saw, with no interference from anyone, including her son.

The only thing that seemed to make his prison cell even mostly tolerable was seeing Ari on a frequent basis, if you could call the glimpses he got of her as seeing her. She was like a ghost, but one he wanted to track down and get to know much better. He closed his eyes, let the sounds of the castle fade away and just drifted there, dozing as he continued to imagine ways he could get to know Ari.

He was still lying there nearly two hours later when Danril finally returned from the order's sanctuary and found Finn still in his chambers. He looked at his charge, who had his eyes half closed, seemingly oblivious to everything around him.

"Were the meetings that mind numbing?" Danril asked, sitting on the edge of the bed. "Or are you just moping because a certain someone is out of the castle again?"

"Who says it can't be both?" Finn asked, not moving.

"Never said it couldn't be," Danril said with a chuckle. "She'll be back, you know."

"I know. Maybe I should stop pining in secret and just tell her how I feel."

"First bit of sense I've heard come from your mouth about this in a long time," Danril said. "But be prepared for her to either have no idea what to do or instinctively shut you down. She's never known affection."

"It's well past time for someone to show her then," Finn said, sitting up. "Do you know how long she expects to be gone?"

"I do not," Danril said, "we can never put a timeline on how long a mission takes. There are too many factors to be considered."

"I was afraid of that," Finn said with a sigh. "Never the mind, I'll just plan something nice for her after she returns."

Danril laughed, already looking forward to seeing Ari's reaction to this. "Good luck with that," he said, getting to his feet. "Now, are you planning to continue moping or shall we go walk around town and get some fresh air? I heard the marketplace received a new batch of fresh gingerfruits today."

"You think a gingerfruit will cheer me up?" Finn asked.

"Not completely, but it's a nice start. Grab your cloak, let's go. You're not allowed to just mope until she returns."

Finn grumbled but did what he was told and the two of them were off, soon eating some of the freshest gingerfruits Finn had ever had as they walked through the market mindlessly.

Ari rode into the Stuttgadian capital just as the sun's last rays were fading. Like Thannid, the closer she was to the wall, the shoddier the houses were. Ari smiled at the comfort that sight brought as she found herself an inn to inquire about a room. The great room wasn't busy, which bothered Ari, especially since they all stopped talking as she walked in. One of the regulars sized her up, decided she wasn't harmless, and approached.

"Pretty girl like yourself shouldn't be all alone in this part of town," he said, his hand trailing down Ari's back before coming to rest on her hip.

"If you don't want to lose your hand, I suggest you move it," she said sweetly, turning to look at him. He didn't move his hand, instead he tightened his grip on her and spun her to face him.

"Such a pretty thing like you, couldn't hurt a fly," he said with a sneer.

"Would you like to test that theory?" she asked, losing all sweetness. Every fiber in her body tensed, ready to strike. The man watched as the softness melted away, her eyes going from round and innocent to cold and deadly. He took a step back, but still didn't let go.

"Thommy, let her go," called the innkeeper, but the man still held on to Ari. "Quit harassing my patrons."

"Little bitch here needs to be taught a lesson about manners," he said, looking up at the innkeeper.

"It's not me who needs a lesson in manners," she said, tired of waiting. "Move your fucking hand."

The entire great room watched in shock as Ari reached over, grabbed Thommy's hand and twisted it off her hip, the cracking bones echoing through the room. Thommy howled as he sank to his knees, holding his now broken wrist in his lap. Ari stepped over the blubbering mess and approached the innkeeper, who looked at her with wide eyes.

"Ca.... Ca.... Can I help you?" he finally sputtered out.

"I need a room and a stall for my horse in the stable please," she said, all trace of the hard assassin that had briefly appeared gone, leaving a sweet, innocent young woman in its place.

"Of course," he said, over the initial shock. "Do you know how long you plan to stay?"

"A couple weeks to start, I think," she said, pulling out the coin. "This should cover my stay, correct?"

"Enough for a month, child," he said, eyes bulging. "You sure you don't plan on staying longer?"

"Remains to be seen," she said. "But consider the extra my apology for the scene caused."

The innkeeper had been doing this long enough that he knew when someone was looking to keep their profile low. He nodded and took the coin, the extra would go a long way to clearing up some debts to his suppliers and getting some much needed necessities for his family. He pulled a key from under the counter and held it out for her to take.

"Welcome to The Rocking Horse, miss," he said. "We serve meals at sun up, midday, and anytime from sundown to final curfew."

"Final curfew?" she asked, looking at him with her head tilted. Thannid had no such thing, even in the slums.

"Yes. There's a final curfew, it makes sure that citizens cannot will not be attacked in the streets, or in theory, it's supposed to." Ari noticed he sounded bitter about it. "If you have any other questions, you can ask anyone here. Aside from Thommy, who fancies himself popular with the ladies, nobody else there will bother you like that."

"Appreciate it," she said, recognizing the brush off. "Thank you for your hospitality." The innkeeper snorted as she went out and stabled her horse. She spent extra time with her, making sure her horse got combed out, rubbed down and well fed before she took her things inside to her room.

She wanted to give the great room time to fill up more. The more people in the tavern, the fewer people who would pay attention to her. As she listened to the noise grow louder, she pulled the band holding her braid in place and shook it out; the hair falling out gracefully into waves that framed her face. In the grimy glass above the sink, she stared at her reflection and sighed. Gone was the assassin, the sweet innocent little woman, and in their place stood the tired girl looking back at her. Hollow eyes, blank expression, a girl without anything tethering her to anything or anyone, a girl whose emotions didn't exist. She slowly brushed her hair out, the repetitive motion coming automatically as she let her mind empty. The noise grew loud enough that she could almost clearly hear things in her room. She pulled the brush through her hair one last time, set it aside and pulled it back away from her face, deciding a braid was way too much work. She changed from her travel clothes into a fitted dark red tunic and black pants, pulling her boots back on, and went to join the ruckus in the bar.

The atmosphere was lively, and Ari adjusted her mood to fit. She took a seat at a small table near the window, closest to the group of soldiers who seemed to be bitching about something. She waited until she'd gotten her food before she studied the conversation intently. As she took a bite, she closed her eyes and let the sounds of the soldier's conversations wash over her. Her interest piqued when she realized they were talking about her target.

"Minster Henrich seemed to step in it with his wife again today," one of them said as he downed his beer. "Apparently the shark he owes a large debt to stopped by the house while he was in council today. Lady Henrich was absolutely a wreck when she arrived at his office over it."

"The man is going to wind up dead in a back alley if he keeps racking up debt to that particular shark."

Ari's nose crinkled in disgust at the mention of the shark. She and Danril had made a fair few of them disappear in the time they'd worked together. She continued her stew while she listened to the two soldiers gossip some more.

"Don't I know it," the first replied. "It's a pity too. That pretty little daughter of his being sick and all."

"How terrible," Ari chimed in from next to them. "Is this chair taken?"

Both men looked up and felt their jaws drop at the sight of Ari. She repressed a sigh of disgust as they both scrambled to pull out the chair for her.

"Sorry if we were too loud," the first one said. "Job stress really takes it out of a guy."

"No, it's fine. I just arrived today and was curious about what you were talking about. I confess I'm a tad nosy when it comes to political gossip."

"Won't find anything juicer than Minister Ernst Henrich gambling away the sorely needed cash to take care of his ailing daughter."

"Why would he be doing that?" Ari asked, laying on the dumb blonde act pretty thick. These two, however, were drunk enough that they couldn't tell she was acting.

"Well, if we're to believe what Minister Faolan's detail says, it's because he thinks he can double the funds he has to dig himself out of the debt he racked up for the apothecaries," the second said. "Personally, I think he's doing it to take his mind off how shitty things are at home. He wouldn't be the only minister with a vice."

"Fascinating," she said as she picked up her tea and finished it. "I shouldn't take up any more of your time."

"It's not a problem," they said in unison as Ari stood.

"As glad as I am for the company, I should be getting to bed. It was a long journey here." She put a few coins on the table to pay for the drinks, much to the surprise of the soldiers. "Thank you for the time, and the conversation."

They bid her goodnight as she headed up to her room. From the stairs, she could hear them bickering about who had the better shot with her. She shook her head, knowing neither one of them had a snowball's chance in the summer as she pulled the door open and walked into her room. She kicked off her boots and flopped on the bed, breathing a sigh of relief before pulling out a scared leather journal and a pen from her pack. The journal definitely looked like it'd seen better days. The once sturdy leather now looked like it was a breath away from falling off the pages that Ari had replaced not too long ago. She carefully flipped the book open and jotted some notes down about the town and her target. She finished the last of her notes and closed the book, tucking it back into her pack carefully and then blew out the candle to get some rest. Tomorrow, she had a town to explore and a target to stalk.

Chapter 3

ERNST HENRICH RUBBED HIS face as he looked over another finance report, seeing it but not comprehending it. The numbers on the page blurred together as they reminded him of just how far in debt he was to the shark that ran the card hall where Merchant's Row met the slums. He looked up at the window and let out a sigh before he got up and stretched. If he didn't get a move on it, he was going to be late making his payment to Zarath, which would only add to Illana's aggravation with him. She'd put her foot down yesterday telling him to either pay off the debt or get out of the house. When he'd pressed her for details, she'd screamed at him, telling him that men from Zarath's employ had shown up at the house looking for him and the money. Illana had reason to be pissed, he'd sworn months ago that he'd stopped, only to fall back into his awful habits and put them further in debt, which had done nothing to ease his wife's anxiety. Caya was sick and the apothecaries were on the verge of turning him away until they received payment for the medicines they'd already gotten for her illness. His face was tight with worry as he grabbed his jacket and pulled a pouch from his desk.

"Ayni, I'm leaving for the rest of the day," he said as he passed his secretary's desk in the outer office, "I'll be back in the morning."

"Minister Riterite requested a meeting with you this afternoon," she said, holding out a note for him.

"Send a note that I will have time to meet about the baseless accusations leveled at me by Thenndin in the morning," he said bitterly. "Right now, I have personal matters to attend to." Henrich left the outer office quickly, letting the door slam shut behind him, startling his poor secretary. She wrote out a quick note and then hurried away from her desk to deliver it.

Ari watched them disappear in their different directions from the corner she was hiding in and then slipped into the now vacant office. The desk was an absolute mess of financial papers that meant nothing to Ari, except the one peeking out from under an official looking ledger. She carefully lifted the book and turned her head to see what was on the paper. The handwriting was neat but loopy, like that of a court educated woman, which Ari assumed was written by his wife. . One column labeled gambling debt, the other labeled medicine. They were in a considerable amount of debt, made worse by the next pages she found as she looked through the desk drawers. Death threats against him and his family, how much he owed and how much interest accumulated on the astronomical figure had Ari's blood boiling. She carefully put the papers away and would've snuck out of the office the same way she got in, but she heard the secretary back in the front office. Cursing her rotten luck, she cloaked herself in glimmer and slipped on to the balcony just as the office door opened and the secretary slipped in, placed a note on the top of the mess and left. Ari breathed a sigh of relief as the door closed again. The sun was beginning to set, and Ari took to the sky, leaving the glimmer in place, dropping it when she landed in an empty alley in the slums. She joined the crowds going to their various homes and slipped into the inn with barely a glance at anyone around her.

She skipped dinner in the great room tonight, her mood sour after looking over all the papers that Henrich was storing in his office. She couldn't tell what had angered her more, the fact that he was gambling away any money he had or the fact that the shark was out there preying on desperate people like Henrich. To keep herself from doing something stupid, she pulled her sharpening kit from her bag and pulled a dagger from her boot. She focused her breathing and slowly worked the blade against the sharpening stone, her breathing eventually matching the back-and-forth movements of the stone, the familiar scrape of steel against stone drowning out the desire to go hunt up this shark. As her mind fell quiet, she grew tired, placing the stone and blade aside to rest.

Ari had settled into a routine over the next three days. She'd get up, get dressed, have breakfast, then hide on Henrich's office balcony until he'd leave again for the day where'd he go home and fight with his wife after they'd put their daughter to bed. The fights were always the same. Illana would start cleaning; Ernst would join her and inevitably the topic of money would come up. Ari was sitting under the window, cloaked in glimmer, when they stared in again.

"Shouldn't you be at the card house?" Illana asked as she set a pan down hard.

"Can we not do this tonight?" he asked wearily. "I told you I was paying both off."

"Not fast enough. She needs more medicine, Ernst."

"I need another week, Illana," he snapped. "One more week and the apothecaries' are going to be paid up."

"And Zarath?" she asked. "How long before we're able to walk through town without one of his goons walking in our shadows?"

"I'd have to increase how much I pay him a week, Illana," he said, wearily. Ari recognized his tone. Danril used it on her repeatedly as an initiate, it was the tone of a man who'd already explained something. "And with the cost of Caya's medicine, we cannot do that."

"Then I'll increase my hours down at the shop and I'll speak to my mother," she said, turning to look at him. "I want him out of Caya's life, Ernst. I don't know why you started gambling, and frankly, at this point, I don't care, but it stops. Caya's fragile enough without this danger looming over her."

"I know that," he grumbled, which caused his wife to snap.

"And yet you did nothing but invite this danger into our lives. Figure it out Ernst, or get out so I can make sure Caya gets the help she needs without the added danger of someone wanting us dead."

A door slammed, shaking the house. Ari took that as her sign to leave. She shook out her shoulders, letting her wings flutter out, and took the sky again. Tomorrow would be a week since she started following him and he had yet to lead her to the shark. She'd gone through his appointment books, searched his study in his home while they'd been out, but there was nothing written anywhere as to when he delivered his payments to the shark. She landed near the inn's stables and released the glimmer. The inn was noisy again, which both comforted Ari and set her teeth on edge, so she went into the stables to brush out her horse to see if she could steady her mind and emotions. She was growing frustrated, both with the mission and her mark. In just under a week, Ari hadn't been able to piece together why a minister of finance would be responsible for an attack on Thenndin's northern border, not that she should be caring about that. Ari wasn't a spy; she didn't determine innocence or guilt. No, she was an assassin, a killer, the one who killed those who'd already been determined to be guilty of something. The steady brushstrokes eventually allowed her mind to wander to less serious topics while the noise from the inn slowly died out. When there was both silence in her mind and the inn, she went inside, skipped dinner and went to bed.

Ari finally got her wish the next afternoon when Henrich left his office late in the day abruptly, again telling his secretary he'd be out for the rest of the day. As she followed him deeper into the city, the thicker the crowds got, which meant that she had to release the glimmer to avoid running into people. With a grumble, she continued making her way through the throngs, almost losing sight of Henrich twice. Eventually, the crowds thinned the closer they drew to the slums. Ari quickly threw the glimmer back around her as Henrich looked around him before pulling open the door to the card house and quickly getting off the street, Ari following suit.

The man behind the counter looked up as Henrich entered. No words needed to be exchanged as the barkeep pointed at the stairs. Henrich's stomach churned unpleasantly as he started up toward Zarath's office, his foot hesitating over every stair. The barkeep looked at him and huffed as Henrich made slow progress up the stairs.

"You know he don't like to be kept waiting," the man said in a low voice. Henrich swallowed and picked up the pace, eventually reaching the door at the top of the stairs.

"Took ya long enough," Zarath's bodyguard said as he opened the door for Henrich. "Boss man's gettin mighty impatient." He didn't give Henrich time to respond, instead grabbing the minister and throwing him into the room. Ari barely had enough time to sneak in with the minister before the door shut.

Zarath looked up as Henrich stumbled in, nearly falling on his face. He snorted in disgust and came around the desk to stand in front of the minister.

"You're late Henrich," he said in a voice that Ari could only describe as oily. "Do you have my money?" Zarath held out his hand expectantly while Henrich reached into his pocket and pulled out a small bag and dropped it in the man's hand. The man quickly counted it, snorted in disgust, and tossed it on his desk before turning and striking Henrich across the face. "What kind of fool do you take me for Ernst?" he asked as the minister whimpered.

"I.... I.... don't," Henrich stuttered, holding a hand to his cheek. "That's our agreed upon payment amount."

"Oh, did I forget to give you the news?" Zarath asked with a toothy grin on his face. "I've increased your payment amount. You owe me twice as much as what you've brought this week."

"You said you'd give me until I paid off the other debts," Ernst protested. "Illana won't accept this new arrangement."

"Why should I care what your wife will or won't accept?" Zarath asked, sneering. "I didn't make this arrangement with your wife; I made it with you. Now, you'll get me my money, or I will be sending Bortin out there to visit that pretty little wife and child of yours."

"I need one more week to pay off the tab at the apothecaries. After that I'll pay you what you want, I just need this week. Please, just the week."

His words and tone stirred some compassion within Ari and had she been any other hired mercenary, she probably would've walked away from killing him. But doing so as a member of the Shadow and Blade, that could result in her dismissal from the order, not to mention her death at the hands of the queen. She tamped down her sympathy, knowing full well the man in front of the minister was not about to grant him any clemency.

"You've had ample time Ernst," Zarath said, his voice hard and cold. "I get the increase in payment starting next week or I send Bortin to see your wife and child. It's that simple, Ernst."

"Do what you want with me, but please leave Illana and Caya out of it," Henrich pleaded.

"Then get me my money, Ernst," Zarath said, dismissing him.

Henrich scrambled out of the room, terrified, while a very furious Ari remained cloaked in the shadows, waiting for the right moment to confront the man. If it had been Henrich's life on the line, Ari wouldn't have interfered, but the man had threatened harm to innocents, people who had no business paying for the mistakes of one man. Her oath as a member of Shadow and Blade ran through her mind, and she moved from the shadows, letting her glimmer become visible. As she approached him, he looked up, catching the shimmer out of the corner of his eye. By the time he realized she was there, she was behind him and had his letter opener in her hand and pressed against his throat

"Who... who.... who are you?" he sputtered, terrified, afraid to move.

"Someone who could easily end you in the blink of an eye," she whispered in his ear, casually alternating between pressing the flat portion of the letter opener and the sharp edge against his throat. "Someone who will end you if that woman and child end up dead."

"Ernst Henrich has to be taught a lesson," he said as the blade switched again. He swallowed and gulped as he felt the sharp edge against his throat suddenly. "Why do you care so much?"

"Where I'm from," she hissed, "the innocent do not pay for the mistakes of the guilty. Henrich's wife and child are not to be harmed, or I will slowly cut every vein so you bleed out from every possible surface and watch your life drain away at such a fast past, you have no time to realize what's happened to you."

"All talk," he said, voice full of false bravado. He smirked and was about to say something taunting to Ari when the letter opener slammed into his hand. He roared in pain and turned to look behind him as blood poured from the wound in his hand. "Who are you?" he asked again, cradling his hand as he tried to get a glimpse of his attacker. But where she had been standing, he found only empty space.

"Consider that my only act of mercy," she said quietly, her voice seeming to echo around the room. "If I see any men outside Henrich's home, ready to kill the woman and child, I won't be stabbing a hand, it'll be your throat instead."

"Show yourself" he roared as the door burst open and Bortin rushed in. "You coward, come out and face me proper!" Bortin looked at Zarath with confusion while Ari took advantage of the open door and disappeared.

Ari returned to the inn to finish her plans for tomorrow, but as she stared at the fire in her room, mulling over the plan, she noticed her hands were shaking. She was an assassin, a cold-blooded killer, not someone who should not be acting like this, succumbing to her emotions over two lives. Ari worked to shove them back into the far recesses of her mind as she continued planning, fine tuning her approach, thinking about each possible scenario that her mind could conjure up. The sun was peeking through the window as Ari fell over on the pillow, her head full of plans, death, and fire.

The sun had begun to set on another day, and Ari, who'd dozed off waiting for sundown, bolted upright in bed, her skin feeling like it was on fire. Her chest felt tight, and her hands were shaking as she tried taking a deep breath to settle her racing mind. There wasn't a garden here for her to get lost in, so she fumbled around with half lidded eyes and found her pack. Clothes and various tools went flying as she found the sharpening stone. Her hand closed over the cool rock as she pulled it out of the bag. She grabbed one of her blades and began running the edge of the blade down the stone letting the scraping of metal against stone drown the echoes of the screams in her head.

The sun was completely gone by the time she'd finally calmed herself. She took a glance at the street below and decided there was no better time to carry out her assigned mission. The last fight she'd overheard between Ernst and his wife had ended with her telling him he needed to leave by sundown today. She put the stone back in her bag, changed from her brightly colored loose-fitting tunic to a form fitting black one that matched her pants perfectly. She pulled her boots on and then slowly, reverently, affixed her dagger sheaths to her back and hips and put the fire out in her room. With one last look, she grabbed her things and disappeared.

Ernst was still pleading with his wife from the doorway when the unseen assassin slid through the front garden. Ari hid herself behind the large fruit tree as she listened to the last of their argument

"No, I'm not changing my mind, Ernst," Illana said, crossing her arms. "Until you're out of Zarath's debt, you cannot be in the house. Caya's finally doing better now that I can get her medicines again. I will not have this added danger of our lives being on the line for your mistakes, making her worse."

"You don't get it, Illana; they'll kill you either way." The rest of what he said got drowned out by rustling from a nearby bush. Ari crept toward the noise, dagger in hand, hoping that the disturbance was nothing more than just a small creature who'd wandered into the garden. Leaving more than just Henrich's body in the front garden was going to cause a lot more problems than Ari had time to deal with. A bunny hopped out of the bush in front of her and she let out a sigh before going back to her tree. "This is the last time, Illiana, I swear," he said, begging.

"Ernst, you've said that the last dozen times," replied his wife. "There may not have been anyone watching us in the market today, but that doesn't mean anything. Now, go and do *not* come back here until you've paid off that debt and sworn off gambling for good."

A door slammed and was quickly followed by the sound of the main door opening and closing. Ari adjusted her grip on the handle of her dagger as she listened to the sound of footsteps draw closer. She closed her eyes, slowed her heartbeat and her breathing before sliding out from the shadows and grabbing Henrich by the arm. He startled, opened his mouth to yell, but never got the chance as Ari slid the blade between his ribs, piercing his heart. She pulled the blade out and let go of the minister's arm. He stared at her, his mouth agape, as he fell to the ground in almost slow motion. She wiped the blade clean with a rag as the door opened and footsteps crunched against the gravel walk. Ari had no time to make a silent getaway, so she dove back into the shadow of the tree and pulled her glimmer over herself for good measure just as Illana came down the walk.

"Ernst," she called as she came down the front garden walk. "Before you go..." her voice trailed off as she came across his now lifeless body. "Ernst?" When he didn't respond, she knelt next to him, putting her hand and knee in the blood pool. "Ernst?" she asked again as she held up her hand. In the light from the open door, she realized it was her husband's blood running down her arm. The scream that tore from her lips was enough to make the hair stand up on Ari's neck, but worse was how much it sounded like the one from her dreams. She turned and left, the scream echoing in her ears as soldiers ran into the garden.

Screams were nothing new to Ari, whether they were the screams of anguish from a loved one discovering the dead, to the screams of pain from the children in the orphanage as they cried from hunger. But no matter how much she tried to tell herself these screams were nothing different, she couldn't help but liken them to the scream that haunted her dreams. She cursed the dream as she ran through town to pick up her horse. Once she was atop her steed, she sped out of town, trying to outrun the dream and Illana's scream.

The servants were all buzzing about the rider the guards had spotted early in the morning. Danril was only half paying attention over a muffin while Finn was staring at the coffee in his mug, not hearing the conversation around him at all. Danril had just taken another bite of his muffin when he heard the conversation behind him.

"Oh yeah, you should've heard Crispin tell the story. A blonde-haired rider dressed in all black came tearing back into town this morning. According to him, she looked like she was trying to outrun a spicewolf or something from the woods."

"Spicewolves haven't been seen since King Taprin was on the throne," the second servant said, snorting in disbelief. "She probably got spooked by her own shadow. You know as well as I do that the dead branches on the road leading toward Thiamult cast eerie shadows." The servant shook her head. "Spicewolves, what a load of horse shit," she muttered again as she wandered off.

Danril paused mid bite of his muffin and looked up. Ari had headed off that way two weeks ago. He set the muffin down and disappeared from the table. Finn barely looked up from his coffee. He didn't quite get what was happening. He needed more coffee, it seemed, as he reached for the pot and refilled his cup.

Ari was in the stables, brushing her horse, the rhythmic activity doing nothing to calm her shattered nerves. As Danril approached, his foot caught a rock and skittered it across the floor. He barely had time to blink as Ari's instincts kicked in and she leapt toward the sound, dagger in one hand. Danril found himself pinned against a wall, his hand around hers to keep the blade in her hand away from her throat.

"You could've just said you missed me," he joked in Old Thenndin. She blinked and let him go, stepping back. "Someone's on edge."

"Just a bit," she said, putting her knife away and picking up the brush.

"Ari, are you going to make me ask?" Danril looked at her, arms crossed. "I can tell something's off."

"My head got in my way," she said, eventually. "That stupid dream, I keep having it."

"Why don't you consider a sabbatical then?" he asked gently.

"And go where and do what? With you watching the prince, I'd end up being relegated to teaching theory or something at the order."

"What's wrong with that?" he asked, smirking.

"You damn well know I would lose my shit on the first initiate that made me mad."

"It'd be a good lesson in patience," he said as she let out a low growl. "How soon before you report to the queen?"

"As soon as I get a chance to clean up and calm down. I'm not about to go before her like this. That's asking for my head on the castle wall."

"Simeon wouldn't-" he started, but Ari cut him off.

"Lord Simeon wouldn't have time to intercede," Ari snapped, nearly throwing the brush at the wall. Danril raised a brow as she fought to bring her temper back under control.

"Clearly, given how little control you have on that temper of yours, *Fire*," he said, causing her to snarl. "Put the brush down and go relax. I'll see what I can do to keep the queen out of your hair a bit longer."

"Thank you," Ari said after a moment. "Drinks at the Rose later?"

"Only when you're feeling up to it child," he said, patting her shoulder. "Take the next few days and relax. The Rose should still be standing by then."

"Should be," she said with a snort. "Have you seen who frequents that joint?"

"As long as nobody runs into Aermore, it should be fine," he said gently pushing her toward the door. "It's good to see you back in one piece, little one."

"Someone's making you soft," she said lightheartedly. "We both know a couple years ago you wouldn't have said anything like that upon my return."

"With time, things change Ari," he said as he followed her out of the stables. "There is change in the wind. You should consider embracing it."

"I'll consider it," she said quietly as she headed inside.

Danril watched her go, a little voice in the back of his mind nagging him that something wasn't right with her. He pushed it aside, knowing that if he forced her hand right now, it would end badly for everyone. He said a quiet prayer to any god that might be listening and decided to take his own advice about relaxing, but only after he managed to get the queen out of Ari's hair.

As she walked into her room, she became acutely aware of just how tired and achy she was from the ride back to Thannid. Her legs felt like lead, which made every step she took seem like it required twice as much effort. She stumbled into the bathroom and turned on the tub, deciding that she needed a long soak, and an even longer nap before she went and spoke to the queen. As the tub filled, the air became thick with the scent of eucalyptus, lavender, clove and ginger, the scents already beginning to work on soothing the exhausted assassin. She carefully worked herself out of her dirty, sweaty, and bloodstained clothes, before easing herself into the tub and closing her eyes, getting lost in the scents and steam that whirled around her.

She'd only barely begun to relax when the door to her chamber burst open and the sounds of heels clicking across the stone floor reached her ears. Ari sighed and internally braced herself for the verbal and potentially physical lashing the queen was about to give her. The bathroom door burst open not long after and the queen stormed in, fuming. Ari opened one eye part way and stifled the laugh that bubbled up as she saw the queen's bright red face.

"I figured you'd be here a lot sooner, Your Majesty," Ari said, sinking deeper into the tub. "To what do I owe this interruption that is sure to be unpleasant?"

"You expect that a messenger will suffice when you know to report to me right away?" Tatiana snapped. From the tub, Ari rolled her eyes. Danril hadn't managed to keep the queen out of her hair for long.

"My reporting to you right away would've ended badly for both of us, Your Majesty," Ari said, fighting off a yawn. "However, if you insist on a report, the minister you wanted dead, is most certainly dead."

"Were you able to find anything else out?" Tatiana asked, crossing her arms.

"I will again remind you that I am not a spy, merely an assassin. He's dead, as instructed. Now may I finish bathing in peace?"

For the first time since she entered the room, Queen Tatiana finally seemed to realize where she was. With a low growl, she turned and left the room, heels clicking on the marble floor. Ari leaned her head back against the cool metal edge of the tub and sighed, knowing she was going to pay for that comment later. It was the last thing on Ari's mind however as she finished her soak, dried off, changed into a dark green sweater and loose-fitting black pants before she flopped on her bed, falling asleep even before her head hit the pillow.

Chapter 4

A RI AVOIDED MOST EVERYONE and everything around the castle and around the town for well over a week. Danril had attempted to check on her but had been told to piss off repeatedly by the grumpy voice on the other side of her door. He'd decided to give her as much space as he could, but when another week went by with her not emerging, he began to get worried.

"Ari?" he asked, knocking on her door. Instead of the usual growl telling him to piss off there was silence. "Ari," he said, knocking again. When there was only silence, he carefully opened the door and walked into a mess. "For the love of the gods, child," he muttered under his breath as he picked his way across the floor."

From her bed, Ari looked up and glared at him as he crossed the mess and sat on the edge of the bed. "What are you doing here?" she asked, not bothering to get up.

"Trying to decide if I drag you into the land of the living or not. You look like shit, child."

"Just what every girl wants to hear," she muttered dryly. "I'm not leaving this room."

"You've had two weeks to sort yourself," he said, chiding her. "Enough is enough. You need to get out of this room."

"And do what?" she snapped, burying herself in a pillow. Danril reached over and pulled it out from under her head. "Can you not?"

"No. You owe me a drink or two. I'm cashing in on that. Get dressed. If you have anything clean to wear that's not scattered across the floor, let's go." When she didn't budge, Danril got up, found some clothes that looked mostly clean and threw them at her. "Let's go, Ari Penndra."

"Can't a girl mope in peace?" she grumbled pulling the clothes off her and dropping them next to her.

"You have for two weeks, enough is enough. Now get dressed. Cheap whiskey and good times await us at The Blue Rose."

"Ugh, do you really think I'm fit for company? Especially for the assholes that frequent the Rose?" Danril laughed as he reached over and pulled her to sitting. "You're really not going to let this go, are you?" He shook his head. "Don't you have a prince to babysit?"

"Unluckily for you, the prince is busy with other things tonight, which means I am free to do whatever." Ari groaned and grabbed the clothes. "You have needs, which include human connection Ari, so quit ignoring them. You need to go out, let go, have fun, hell, get laid." Ari twitched a little. "When's the last time you did that huh? Just let go, let your brain get scrambled by a good fuck?"

"Fucking hell," Ari said, her face turning red. "You're like my brother, you really think I'm going to discuss that with you?"

"Then it's been a while," he said, laughing at her reaction. "Take tonight to just let loose."

"Because that will end well," she said, finally going to change. "Remember the last time I *let loose*? I broke Aermore's nose and couldn't come back to the Rose for two months because of the fight that broke out after that."

"So don't try to solve your problems with violence," he said, tongue in cheek. Ari groaned from behind the screen and threw her shirt in his direction.

"That's rich coming from you," she muttered. "I've seen you when you finally lose control of your emotions."

"That was one time, and you were very much complicit in that," he said thinly, pissed that she'd even brought that incident up.

"Only because you asked me to help after I tried talking you out of it," Ari replied as she came back around in a fitted red shirt, black vest and black leather pants.

"You didn't try very hard," he said quietly. "But then again, you liked her as much as I did."

"She was the sister I never had," Ari said sadly. "I won't ever forgive her father for those sins."

"Jenna would want us to, but I can't either. Not when his sins caused her death. What happened to get you to bring this up?" he asked as she began working on untangling the knots in her hair.

"I watched a man put his family at risk with a shark while in Stannard, incurring multiple death threats against his wife and sick child." Her hands shook as she tried to work a knot out of her hair. Danril came over and took the brush from her hands and worked the knot out like he had when she had been a small weak teenager who'd been given to the order when the orphanage shut down.

"This job was nothing but bad memories for you, wasn't it," he said, looking at her face in the mirror while she nodded. If anyone else was looking at her all they would've seen was a stony expression, but Danril had known her for twelve years, knew that under the stone was a young woman trying to keep from bursting into tears.

"Bad memories and bad dreams," Ari said eventually, her voice rough.

"Then let's go erase them for a bit," he said, setting the brush aside and braiding it for her. She nodded, forgoing the usual protests she put up when he did things like brushing or braiding her hair. When he was done, he held out his arm for her and together they headed off into the heart of Thannid's slums and for The Blue Rose.

The Blue Rose was the shabbiest building in the row, with the paint peeling from the sign and the side panels looking like you could see through them. Various boards and rags covered the windows from the sheer number of times the panes were smashed out, both Danril and Ari responsible for a fair few of those broken panes. The door barely stayed on its hinges, threatening to fall off as he pushed it open.

As they entered, the tavern keeper looked up from the chipped glass he was polishing and sighed. Danril raised his hands in a gesture of peace before glancing around, looking for an empty table. The barkeep narrowed his eyes at them but didn't say anything as they picked a table toward the back of the bar, theoretically out of the way and where they wouldn't cause trouble. They sipped the first drink in silence, as was their custom, silence for the victim, silence for the lives affected, and silence for a prayer for their souls and the souls of those gone on. Ari probably would've sipped her second beer in silence too, but a roar from the very back of the bar broke through her thoughts.

"Aermore's found himself a new victim it seems," Danril said sourly as he downed his shot of cheap whiskey.

"Yep. Though you and I both know that if we get involved, we're likely to get banned from the Rose for life this time." Ari glared at the back bitterly as another loud roar came from the back. "Though beating the shit out of that fucking asswipe might make me feel better."

"How about you just go," he said as two more shots were brought over. "I'd rather not brawl tonight."

"Your loss," she said, downing her shot and grabbing her beer before swaggering off to rescue Aermore's most recent victim.

The scene in the back was a rowdy affair. Crowded around the dartboards was Aermore, a dark-haired man Ari didn't recognize, and Aermore's usual crowd of lackeys and bimbos. She paused just behind the crowd gathered around the dark-haired man and listened to Aermore be a blowhard like usual.

"Come now laddie," he said mockingly, "surely you could do better than this."

The man would've responded, but Ari stepped in. "I'm sure everyone would have a sporting chance, Aermore, if you didn't weigh the competition's blades down."

A collective gasp went around the group. Finn's heart nearly stopped when he recognized Ari's voice. He slowly turned and looked at her. She had a bland grin on her face, like she was trying to hide how much she was enjoying the effect her words were having on the man. Her eyes scanned the group, her eyes skipping across everyone but pausing to linger on him. She gave no indication that she recognized him, which both pleased and saddened him. She crossed one arm across her chest and took a sip of her beer while Aermore struggled to keep his temper under control.

"How would you know?" he growled, crossing his arms.

" Pick up that blade," she said to Finn while she drew her own. "Compare its weight to this one." Finn did as instructed, taking the blade Aermore had provided and comparing it against the one Ari handed him. His eyes grew wide as he looked up at the burly Fae.

"You fucking cheated," he said, handing Ari her knife back.

"Sounds about right," Ari said, handing Finn her beer. "Hold this."

"Why?" he asked, confused as she shoved the mug into his hands.

"How much does he owe?" she asked, looking up at Aermore.

"What's it matter?" Aermore asked, looking down at her with a scowl.

"How much, Aermore?" she asked again.

"A hundred and thirty crowns," he said eventually. Ari raised a brow at the amount and shook her head.

"New bet," she said, putting her hands on her hips. "You beat me, he pays his debt and learns a hard fucking lesson. I win, you wipe the debt and leave poor Sir Gullible here alone any time he comes into the bar from this point forward."

"Only a fool would take that bet against a Blade from the Shadows," he spat.

"Then he can just walk away, and you never see your crowns," Ari said, nudging Finn to leave. "Or I can even the odds and use your weighed down blades."

Aermore considered it for a moment before he shrugged and nodded. "If your delicate little hands can lift them."

"You're gonna eat those words, bastard," she said, picking up the weighted blade and throwing it at the target. The crowd gasped as the blade found its mark in the center of the target. "Your move fucker."

Aermore growled as he lined up his toss. It was good, precise, but Ari's perfect shot with a blade she shouldn't have been able to throw with that much accuracy had thrown him off. His blade barely stayed on the target, the tip burying itself as close to the edge as possible. Ari let out a snort as she took her beer from Finn and drank half of it.

"What's wrong with you Aermore? Are you off your game now?" she taunted, shoving the mug back at Finn.

"Shut yer fuckin mouth," he said as their blades were brought back. "You haven't won yet."

"How many rounds have you gone with pretty boy here?" she asked, gesturing to Finn with her thumb.

"Four." Aermore looked like he'd rather eat glass than go another three rounds against Ari, but pride had him picking up his blade again. "Ladies first," he said with a grimace.

"Insults Aermore?" she asked, lining up her throw, landing the blade right where it needed to be again. "At least be creative with them."

From his table, Danril sighed as he listened to Ari taunt Aermore. The taunts flew fast and thick as Aermore continued to miss his marks. The crowd around them was laughing and cheering. Ari was just adding to Aermore's growing frustration. Danril finished his beer and joined the crowd as Ari's final throw hit the mark yet again.

With a growl he slammed his knife into the table and picked Ari up by the throat. She gasped and kicked at him, but his longer arms prevented her from actually doing more than tapping him with her toes.

"Put me down," she gasped as she struggled.

"No," he snarled as he pinned her to a wall. "You conned me bitch so now you're going to pay for it."

"I've done nothing of the sort," she said, gasping for air. "You watched me use the blades you weighed done, you know I didn't cheat."

"Uh huh, sure you did," he snarled, getting inches from her face. "I have a hard time believing that when you trained under the head bastard of the blades himself."

"If you know that, then you should probably let her go," Danril said, voice quiet, yet angry. "I don't appreciate having my student manhandled in that way."

"Was wondering if you'd be man enough to show up," Aermore said with a sneer.

"I've been here," he said, "wondering how I could get your ball served up on a plate. Might just have to do it myself if you're not going to take your hand off Ari's throat."

"Bitch owes me for cheatin," he growled, as he used his free hand to trace the shape of Ari's jaw. "I intended to collect."

Ari reached up and grabbed his fingers, snapping them as they trailed over her cheek. He yelped and dropped her, leaving her gasping for breath on the floor. The man she thought of as a dark-haired stranger ran over to help her get up and out of the way.

"Are you ok?" he asked as she took his hand.

"Fine," she said hoarsely, rubbing her throat. "We should move though."

"Oh, I don't fuckin think so," Aermore said moving to block them. "Bitch owes me for cheatin and laddie here owes me a hundred and thirty crowns."

"That's not the deal I heard you make," Danril said in a low tone. "I suggest you honor it or it's me you'll deal with next."

"I ain't scared of you," Aermore said with a sneer.

"Ari, it might be time to take your new friend and leave," he said, glancing over his shoulder. "The Lily might be a better place to frequent from now on."

"Sounds good to me," she said, pulling Finn along with her. Danril watched them go and as he did, he realized who Ari was tugging along behind him.

"Aw, you took away my toys," Aermore growled. "You're going to pay for that."

Aermore was fast, the dagger he'd slammed into the table was in his hand faster than most people could blink, but Danril, who was a few years younger, who'd honed his skills, was faster still, the knife he always kept on his back was suddenly in his hand and buried in Aermore's shoulder. The scream of pain he let loose echoed through the bar, causing silence before the remaining patrons whipped themselves into a frenzy. Danril pulled his knife from Aermore's shoulder and quickly made his way through the brawling crowd. He barely heard the barkeep yell at him to not come back as he slipped out the broken door.

Over at the Gilded Lily, Ari was sitting in a corner of the bar still unaware that she was having drinks, and flirting, with the prince of Thenndin. Had she been sober, she probably would've seen right through the glimmer around him, but by this point, she'd had quite a bit and completely missed the glimmer around him. As they continued to talk, drinks flowing freely, Ari did something she wouldn't have done sober, she leaned over, grabbed him by the collar and kissed him.

Finn was taken aback, but he didn't stop her. Instead, he reached over and tugged her closer, moving her into his lap. They were still like that when Danril walked in a few minutes later.

"For love of the gods," he snapped, grabbing both of them by the collar and pulling them apart. "Do you both have a death wish?"

"Huh?" Ari asked, looking up at Danril, completely confused.

"Look closely, child," he said. "Tell me what you see past the glimmer."

Ari squinted, forcing herself to see past the haze that she now realized surrounded the man she'd just been kissing. As the glimmer faded out of view, her face grew red and her eyes grew wide.

"Oh fuck me," she muttered.

"Probably would've happened had someone not interfered," Finn said irritably, causing Ari to turn even redder.

"Not funny," Danril said. "Back to the castle, both of you." They got up, and filed out of the bar, Ari still reeling from embarrassment and Finn torn between irritation and relief. Nobody said anything until they were behind the closed door of Danril's room. "Good gods, what were you two dumbasses thinking?"

"The point of this evening was to not think," Ari said, refusing to make eye contact with Finn, her cheeks still red.

"I would've expected you of all people to check for glimmer around a person. How many times has Aermore nearly had his way because you failed to look for it?" Danril was fuming. "And you, you know damn well your mother has spies everywhere. You want to let loose, fine. But do it with someone not known to the court."

Both Ari and Finn began to argue with each other and Danril, who just let the conversation fade into background noise.

"What do you think you're playing at out there?" she snapped at Finn. "The wrong person sees through that glimmer, you're dead."

"If one of the greatest assassins can't see through my glimmer drunk, you expect the average resident, also drunk, to see through it?" he shot back. "Besides, you seemed to be enjoying yourself, glimmer or no."

"You son of a bitch," she snarled, "you tricked me. You knew who I was, you led me on."

"All you had to do was open your eyes," he said, shrugging. "You chose not to." He smirked. "You even agreed to dinner with me."

"Gods dammit Ari," Danril inserted. "Are you kidding me?"

"No. But it shouldn't be enforceable since I did so under the influence of hard liquor and enchantment."

Danril opened his mouth to agree with her but remembered Simeon's words and stopped. "No. If you agreed to it, honor your commitments, Ari. You failed to realize you were being played, now deal with the consequences."

Ari wanted to protest, but she knew that ultimately he was right. She'd been remiss in checking her surroundings and now she would have to pay for her mistake. "Fine," she said eventually, her teeth clenched.

"Perfect. How about we have dinner now?" he said, beaming. "What? It fulfills your obligation to me and gets it out of the way."

"Fine," she said. "I'll meet you..." she trailed off, letting him finish the sentence.

"My room, half an hour," he said, smirking. "Don't be late." Ari had a sudden urge to knock the smirk off his face as he left. As soon as he did, Ari turned and looked at Danril.

"What, pray tell, the fuck was that all about?" she snapped.

"You fucked up, now pay the piper," he said, patting her head. "Just don't be stupid about it."

"Stupid how?" she asked, eyes narrowed. "Because I have half a mind to finish what I started back at the Lily."

"Just don't get caught, child," he said, giving her a shrug and a smirk. "And don't toy with the boy's heart."

"Me, toy with a heart? Like I know how," she said with a snort. "Why aren't you stopping me?"

"Why should I?" he asked. "You're both grown, consenting adults, why would I interfere?"

"I hate you some days," she grumbled as she left the room. He smirked and snorted as the door shut hard. Ari fumed all the way from Danril's room to the prince's. All the beer and whiskey were finally catching up to her and by the time she reached his door, her head was spinning. She'd barely knocked when the world tried to rush up to meet her. Finn chose that moment to open the door, and she tumbled right into his arms. "I can walk," she grumbled as he scooped her up and carried her in the room. "Put me down."

"Oh, I will, in a moment," he said, nudging the door closed with his foot. "You really should work on being nicer, especially to someone who went to all the trouble to make sure you had dinner."

"I am more than capable of getting my own dinner," she said as he walked into the sitting room where a fire roared in the hearth and with a small dinner laid out in front of it. "I remember agreeing to dinner, not whatever this fancy stuff is."

"There are no expectations," he said and from against him, she could feel his heart racing.

"You're a terrible liar," she said as he stopped near the fireplace. "Are you going to put me down now?"

"Your wish is my command," he said dryly, dropping her onto some of the cushions. She yelped as she thudded into them before giving him a glare. "You didn't say I had to do so gently." She stuck her tongue out at him. "Now where were we?"

"What makes you think we're picking up where we left off?" she asked, raising a brow as she eyed the plate and picked up a sandwich.

"Because I know two things," he said, pouring some tea and handing it to her. "You never leave things unfinished and two, you could've easily gone back on your word or showed up, told me off, and then left."

"True," she said, making short work of another sandwich. "Although neither of those mean that I plan to pick up where we left off."

"Your choice," he said. "I'm not here to force you either way. For all I care, you could eat and leave."

"What are you playing at Finnian Ophir?" she asked, wrapping her hands around the cup of tea. "What's the end game here?"

"I'd say no game, but you'd call me a liar. I just want some of your time," he said, "How we spend said time is up to you."

"My time? Why? There's nothing special about me. I'm just the broken toy assassin the queen fails to keep a secret."

"Lies," he said. "You're more than that. You have meaning beyond being my mother's puppet."

"I do nothing more than take lives," she snapped, causing him to recoil. "I am death, I bring ruin and despair wherever I go."

"There's more to you than just death and ruin," he said, quietly. "There's a woman in there who can laugh, cry, and smile. She may not know it but she brings happiness when she's around."

"Nobody is happy when I'm around," she said, shaking her head. "Danril might be pleased to see me, but I wouldn't say I bring happiness to him."

"Maybe he's not the only one who's pleased to see you come back safely," Finn said, exasperated. "Open your eyes and realize there's more to the world."

"More to the world?" She snorted. "Your privilege is showing, Prince Finnian." He bristled as she used his proper title. "For people like me, there's never more to the world. We're lucky to get what we have. Most of the children I grew up with in the orphanage would kill for the little I have."

"That's not fair," he said quietly.

"No, what's not fair is watching two children I considered to be my family slowly starve to death because the orphanage couldn't get enough food to feed us all. What's not fair is me starving myself to try and save them, only for it to be in vain. The world isn't as fair and good as you think it is," she said, getting to her feet. "It's cold, harsh, and unforgiving."

"Just because your experience with the world has been cold and harsh, doesn't mean you can't begin to see the beauty in it," he said. "Just look around, see the good."

"See the good?" Ari snorted again. "There's never been any good as far as I could tell. Thank you for the sandwiches." She moved to the door and pulled it open.

"Ari, stop," he said, getting up and going over to her. "Why do you choose to see the world in such a terrible light?"

"Because it's been terrible as far as I can remember," she said, not stopping him as he pushed the door shut. "When your first memory is of the master of the orphanage telling you that you shouldn't have survived, it tends to sour your outlook on life. From that point on, I had no faith in my fellow man and no hope. I've gone through life being numb, because numb keeps you from getting hurt."

"That's no way to live," Finn said eventually, reaching out and taking her hand. "Living numb, hiding your happiness, sadness, even your anger and pain doesn't let you experience the world at large. There's so much more to enjoy when you feel the world, rather than just simply existing in it."

Ari looked at him, eyes narrowed, mouth twisted in a bit of a frown. The expression crinkled her nose up and Finn suppressed the urge to tap it like he might a kitten or a puppy. "You sound like Danril," she grumbled.

"I'll take the compliment," he said, causing her face to scrunch up even more. Finn laughed and used his other hand to cup her chin. He gently tilted her head up to look at him before he kissed her with the same intensity that he had at the bar just a few hours ago.

"You're lucky you have such a pretty face," she muttered after he pulled away, "otherwise I might've broken it."

"Did you just admit you like my looks?" he asked with a smirk.

"Don't push your luck buddy," she said with one corner of her mouth turned up in a smile, causing him to laugh. "I should be going."

"You could stay," he said, sounding a little hopeful. "After all, it is late."

"I cannot afford to incur your mother's wrath," Ari said, patting his cheek. "As much as I'd love to upset her, I do like my head attached to my shoulders."

"Then I will take all the blame for it," he said, but she shook her head.

"Your head needs to stay attached to your shoulder too," she said, rising up to kiss him one last time. "Otherwise, I couldn't do that. Good night, Finn." She turned and left, leaving him standing in the doorway.

Finn stared at the door before going to sit in front of the fire. He watched as it dimmed, looking at the spot she'd occupied, unable to shake how she'd felt in his arms, strong yet so delicate, and suddenly he felt so empty and alone. Not bothering to deal with the remains of dinner, he left the sitting room and flopped on his bed, feeling like he'd let a piece of him walk out of that door. Eventually he fell asleep, dreaming of her, wishing she was still there with him.

Chapter 5

A RI COULDN'T TELL WHICH pounding woke her, the pounding in her head from too much booze and too little food, or the pounding on the door. All she knew was her head felt like lead and that it was very difficult to pick her head up from the pillow. The pounding eventually stopped, but it was short lived because the door to her room burst open and Danril stalked in, slamming it behind him.

"A closed door usually means do not enter," she grumbled from her pillow.

"You'd live your life behind a closed door if given half a chance. Why's Finn moping around like you kicked his puppy?"

"Because clearly I went back to my own room last night." Ari forced herself up and squinted at him. "For as much as I'd love to piss off the queen and hook up with her son, I like my head attached to my shoulders more." She put a hand to her face and rubbed her eyes. "He seemed to understand last night."

"Crickey, you are so bloody dense," he grumbled.

"What now?" she asked, finally forcing herself off the bed. "When did this room get so messy?"

"Sometime when you decided to hole up in it for two weeks," he said, shaking his head. "Are you really telling me you don't get why he's upset?"

"Are you really going to make me answer that or would you like to draw upon your knowledge of me?" she asked, locating a blue shirt and some brown pants that looked and smelled reasonably clean.

"He has feelings for you, though heaven knows why," Danril said, tired of trying to make her figure it out. "Has for at least three years as far as I can tell."

"Kid needs a new hobby," she said, swaying slightly as she went to change from her bar clothes last night.

"Need I remind you child that he's not much older than you?" Ari didn't say anything. "Look, I don't necessarily like this either, but Lord Simeon doesn't want me to interfere."

"Then I'll speak to him," she said, coming back out. "He's the crown prince, heir to the throne if or when Tatiana kicks the bucket. He does not need to damage himself with the likes of me."

"Good luck. The kid's been pining for three years, Ari. The only way he'd stop is if you took sabbatical and left Thannid."

"If that's what it comes to," she said. "He's lucky he still has that pretty face of his on those broad shoulders of his," she said, shaking her hair out of the braid and brushing it. "If his mother knew about his jaunts..."

"Pretty face and broad shoulders, someone was paying more attention than she let on," he said, teasing. She stopped and looked at him, her eyes wide. "Admit it Ari, you find yourself attracted to him."

"Physically, maybe," she said, blinking owlishly. "But we both know it runs deeper for him. It wasn't hard to tell last night. He's got such expressive eyes."

"I'd never thought I'd see the day when you'd get hung up on someone's eyes," he said with a laugh before dodging the brush she threw at him. "Oh, lighten up about it, child. You know Simeon's married. I was serious with Jenna for close to two years. There's nothing that forbids it."

"He's also the lord councilor and a prominent figure in Thannid society," she said going to retrieve her brush. "Expected for someone who runs Thenndin's oldest spy organization."

"Who leads by example, Ari. What's ok for him is ok for us, you know that."

"I also know that romantic entanglements are viewed as weakness. Do you know how many of the order think Simeon is weaker because of his marriage?"

"I'd argue he's a stronger leader. You cannot have strength without softness."

"Physical relationship, fine. We all need to let off steam, but romance? It tends to end badly."

"You don't need to continue down that path," Danril said, quietly. Ari felt a little bad about making him remember how he'd felt after Jenna died. "Romance is a double-edged sword among us, yes, but that doesn't mean we can't pursue it."

"Others can pursue it then," she said, as she re-braided her hair. "I see no reason for it."

"Only because you persist in believing yourself unlovable," he muttered. Ari spun around and looked at him with narrowed eyes. "Oh, don't give me that look. You've said it yourself repeatedly."

"Cause it's true," she said with a shrug, deciding his throwing her words at her wasn't a cause to get upset. "The broken assassin from the slums, who would want that?"

"I can think of one," he said, staring at her with a blank expression. She let out a groan and rolled her eyes. "Fine, whatever Ari. I don't feel like going rounds with you on this today." He sighed. "And you're not staying cooped up either."

"I wasn't planning on being cooped up," she said. "I was going to go sit in the library."

"Nope, nice try," he said, grabbing her arm before she could waltz out of the room. "We're going into town and then we have plans this evening."

"We do?" Ari looked confused.

"It's the night of the full moon child, yes we do." He held on to her as he guided her to the door. "Official order business and all."

"Ah, the one time Queen Tatiana cannot yell at me for not being at her beck and call." Ari smiled. "But why are you dragging me into town?"

"Because you need to see life differently for a while. The world is not just full of Aermores and Steins; there are good people, hard working, honest ones out there."

"Why do I feel like I'm an initiate again?" she asked with a slight groan.

"Because you haven't ever learned this lesson. Simeon thinks you need to figure it out on your own. I think you just need to be shown how people truly live and act."

"Who's right?" she asked as they made their way through the castle gates and into town.

"Only time will tell. But try to enjoy yourself. Quit looking like you have a stick up your ass." She harrumphed. "Don't get grouchy at me. You're the one that chose to walk away last night."

"You act like you wanted me to sleep with the prince," she said, shaking her head as they headed into town.

"It's a basic human need, Ari," he said, shaking his head. "Something you ignore far too often."

"Might be a basic need but the last time I checked, we weren't human," she retorted.

"Dammit child," he said, shaking his head. "Nitpick over words all you want but the point stands, you ignore your needs too often."

"And when's the last time you went and got laid yourself?" she asked, nudging him with her elbow. Danril grumbled and glowered as his face turned red. "See how it feels when you bring it up to me now?" she asked, laughing as she let go and procured some fresh steamed buns.

"Fine, you win, little one," he said eventually. "There's nothing worse than your little sister asking you when you got laid last." He shuddered as she laughed again. "Oh, yuk it up," he grumbled as they walked into the large gardens in the center of town. "What did you see out there?"

"People going about their day. Merchants hawking their wares, townspeople getting their needs and wants fulfilled."

"Think about how they were doing it," he prodded, easily slipping back into the role of her teacher. "Think about their expressions, the atmosphere in the market."

"They're laughing and smiling," she said, closing her eyes to listen. "Nobody feels like they're mad or scared or on edge." She opened her eyes and looked at Danril, who promptly choked on his bite of his pastry at the confused look on her face. "Do people really go through their days not wondering when their next meal will be? Or for fear of getting close to someone only to have them taken away by sickness or starvation?"

"Not everyone has experienced life the way we have," he said. "But even those who worry that their next meal will not come for some time, or that they will not see a friend or loved one again choose how they live. If they want to live in fear, they can but they will find themselves lacking."

"Are you saying my life is lacking?" she asked, biting into her bun.

"You made the connection, not me," he said, secretly pleased she'd caught on. She let out a harrumph and chewed on the bun while the sounds of the market washed around them. Eventually, a guitar thrummed outside the garden. Danril smiled, letting a pleasant memory replay. "What are you thinking about?"

"The same thing I always do when you force me into one of these lessons," she said. "Why?"

"Because life cannot be taught, Ari," he said, standing up and holding out his hand. "Life must be experienced." A second guitar joined the first, followed soon after by the sound of a drum. "We should go experience it."

Ari shrugged and took his hand, and together they left the garden and melted into the throngs of people. The crowd was lively, with music filling the air in the square. Eventually, the merchants moved their stalls back as far as they could, and the square filled with people dancing. Ari watched as the afternoon shoppers stopped what they were doing and indulged in a moment of frivolity. Eventually, Danril pulled Ari into the fray, and it wasn't long before she was dancing and laughing with the rest of the crowd.

The afternoon passed into evening, finding Ari and Danril outside the gates as the sun continued to dip past the trees. Her cheeks were flushed. There was an unusual sparkle in her eyes, and she still sported a big grin on her face. Danril couldn't help but smile as well, happy to see her relaxed for a change.

"Somebody enjoyed herself," he said as they walked into the trees.

"Maybe a little," she said, shaking her shoulders, letting her golden wings flutter freely. "I don't think I've ever felt like that."

"That's what happens when you let yourself experience life, Ari," Danril said, shaking out his wings. Next to hers, the blue looked icy and cold to the touch, earning them the nicknames Fire and Ice. "And I've seen your face after the Moon Dance, you can't tell me you don't feel light and free then."

"Well, yes, but not in the same way," she said as they came to an opening in the trees. "That makes me feel free and powerful. This...." she took off, Danril joining her moments later, "this is a different freeness, like the world's burdens have lifted."

"Remember this feeling, Ari. Hold tight to it and try seeking it out." He went silent, his mind on Jenna.

"You were thinking of her, weren't you?" she asked. He nodded, but didn't say anything else until they reached the clearing.

"I was yes," he said, stretching his arms. "Thinking about how much she would've loved the scene in the market this afternoon."

"Is she why you live life the way you do now?" she asked, turning away to wipe her face.

"Yes," he said, looking up at the sky. "No more words for now. The moon is waiting for us." Ari nodded and looked up, feeling the rays of the moon lighting up her skin. "Shall we dance, little one?"

Ari took his hand, and they moved to the center of the clearing. As the moon moved about the sky, they moved through the glade, performing a dance as old as the Fae themselves to honor the moon, from whom they drew their power. They moved and twirled around, the glow of their wings trailing through the night sky like shimmery butterflies. They continued their fluid movements, eventually both of them rising into the night sky where they ended the dance.

As they sank back toward the world, Ari closed her eyes and wondered what it would be like to have a person change her like that. The thought clearly had her face twisted up in puzzlement and she wasn't fast enough to shove the thoughts into a box before Danril noticed.

"What's that look for?" he asked as their feet touched the ground. Ari shook her head and let herself sink into the soft grass. "You've always been terrible at hiding things from me Ari."

"Just wondering what it would be like to share a moment like this with someone special," she said, looking up at the moon and the stars.

"It's an absolutely wonderful feeling," Danril said, sitting beside her. "Because it becomes something for just the two of you, a special moment you share. While I do enjoy spending time with you little one, I won't lie and say it's the same as sharing this Moon Dance ritual with Jenna, even if we had you tagging along."

"Only because Simeon told you not to leave me unattended at the order."

"It was two hours, and you nearly burned down the storage shed. I still don't understand how you managed that."

"I miss having her around," Ari said, looking up at the moon again.

"As do I," Danril said, putting his arm around her shoulders. "What else is on your mind, Ari?"

"How'd you know?" she asked, leaning against his shoulder. "You know what, don't answer that." She sniffled and wiped her face with her hand again. "Do you ever think it's my fault Jenna died?"

"What do you mean?" Danril asked. "Ari, are you asking me if I hold you responsible for Jenna's death?"

"Well, yes," she said, a sick feeling in her stomach forming. "You were supposed to meet her the night she died."

"Ah, yes, you were having one of your episodes that night, I remember." He gave her shoulder a squeeze. "You had no control over that, and if I'm not mistaken, Matron said that one nearly killed you."

"It was the one that made it impossible for me to even conceive a child. Why didn't you go anyway?"

"Because you needed me. Your body rejected four other blood donors that night. Only two people in the order are compatible, me and Simeon and he was visiting Pertina that week. Jenna would've understood little one. I don't blame you. I solely blame the man who put her in that position in the first place." He stroked her hair. "Now, if you ask me if she's the reason I'm on sabbatical, the answer is yes."

"Will you ever go back?" she asked, looking at him. "Or would you stay on sabbatical forever?"

"I haven't decided," he said after a while. "Retirement isn't an option for us, so I may just choose to live out my time protecting the prince." He looked down at Ari. "One thing is for sure, that whatever you choose to do in life, I will probably go with you."

"Why?" she asked, confused. "You have a chance to be rid of me. I've done nothing but give you those silver streaks in your hair."

"You'd be surprised how many women like the streaks," he said, causing her to groan. "But for as much hell as you've put me through and that I've put you through, we need each other."

"We do?" Ari looked even more confused than she did a minute ago. "Nobody's ever needed me."

"Yes. I needed you. I needed you to show me what I was like, how to better myself. But most importantly, I needed you to become the missing piece of my family. The one I'd created for myself where I had none. The sister I never had that I didn't know I needed." The dam burst on Ari's tears for the second time in two days. Danril put an arm around her shoulder, and they sat there for a while until she'd let the tears run their course. "People find value in you, just remember that."

"Thank you," she said, a little hoarsely. "I didn't realize how much I truly meant to someone until just now and I don't know what I would do without having you around. I...." she stopped, feeling like she'd be opening herself up to the world's biggest cosmic joke if she continued.

"You what?" he asked, squeezing her shoulder. Ari decided to throw caution and common sense to the wind and continued on.

"I feel like I gained a small piece of family too," she said timidly. "Thank you for not giving up on me." He smiled and stood, pulling her to her feet.

"We should get back. Heaven knows what kind of mood the queen will be in should you ignore a summons."

"She will get over it," Ari said with a deep sigh. "She'd have to, Shadow and Blade business and all."

"That's a bold claim to make, little one," he said as they flew up over the trees and back towards Thannid. "Though not wrong. What if you have no summons?"

"Then I supposed I shall go sit in the gardens. The night is clear, and not too cold. I would like to enjoy the fall air for a while."

"Don't make yourself sick, though," he said. "Wear a sweater."

"You sound just as a father should," Ari said, with a light laugh. Danril's nose crumpled in irritation.

"Ari Penndra, I am not that old, you take it back," he called as she sped away from him, laughing.

The moon was still high in the sky when they returned to the castle. Danril bid her a good night and headed inside, exhausted. Ari would've teased him, but she too was feeling sort of sleepy, even though her brain was running a million miles an hour again. She headed into the garden and ducked through the lilacs to a small patch of grass just big enough for one person to sit. However, much to her surprise, she found Finn there.

"Oh, I didn't know someone else knew of my spot," she said, going to crawl back out. He reached out and grabbed her arm, tugging lightly.

"No, stay," he said quietly. "I'd be glad for the company."

"I'm not sure what kind of company I am, especially after leaving you hanging last night," she said. "I should probably apologize for that."

"Why? You did nothing wrong, though I would've rather liked the company last night." He moved slightly so she could fit herself in there better. "But I understand why. I did act spoiled and dismissive of your experiences, and I'm sorry."

"I reacted harshly when I shouldn't have," she said, folding herself into a position most wouldn't call comfortable. "My experiences are usually not the same as the world at large. I often forget that." She adjusted to get a branch out of her back. "And I often come at the world with a chip on my shoulder, angry when I shouldn't be because someone didn't have to fight to stay alive as I did."

"Everyone fights differently," he said, looking at her. "Even someone who shares your experiences fought differently to stay alive." Ari looked at him and blinked repeatedly, going from shock to puzzlement to eventually anger, Finn was suddenly wishing he'd kept his mouth shut. "I didn't mean to upset you. I'm sorry if I did."

"No. I never saw it that way and I'm mad at myself for thinking selfishly," she said, placing her hand over his to reassure him, only to immediately pull it back when she felt a shock on her hand. "Ouch," she said, shaking it.

"Are you ok?" he asked, carefully reaching out and taking her hand. She braced herself but there was no shock.

"I'm fine," she said, looking at her hand in his. "Just felt like something shocked me." She made no effort to move her hand from his as she looked at him. "Where was I?"

"You were talking about thinking selfishly," he said, placing her hand between his to warm it. "You're also chilled."

"I'll be fine," she said as the breeze came by and sent shivers down her back.

"Oh, don't be a martyr," he said, carefully working out of his sweater and handing it to her.

"Won't you get cold?" she asked, shrugging it on. He laughed and held out his hand.

"Not likely, since every Ophir is a fire Fae," he said, conjuring a small flame in his hand. "Though nobody can tell you why mine are black and red."

Ari stared at the flame in fascination, her hand moved on its own toward it. The searing heat against the tips of her fingers brought her back to reality very quickly.

"Fuck," she said. "Those are hotter than any conjured flames I've ever encountered."

"Are you ok?" he asked again, taking the injured hand. "It doesn't look like they'll blister, but we should put some salve on them just in case."

"Trust me to go playing with fire, literally," she said, tongue in cheek, causing him to snort as he started out of the little cove of lilacs. "Oh, you were serious about the salve."

"Uh, yes," he said, motioning her out. "Do you want to be the one to tell my mother you can't go do her bidding because you can't hold a knife properly?"

"You win this round," she said, following him out. "Why were you out here anyway?"

"Mother was on another one of her ragers. I decided I didn't want to be easily found. So I snuck out here."

"Is she still raging?" Ari asked as she straightened up. Finn shrugged. "She rarely comes to my room if you want to avoid her."

"How scandalous," he whispered, "inviting the princeling back to your room."

"Do you want to get caught up in her tirade?" Ari asked as they entered the castle. Finn shook his head. "Then hush up and follow me."

Finn learned a surprising amount about the secret passageways in Tena Castle as Ari guided him through them to her room. With a quick check to make sure nobody was watching, she ushered him into her room and shut the door.

"Interesting organization style," he said, picking his way through the mess of clothes. "Though I do know most people prefer to keep their clothes in the wardrobe."

"Yeah, yeah, it's a mess," she said, grabbing a couple of piles. "But at least the couch is clear."

"Ignore the piles and bring me the salve," he said. "Or better yet, sit your ass down and tell me where it is." When she didn't stop, he walked over, took the clothes out of her arms, dropped them, and then picked her up and dropped her on her bed.

"Excuse me," she said, a bit breathlessly, "what the fuck was that?"

"You don't listen well, do you?" he asked, as he wandered into the bathroom.

"What gave you the impression I did at all?" she asked as she sat up. He came back from the bathroom with a jar in hand.

"Give me your hand," he said as he sat next to her. She held out her hand so he could carefully apply the salve. She flinched slightly as his hand brushed over the burned skin. "Sorry," he said as he finished. "Does it feel ok?"

"It'll be fine," she said as he closed the jar and put it away. He returned with a roll of bandages and wrapped it around her hand. "What are you doing now?"

"Taking care of you. It was my flame that burned you."

"But it was my stupidity that burned me," she argued.

"So?" He finished with the bandage and looked at her. "It's not too tight, is it?" She shook her head. "Good. Are you hungry?" She was going to say no, just to get him to stop asking questions, but her stomach rumbled. "I'll be right back."

"Finn, it's fine," she called but it was too late. The door closed, and she slumped against the pillows. After a few minutes of grumbling, she sat up and tried pulling his sweater off. She was halfway out of it when the door opened, and he came back in.

"Are you planning to pick up where you left off last night?" he asked, forcing himself to look away.

"What are you talking about?" she asked as she finally disentangled herself from it and looked at him.

"Might want to fix your shirt, sweetheart," he said, eyes flicking back to her and away again quickly.

"Wha..." she looked down and quickly fixed her shirt so everything was covered. "That didn't happen."

"Uh huh," he said, unable to erase the image from his mind. "Four years I've wondered. Guess I don't have to anymore."

"That's not funny, Finnian Ophir," she said, lobbing a pillow at him. He dodged it and laughed.

"Says the woman who was two steps away from taking me to bed last night," he shot back, setting a plate of food on the bed between them. "My mother aside, what else stopped you last night?"

"Honestly," she said, picking up a piece of cheese, "I saw more than just physical attraction when you looked at me. Fear of your mother is a key factor, but we both know I don't feel the same way you do."

"So?" He took her unbandaged hand and laced his fingers with hers. "Kind of sounds like that's my problem to figure out."

Ari sighed and looked at her hand, unable to stop herself from noticing how soft it was against her calloused palm. "Are you sure? I don't want you to go into this thinking you'll be able to sway my mind, make me want something I don't."

"I'd be lying if I didn't say I'd hope for a different outcome, but I'll be satisfied with what I can get for now," he said, reaching over to brush her hair out of her face. "But you don't seem very sure of this right now."

"Because I'm not. I don't know what I want. What I do know is how everything felt last night, how badly I wanted to stay and finish what I started, and I cannot tell you why." She blew out her breath and ran her bandaged hand over her hair.

"Would you rather go slow? I don't have any expectations, Ari." He squeezed her hand as she leaned against his hand.

"I don't know," she said as he slid the plate out of the way. "I'm never unsure about anything, so why am I now?"

"I can't answer that," he said as he laid back, pulling her onto his chest. "What I can tell you is that if you're unsure, you shouldn't be doing this."

"Says the man who just pulled me onto his chest," she retorted, though she couldn't help but notice how sturdy yet soft he felt. "You make a good pillow."

"Do I now?" he asked as he curled his other arm around her. "I'm always amazed by how tiny you really are."

"I'm not that small," she protested as he picked her up and moved so he lay stretched out on her bed.

"Ari, you are a finely honed assassin but you're a foot shorter than me and you weigh at least fifty pounds less than I do. You're tiny. You just have a personality that makes you seem so much bigger than you really are."

"Hey, just because I'm short doesn't mean I cannot do the job. It's actually beneficial at times."

"I have no doubt of it," he said, pulling her hair band out and tossing it on her table. They lapsed into silence, Finn just stroking his hand along her back. She had nearly fallen asleep when he ran his fingers along her spine just right, causing her to twitch in such a way that her wings extended, covering them both. "Whoops," he said, as they were suddenly bathed in the golden glow of her wings. "Though I'm not surprised your wings are gold. Everything about you shines."

"Flattery will get you nowhere," she said, shaking her shoulders so they disappeared again.

"But it does get you to lower your defenses enough for me to do this," he said, cupping her chin and pressing his lips to hers. She stiffened momentarily and then relaxed, her bandaged hand coming to rest on his cheek.

"You know your mother would kill us if she caught us," she murmured sleepily as he pulled back.

"Let her try," Finn said. "In fact, fuck what she thinks. I'm happy right now, probably the happiest I've ever been. She's not taking that from me."

"You can afford that luxury," Ari said with a yawn as she laid her head against his chest. "No matter who said what, I don't think I could count on the Shadow to save me."

"So, then we keep it a secret," Finn said. "This," he said, wrapping his arms around her, "this is something I've wanted for quite some time."

"I wouldn't mind more of this," she said, her eyes finally drifting shut. "But do you really think we can keep her from finding out?" She was too tired to add how, for the first time in a while, she felt safe.

"For a time, yes," Finn said, brushing a strand of hair that had escaped. "Hopefully long enough for me to convince you to give me a chance beyond something just purely physical."

"I admire your optimism," she said, her voice trailing off. Finn laid there as she fell asleep, letting the gentle rise and fall of his chest lull her into a deep, peaceful sleep.

The fire crackling in the hearth was the only sound in the room, and it kept Finn company as he watched the sleeping assassin on his chest. He knew his mother could make their lives difficult, hell in his mind she already made it difficult for Ari, but as he looked at her, taking in how small and vulnerable she looked, he knew that there was no one else he would rather be with. As the first rays of sun peeked through her curtains, his eyes finally drifted shut, falling asleep with his arms curled around her protectively.

Chapter 6

IT WASN'T THE MIDDAY sun that woke Finn, it was the muttering and tossing Ari was doing in her sleep, almost as if she was trying to get away from something. With an inadvertent elbow to his gut, she sat up and patted her arms, like she was trying to put out a flame. He groaned and sat up, rubbing his stomach as she was still reeling from the dream.

"Ari," he said quietly. "Is everything ok?"

"Huh?" she asked, turning around to see who was there. "Finn?"

"Yeah," he said, putting his arms around her and pulling her next to him. "What was that about?" He could tell she was still trying to calm herself down. "Don't you dare tell me it was nothing. Your heart is racing, you're breathing like you just ran for your life and you're shaking."

"Just a nightmare," she whispered eventually. Finn didn't press for details as he just held her close. Ari would've fought to get free and get her sharpening stone but every time she looked at her hands, they were shaking too much.

"Just breathe, it's just a dream," he said in a low voice to calm her. He continued to murmur softly until she eventually fell back asleep.

The sun had nearly set when a soft knock came at her door, causing Finn to look up at it as it opened and Danril slipped in. Finn held a finger to his lips and pointed to the still sleeping Ari. Danril nodded and lit a fire and a lamp before coming to sit on the bed.

"Is she all right?" he asked, looking at her with some concern.

"Exhausted from what I can tell," Finn said, gently stroking her hair. "She woke up around midday from a nightmare."

"I wonder how often she's been having it again," Danril said, watching her chest rise and fall softly. "Nobody knows what it means either. It's not some sort of prophetic dream as far as anyone can tell."

"Memory of the past?" Finn asked as she stirred a little but didn't wake. "It's a common theme in stories."

"It's possible, but if it's a memory from the past, it's from before she was at the orphanage and the only event that occurred that would match the dream happened when she was a mere infant."

"It's worth considering. She's clearly struggling with it." Finn squeezed her hand as she mumbled something. "Could I ask you a favor?"

"You want me to lie for you, don't you?" Danril asked, looking at him. Finn's eyes narrowed. "I've been your protector and friend for four years, child, I know when you want me to lie for you. Why this time?"

"Because I'm going to be wholly irresponsible and steal her for a day or four," Finn said with a small grin.

"Finn, you're supposed to be in meetings with advisors and the merchant's guild tomorrow," Danril said, shaking his head. "What are you planning?"

"Getting her out of Thannid, maybe going to Tarka. They have that lively dance festival every month."

"Tarka huh?" Danril asked. "You know that's at least a day's journey. How long are you planning to be gone?"

"Three, four days," he said as she let out a small groan and stretched. "Little late to be waking up, isn't it?" he asked teasingly.

"Ugh, how late is it?" she asked, blinking. "What are you both doing here?"

"Well past sundown, little one," Danril said. "Nobody had seen either of you all day, which caused more than a few eyebrows to be raised, but nobody said anything to the queen." He paused while she yawned and got up to change from her town clothes into loose fitting cloth pants and Finn's sweater. "Ari, are you ok? You've been spending a lot more time sleeping through the day again. You're not...?" He stopped and looked at her, not sure if he should continue.

"No, I'm not on the verge of an episode," she said, tying her hair back in a loose ponytail. "I thought Matron Crifveiw made it so I wouldn't have another."

"She said there would be a slight chance one could happen as you got older," he said, while Finn looked on, confused. "You're acting like you used to before you had one. Withdrawn, sullen, sleeping a lot. It's got me worried, little one."

"Danril, I'm fine," she said, sitting back down. "I'm a little hungry, but fine. My last mission really took it out of me, that's all."

"I'm gonna keep an eye on you," he said, looking at her with narrowed eyes.

"You can do that, after I eat," she said, pulling on a pair of soft bottomed shoes. "I'm absolutely starving."

"How about I go grab you something and you rest. I'm not taking chances with you Ari," Danril said, getting up. Ari looked at him but decided not to argue. "Good. I'll be back in a bit. Behave you two." He left before Ari could even stick her tongue out at him while Finn waited for him to leave before speaking.

"What is he talking about, your episodes?" Finn asked as she sat on the bed beside him.

"You know how I told you I'd give up my food for two other kids last night?" she asked as he took her bandaged hand and slowly began to unwrap it. He paused and nodded before returning to the task. "Well, apparently doing that too many times messed up how parts of my body function, from my magic never manifesting to that monthly time all women get happening in a way that nearly caused me to bleed out repeatedly."

"When's the last time that happened?" he asked, examining her hand.

"My twenty-second year, so four years ago." Ari looked at her and then at Finn. "Seems you were right about the salve." Finn didn't say anything. "What's wrong?"

"What does that mean for you, about kids?" he asked slowly.

"Whatever Matron Criftview had to do to save my life the last time made it so I wouldn't be able to," Ari said. "And before you drag out the pity, don't. I never wanted a child."

"Because of how you were raised?" he asked, carefully lacing his fingers with hers. She nodded. "I understand that. I don't want to have a child either."

It was Ari's turn to stare, almost dumbfoundedly as Danril came back in with a meager meal for the both of them. She barely acknowledged his presence as she blinked repeatedly, letting Finn's words soak in.

"You're the heir of Thenndin. What do you mean you don't want a child?" she asked eventually.

"Ah, I see we're having this conversation," Danril said. "Ari, where's the whiskey? I know you keep some in your room."

"Wardrobe, second shelf, next to the sharpening kit," she said, still looking at Finn as Danril brought the bottle over. "Well?" she asked Finn again.

"I know my mother, she isn't going to give up the throne. Even if I do get my turn, I don't want it. I don't want to have all that pressure and fuck if I want to pass on my mother's legacy."

"That makes a lot of sense," Ari said, taking the bottle from Danril and taking a swig.

"Yeah so it's a pass on an heir for me," he said as Ari passed him the bottle. "What about you Danril? No kids?"

"No. Once I thought maybe, but not now." He took the bottle from Finn and took a large swig. "Enough depressing talk. I've managed to convince a few servants to spread it around that you're not feeling well and are heading south for a few days."

"Oh, really?" Ari took the bottle back and looked at Finn. "Avoiding your royal responsibilities for a few days?"

"Well, yes, but I was also planning to make you come with me," he said, causing her to choke on the swallow she took.

"Excuse me?" she sputtered. "Me? Your mother will have my head."

"I've already been in contact with Lord Simeon. He's agreed to concoct some official order business to get her off your back."

"You what now?" Ari raised a brow and looked at the two of them. "Were you planning on asking me or just dragging me off?"

"I think just dragging you off is the proper answer," Danril said, "since you wouldn't have gone anyway. Eat something child." Ari glared but scarfed down her plate. "Think of it as training on being normal."

"Fine, but we should hurry before the queen gets wind of this and shuts us in." Danril and Finn nodded and stood to leave. However, before he left, Finn put his hands on either side of Ari's face and kissed her and then patted her cheek and left with Danril. Ari blinked and stared, trying to figure out why her stomach had just dropped to her knees.

Finn had just finished packing when a knock came at his door. Believing it to be Danril, he bade them enter, only to be surprised when his mother walked in.

"To what do I owe this unwanted intrusion?" he asked as he closed and secured the flap on his pack.

"A little bird told me you were leaving. I had dismissed it as pure foolishness but now I see there's truth to the rumor."

"I'm going to Tarka for a few days because I don't feel well," he said irritably. "I need some time away, a change of scenery, anything, anywhere is better than this gilded cage."

"Gilded cage?" Tatiana raised a brow. "You know why I keep you at the castle."

"And I'm not a child anymore mother," he shot back. "I'm approaching my twenty-ninth year. I am more than capable of making my own decisions. So, if I want to spend a few days in Tarka without you breathing down my neck, that's my choice."

"And I'm to believe that is pure coincidence that The Shadow and Blade suddenly has an urgent mission for my assassin down in that area?"

"I have no control over what the lord of The Shadow and Blade does with his people," Finn said evenly. "If you have an issue with it, I suggest you take it up with him."

"Do you really think I don't see what you all are playing at? That I can't see through Simeon's ploy to undermine me?"

"I think you need to be less paranoid," Finn said, grabbing his pack and a jacket.

"Finnian, you are not leaving this castle," she yelled as he put his hand on the doorknob.

"I'm a grown man and I am doing this," he said as she began to rage and throw things. "I will do whatever and whomever I want, and I'm done letting you control me."

"You're going to regret that decision," she said as she picked up the dagger-like letter opener from his table and flung it with an accuracy that even Ari would've marveled at. He grunted as it landed in his shoulder. "Enjoy Tarka."

"I will. And I highly doubt I will ever regret this decision. I do regret not doing it sooner," he said, pulling the letter opener from his shoulder. "I'll be back in a few days." The letter opener fell to the floor with a clatter, and he left, closing the door hard.

"Do you think he's ok?" Ari asked as the first tinges of pink graced the sky. The early dawn hours were cold and even in a warm jacket, she shivered against the chill.

"I'm sure he's fine," Danril said as he rubbed his hands together for warmth. "Are you concerned?"

"What?" Ari looked panicked. "No, of course not. I mean…" she trailed off as Danril laughed. "What's funny?"

"You grappling with your emotions. It's ok to be concerned. Especially if Queen Tatiana found out." Finn chose that moment to walk toward them with his pack in one hand, his other held close to his body and a pained expression on his face. "And I'd say she found out."

"Shit," Ari muttered as they rushed forward, Danril taking Finn's weight and Ari taking his pack. "What happened?"

"You're bleeding," Danril said, feeling the sticky blood. "In the coach."

"It's not as bad as it looks," he muttered as they climbed in. "Just a scratch."

"Shut up," Ari said, rummaging through her pack. "Danril, light?" A blue flame illuminated the inside of the carriage as Ari located her field kit and a bottle of clear liquid.

"What are you doing?" Finn asked as he felt part of his shirt fall away.

"Field medicine," Ari replied as she examined the puncture. "This wasn't a knife, was it?"

"Letter opener," he said. "What do you mean by field medicine?"

"Let her focus," Danril said before answering the rest of his question. "My healing abilities extend to superficial wounds only. Ari's magic is limited to glimmer to conceal herself and occasionally a light if she focuses hard enough. However, you're looking at the best field medic the order has."

"You can pass out after I'm done," she said as she dipped a rag in the clear liquid. "Hold him." Danril held the prince down with his free arm as Ari placed the rag to the wound. Finn howled in pain as the liquid burned.

"What the fuck was that?" he asked as the area slowly went numb.

"A cleaning and numbing agent. Matron Criftview created it for me specifically."

"Why?" he asked as she threaded a needle. "What are you doing now?"

"Sewing the wound shut, now let me focus." Ari went silent as she began to sew. It was Danril who answered Finn's other question.

"Paired teams with Shadow and Blade are meant to complement each other. Because of Ari's upbringing leading to her inability to access the magic she may or may not possess, special measures had to be taken. Ari learned field medicine to compensate because my own healing magic lacks."

"Fascinating," Finn said, looking at Ari as she concentrated. Her face scrunched up in deep thought as she meticulously placed each stitch. Eventually, she put the needle aside and grabbed the bandages.

"I'll need to check it and probably change these when we get to Tarka. For now, you should rest."

"Thank you," Finn said, letting his eyes close. The gentle rocking of the carriage eventually lulled him to sleep. Ari sank against the carriage wall and blew out a breath.

"How bad is it really?" Danril asked.

"Either Tatiana knows about as much as we do when it comes to where and how to stab someone, or she got incredibly lucky. The letter opener missed major vessels. It's gonna hurt, but he wasn't bleeding enough to require the intervention of a healer."

"That's good news," Danril said. "And given the rumors that circulate around Tatiana, I wouldn't be surprised if she knows how to inflict maximum pain without excessive bloodshed."

"Either way, the fact that she's willing to do this to her own son, what would she do to me?" Ari looked scared. "I can't have Shadows watching my every move while I'm on a mission."

"I think you're reading too much into things," Danril said. "Unless there's something you're not telling me." He watched as her face crinkled up in a frown. "I'm teasing, child."

"I know," she said as she stretched out a leg, leaving one knee bent with her hands resting on her knee.

"I sense you have questions, but I don't think I'm the person you need to ask," he said. "Try and get some rest. We'll be in Tarka by nightfall." She nodded and closed her eyes, not sleeping but just letting the sounds calm her racing mind.

Tarka loomed on the horizon, but the lively sounds of a festival woke Finn long before they entered the city. He groaned and tried to sit up, only to let out a growl of pain as his shoulder suddenly reminded him of the injured area.

"Fucking gods," he muttered as Danril leaned over to help him up. "That fucking hurts."

"You were lucky," Ari said, eyes still closed. "Another two inches and it would've needed a healer. I'll look at it after we get settled and give you something for the pain."

"You speak like you've done this on more than one occasion," Finn said as he worked his jacket on.

"I've patched my share of people back up," she replied as they rolled into town. "Enough that Matron would send people to me that didn't need more than a few stitches."

The carriage rolled to a stop in front of their destination, leaving Finn with little time to ponder this new facet of Ari. Voices outside the carriage had them both cringing because they had no good way to explain the blood that covered Ari's hands or the specks of it that dotted the carriage seat. The door opened, and a footman appeared.

"We had no time to prepare the villa for your arrival, Master Finnian," he said in a deep voice.

"I'm sure my companions and I will manage just fine," Finn said, trying to hide how much pain he was in. "I don't mean to be pushy Darion, but we've been traveling all day and we're road worn and hungry."

"Of course, sire, the maids have prepared a light dinner when your carriage was spotted. Can we do anything else?" Darion asked.

"No, thank you Darion," Finn said as he climbed out and held out a hand for Ari, who took it and climbed down next to him, causing Darion to step back.

"Your Highness this is highly improper," he said, taking in Ari's appearance.

"Stick a cork in it, Darion because I don't give a shit," he said as Danril climbed out. "We'll be here for at least the rest of the week."

"Very well, sire. I am obligated to send word to your mother."

"You're not obligated to do shit for her when she's not here," Finn called after him. "Plus, it's just a waste of time. She's aware of all of this."

"Then I shall leave you to your own devices," he said as they went in separate directions.

"The whole town is going to know I bought a paramour by the end of the night," he said, shaking his head as they headed down a hallway toward a couple of rooms. "I'm sorry."

"We'll figure it out after I look at that shoulder," Ari said. "You can be an ass when you're in pain."

"I'm sorry. I'm tired, hungry and this hurts," he said as he stopped in front of a door. "And now I've put you in an awkward position."

"And like I said, we'll talk about it, after I look at the shoulder," she said, opening the door and nudging him in. "Of course, Danril disappeared."

Finn let out a wry chuckle as she shut the door behind them. The room flooded with light moments later and a small fire was started to chase the chill from the room. Ari went to clean her hands of the blood from earlier while Finn struggled out of his jacket before he, too, went into the bathroom to look at it for himself.

"That shirt's completely ruined," she said as she finished drying her hands. "I'd burn it if you don't want sir stick in his ass to find out about it."

Finn laughed and nodded before he tried taking it off. After watching him struggle, Ari came over and helped him out of it. She balled it up, trying to keep the red from rising in her cheeks as she took it and threw it in the fireplace where it quickly burned. Ari wasn't a prude, she'd seen her fair share of chests, but his was chiseled and defined in a way that didn't scream hard labor, but dedication to training, something she couldn't help but appreciate. When she returned, she kept her gaze neutral even though her head was racing with various thoughts.

"Something wrong?" he asked, watching her as she moved behind him to look at his shoulder.

"Yeah, you're too damn tall," she said, shaking out her wings before she rose the few inches she needed to get a good look at the wound. "Let me know if it's uncomfortable," she said as she carefully peeled off the bandages. He hissed as the adhesive tugged at his skin but held still as she examined the stitches, occasionally poking at them. "The stitches are going to hold. They'll be ready to come out sometime after we get back to Thannid," she said, sinking down. "I'll leave them uncovered if you want to clean up."

"I hate to ask, but could you help me clean it up back there?" He looked a little sheepish at having to ask.

"Tall ask," she said, teasing as she went and got a clean rag and some warm water before she rose those few inches again and carefully wiped the blood away from the wound. Finn shuddered lightly as her fingers occasionally brushed over his exposed skin. She eventually put the rag in the basin and began to sink back down when he turned and wrapped his arms around her waist, pulling her close to him. "A simple thank you would suffice," she whispered, her heart beating rapidly.

"It would, but that's not what I'm after," he whispered huskily before he kissed her. There was no softness, no tenderness. It was all primal need, a need Ari shared because she found herself matching his intensity. He paused to catch his breath and looked at her. "Are you sure?" he asked. She nodded and to prove her point, she kissed him again, the need just as intense as it had been. Finn didn't waste another breath as he carried her out of the bathroom and to bed, where they both got lost in need and passion.

There was always that one little sliver of sun, Ari thought as she burrowed under the blanket and against Finn, who barely stirred. She wasn't surprised, given how intense they'd been in bed last night. That coupled with the shoulder wound and Ari wasn't expecting him to be up anytime before midday, which didn't bother her any, if she was being forced to take a few days off, she was going to make the most of her ability to do absolutely nothing. Or that was her plan until someone started pounding on the door. She groaned, disentangled herself from both Finn and the blankets, and found a robe in the closet before she went and pulled the door open to find Danril there. He stopped for a moment as he took in her appearance, his mind trying to make sense of what had happened.

"What Danril?" she asked, crossing her arms in front of her.

"Ari, who's at the door?" Finn asked sleepily as he too appeared, wearing a robe. "Oh, Danril. Did we miss some plans?"

"No, but I think I interrupted something," he said, rubbing his forehead.

"Just me sleeping in," Finn said with another yawn. "Is something the matter?"

"Only that you're about to miss breakfast. But judging by what I'm seeing, that's probably not an issue."

"Maybe you should take these few days and find some of your own," Ari said, teasing him.

"I swear, you are going to make me regret ever bringing the subject up around you aren't you," he said, cringing a little.

"Serves you right," she said as he came in and closed the door. "What's really going on? You don't try to break down the door like that unless something's going on."

"Oh, nothing's wrong, I just know if nobody gets your ass out of bed, you'd spend all day in it," Danril said, looking at her with a raised brow. "You're here to experience life, not stay in bed for three or four straight days."

"Spoilsport," she grumbled, going to her pack. "Fine. Give us twenty minutes and we'll be down for breakfast."

"Anything past that and I'm dragging you down to breakfast myself," he said, turning to leave.

Finn waited until the door shut before looking at her. "We were supposed to have a conversation last night weren't we," he said with a sigh. "I certainly screwed that up."

"It's safe to say the blame lies with both of us for that," she said, pulling out a change of clothes. "But yes, we were supposed to have a conversation."

"We really only have a couple of choices. Either we pretend last night never happened and somehow convince the town we're really not lovers or we lean into it."

"What's going to be easier, for you?" she asked, putting her clothes aside as she pulled out her field kit again and grabbed a small vial. "Take one of these, it'll ease the pain you're about to feel in that shoulder."

"Easier for me? Lean into it, but you've known my feelings since the night we met in the bar." He swallowed the capsule and grimaced. "I sense you have questions about that too."

"Just one. You answer it, and I'll go along with pretending to be your partner for the duration we're in Tarka. Maybe longer if you're really wanting to piss your mother off."

"The longer we do it, the more likely I will grow too attached and that could lead to other problems," he said. "If by the time we leave Tarka, you're still only on a physical level, then I will not expect anything else. Now, your question?"

"What is it you see in me that makes you feel the way you do?" she asked. "I've never presented the court with anything other than the cold, heartless assassin who would rather not be serving the queen. I purposely make myself cold and uncaring, so I don't get attached and people can't get attached to me. When did I present myself as anything but?"

"You realize you asked me more than one question right?" he asked with a half smile.

"Fine, I had two questions. Now, how about you answer them?"

"That makes three," he said, dodging her swat. "But since you asked so nicely, I'll answer. Have you ever seen yourself when you're around a person you trust, which I realize is simply Danril, but you're not that cold person you sell the rest of the world. You laugh, you smile, you crack jokes, it's amazing. That's the person I want to be with, that's the person that makes my heart beat faster every time I see her."

"I thought Danril was the only person who'd ever seen that side of me," she said quietly. "I didn't know you'd seen it."

"I'm really good at being quiet and staying out of sight. Had to with my mother, especially when she would lose her temper." He carefully put his hand to her face, caressing her cheek with his thumb. "It's the Ari the whole world should get to know, it's the Ari I want to get to know more of."

"It's not a side I let out very often. It requires a level of trust that doesn't come easily," she said quietly, leaning against his hand, enjoying the feel of his soft skin against her cheek.

"I understand. I had hoped that some day I might be one of those people," he said, brushing his lips over hers. "For now, if I've answered your question..."

"You did," she said, "satisfactorily as well. For the duration of our stay in Tarka, I will pretend to be your partner." He smiled at her and kissed her forehead before going to change.

Ari watched him disappear into the bathroom while she grabbed her clothes and changed, his words racing around her mind. Could she allow herself to trust yet another person? The question weighed heavily on her mind as they went down for breakfast before they left to go to explore the town for the day.

Chapter 7

A RI HAD BEEN EVEN quieter during breakfast than normal, something that caused Danril to raise a brow. She had barely smirked at his jokes and hadn't responded to any of his teasing attempts. As they prepared to head into town, he pulled her aside and looked her over.

"What's the problem?" he asked, finally getting a good look at her expression.

"I asked a question I wasn't sure I wanted the answer to," she replied. "Now I have it and I don't know how to proceed."

"I'm gonna regret this, but what was the question?" Danril asked, heaving a big sigh.

"I asked Finn what he liked about me. The bastard's as good as we are at sticking to the shadows because he's caught me in a relaxed state goofing around with you."

"Ah, so he likes the authentic Ari, not the shitty facade she puts on for the world, what a surprise," Danril said dryly. "So now what?"

"Fuck if I know. Nobody's seen that part of me but you," she said, "and with good reason. The more people that care about me, the more people I inevitably let down when something goes wrong."

"All two of us," he responded in the same dry tone. "And maybe a handful that would be disappointed at Shadow and Blade. But that's part of life, child. It's all part of the experience. You'll just hurt him by keeping yourself from getting hurt. Give it the three days we're here. If you're not convinced you can trust him to be yourself, then let him down gently." Ari nodded as Finn joined them. She took a deep breath and took his outstretched hand.

"You ok with this?" he asked, moving a strand of hair behind her ear.

"I'm fine," she said, smiling. "You have three days to prove that I can trust you with this part of me."

"Then I best get to work," he said with a grin. Danril rolled his eyes as they headed into town, where the festival was still in full swing.

The mood in town was infectious, and even soon the stoic Ari was laughing and smiling. At some point, Danril slipped away, leaving the two of them alone. Ari knew it was necessary, and Finn was delighted. He was so delighted that Ari couldn't help but liken his mood to that of a giddy schoolboy.

"You're in quite a good mood," she said as they passed by a vendor selling sweet buns. She took a deep breath, letting the scent of them fill her nose. "Those don't smell like the ones in Thannid."

"I don't think I've ever had one," he said, looking at her.

"Crimes," she said, pulling him over and getting two berry filled buns.

Finn took the bun and took a bite, and his eyes doubled in size. "These are delicious."

"One of my favorite snacks," she said, mouth full. "Though the merchants in Thannid usually just have the apple kind. Berry is very rare."

"The climate isn't right that far north for berries," Finn said, having made short work of his bun. "But apples grow nicely."

"That makes a lot of sense, given how close Thannid is to the Pertina border," she said as they continued to stroll down the marketplace. As they walked along, Ari watched Finn carefully, noticing how his eyes darted to and fro, and how he looked like he was having to restrain himself. "You look like I did when I got my first stipend from the Shadow and Blade," she said. "It took a lot of restraint not to buy all the things I wanted to as a small child."

"There's just so much. Until I was in my sixteenth year, my mother kept me hidden in the castle, not allowing me out, even under supervision."

"But you've snuck out," Ari said, looking up at him curiously.

"Routinely, but it wasn't ever the same." She waited for him to elaborate, but he didn't. Her mood became sour, and it took Finn a moment to notice it. "Did I say something wrong?"

"Not really, but you did just assume I knew what you were talking about again," she said harsher than intended. "I didn't grow up royal, I grew up fucking destitute."

"I'm sorry," he said. "I shouldn't have assumed you understood."

"I should not have snapped as harshly as I did," she said as she took his hand. "I'm sorry as well."

"For the happy couple?" a lady asked, holding out a rose.

"Thank you," Finn said, taking it. He broke the stem, removed a thorn, and then placed it in Ari's hair. "There. Red suits you. Most colors suit you."

"It's the light color of my hair. You still owe me an explanation," she said, poking him in the chest.

"Right, sorry," he said as they continued walking. "I may have snuck out, but by no means was I out spending money or anything of the sort. In fact, it was rather hard to enjoy the freedom I stole for myself when I was looking over my shoulder for my mother's guards."

"Stolen moments are only good for so long," she said as they walked along. "That I know."

They lapsed into silence, neither really saying much else. Finn was deep in thought about all the moments he may have lost from his childhood and that Ari may have lost as well while Ari was just strolling, enjoying the music. Eventually, Finn pulled her aside.

"Tell me one thing you wanted to do as a child that you never got the chance to do," he said before she could protest.

"What?" she asked, looking at him with narrowed eyes

"You heard me," he said, "c'mon, one thing."

"Fine, but we need to find a sweet shop," she said. "And a garden."

"Odd choices but ok," he said, grabbing her hand. They went off and found the sweet shop and then found themselves back at the villa, loaded down with boxes of sweets. She led him through the garden before coming to a stop at a large willow tree. "You wanna clue me in?"

"Tika, Cole and I used to sit under the only tree at the orphanage and talk about how when we found our homes that we'd eventually get together on a sunny day and eat sweets with the spending coin we'd get. Tika and Cole never lived long enough for us to do it. I barely lived long enough to be passed off to the Shadow and Blade. But before I left, I promised our tree in the courtyard I'd sit under one and eat those sweets for them."

Finn sniffled and wiped his eyes as he handed her a box. "I never had a friend I could do that with or make promises to. You may have grown up in poverty, but you grew up rich in other ways."

"We were each deprived in different ways," she said as she plucked a chocolate out of the box. "But really, if you think about it, we were both deprived of the emotional connections."

"And we both deal with that in very different manners," he said, taking a chocolate. "But when you've lost those close to you, I guess you'd want to keep yourself from ever hurting again."

"I wonder how much I lost because of that though," she said as she savored another chocolate.

"Maybe," he said as he leaned over and cupped her chin. He gently turned her to face him before leaning toward her, "you weren't meant to find it until you were ready."

"What makes you think I'm ready?" she asked, her golden eyes meeting his blue ones.

"If you weren't, would you have told me about your promise to your long dead childhood friends?" he asked before touching his lips to hers. Her face when he pulled away told him he was right. "You're not very good at hiding your emotions outside of your hard ass persona are you?"

"Shut up," she muttered, grabbing another chocolate and stuffing it in his mouth. He laughed through the bite and though try as she might, the muffled sound brought a smile to her lips. "Thank you for helping me do this."

"I could tell they meant a lot to you," he said as he slumped against the tree and put his head on her shoulder. "I think they'd be happy for you right now."

"Cole would be endlessly teasing me about you, and Tika would want all the dirty details. I miss them. Never realized it til now." She sniffed as tears slid down her cheeks.

"Don't hold it in," he said, sitting back up. "It's ok to grieve." Ari nodded as the tears fell faster. Finn put his arms around her and held her while she cried. The tears stopped eventually, and they gave way to exhaustion. Ari slumped over in his lap, her face tear stained and twisted with grief. "Just rest," he whispered to the sleeping assassin. "Let someone else carry the load for a bit." He stayed there basking in the autumn sun, watching over Ari while she slept.

They were still under that tree when Danril came back as the sun set, a grin on his face. He wandered the gardens, whistling, until he came upon them, a half-eaten box of chocolates next to Finn and a sleeping Ari in his lap. Danril paused, raised a brow, but didn't say anything as Ari's face scrunched in pain. He was about to kneel next to her when she sat up and scrambled away from Finn, her face flushed. Danril recognized the expression and motioned for Finn to wait a moment before he approached.

"What's going on?" Finn asked, looking between them. but mostly at Ari.

"Nightmare," Danril said. "Give her a moment."

Ari wanted to run, escape the heat that the nightmare always left lingering on her skin, but quiet familiar voices kept her where she was. As the fog of the dream cleared, she blinked and looked down at her hands and arms, which were visibly shaking again. Finn carefully reached out and took her shaking hands in his.

"Just breathe," he said quietly, rubbing her hands with his thumbs. Ari focused on her breath and the sensation of his thumbs running across the back of her hands. Eventually, her body relaxed, and she swayed, almost falling forward. Finn caught her and sank back on his heels. "Is everything ok?"

"It will be," she said, resting her head on his shoulder.

"What was that about?" he asked, adjusting them both so they would be much more comfortable.

"Just the same nightmare I've had for as long as I can remember," she said, her voice a little hoarse. "Danril, can you...?" she asked, her voice dropping to a whisper.

"If you're sure, little one," he said. Ari nodded. "Very well. It's the same thing, a raid by soldiers, the stealing of an infant, and the burning of a house. Always ends with her waking up, still experiencing the intense heat from the flames in her dream."

"And you're sure this isn't some deep memory of her past?" Finn asked.

"Like I've said, Finn, if it is, she would've been an infant when this occurred," Danril replied.

"When what occurred?" Ari asked, mustering enough energy to look at Danril.

"The burning of Ruedena," he said. "It's the only major event from your lifetime where a village burned."

"Why would I be dreaming of Ruedena?" she asked, laying her head back down. "It was so long ago."

"Twenty-six years little one," Danril said, patting her leg. "Don't read too much into it. I can see if Simeon can investigate it again if you wish."

"No, don't trouble the lord councilor," she said as the garden grew darker. "You both need to stop letting me sleep through midday."

"The body will take rest when it needs it," Finn said, getting to his feet with her. "That doesn't mean just when you're physically tired either." She harrumphed but allowed Finn to carry her inside to dinner, partially because she knew she was still too woozy from the dream, and partially because for once in her life, she felt safe.

The next day Finn and Ari took it easy, heading into town and just walking past the various stalls, eating fruit buns while talking about the things they would've bought. Danril, who wandered by as they were talking about one of the items at the stall, smiled at the conversation, happy to see her coming out of her shell.

The morning of day three, Finn dragged Ari out of the house almost immediately after breakfast and into the forest just outside of Tarka.

"Finn, what are we doing out here?" she asked as she rubbed her arms. "I didn't even get a chance to grab my sweater."

"You'll warm up in a bit," he said with a grin.

"What are you planning?" she asked, raising a brow.

"Catch me if you can," he said, reaching out and tapping her shoulder before taking off.

"You're going to regret this," she said, smirking as she took off after him. It wasn't long before she caught him and put her hand right on his back. "Your turn," she said, shaking out her wings and flipping around to avoid him swinging around and tagging her back.

"That's cheating," he said as she folded her wings back in and took off running. Her only response was to laugh as he chased her down.

They continued like this for most of the morning, until Finn decided to end the game in a more adult fashion. He waited until she'd gotten him again and gave her a bit of a head start before running after her. As he caught up to her, he grabbed her around the waist, and pulled her to the ground with him.

"Now who's cheating?" she asked as she landed on his chest.

"I win," he said with a smirk.

"Do you now?" she asked, as she tried wriggling out of his grasp. He'd prepared for that and held on to her tightly. "Apparently you do. So what do you want for a prize?"

"This," he said, pulling her head down to his and kissing her. "Though I know full well you let me win Ari."

"How so?" she asked, playing innocent.

"Because had you wanted to, you would've made it so I could never lay a finger on you."

"Hmm, that is true," she said, smirking. "It could be that I like feeling your hands on me though."

"Then darling," he said, cupping his hand around the back of her neck and pulling her closer, "just ask." He kissed her deeply again, enjoying feeling her against him as the rest of the afternoon passed without them realizing it, too absorbed in each other and the moment they'd created for themselves.

****

They returned for dinner that night very disheveled, leaves still in their hair. Danril came in a few minutes later and stifled a chuckle at the two of them as he sat down. He didn't say anything however, because he was thrilled to see Ari looking so happy. The cloud of destruction and despair that usually clung to her had finally disappeared, leaving this carefree young woman in its wake. But that wasn't all he saw, when he looked at her, he saw a softness in her eyes that only appeared when she looked at Finn. He smiled as he went back to his food, thinking about how happy he was for her and how much he missed Jenna.

"Are you thinking about her?" Ari asked, interrupting his thoughts.

"I am. How'd you know?" he asked, looking up at her.

"You have a look. Danril, it's been four years. She wouldn't want you to mourn forever."

"I know," he said, putting his fork down. "It's the last night here, what are you two planning on doing?"

"Probably checking out the dancing in town," Finn said as he finished his last bites. "Unless you had other ideas Ari."

"No, that sounds nice," she said, putting down her fork.

"Then I think that settles it," Finn said. "What are you planning on doing?"

"I was planning on checking the dancing out as well. It does happen to be an old favorite pastime." Danril looked at Ari. "Not just mine either."

"You?" Finn asked, looking at Ari, who just nodded and wished she could kick Danril from across the table. "Perfect then. We should go get ready then."

"Sounds fun," Ari said, as they got up. Danril smirked at her as he fell into step next to her while Finn went on ahead. "I ought to deck you."

"He would've found out eventually. Better to be open about it than hide it child." She snorted but didn't argue, which Danril took to mean she agreed. "And you can't tell me I'm wrong. I've seen your face when we're in the clearing. You absolutely come alive."

"It's freeing ok," she said, grumpy. "It's one of the few times I feel good about myself."

"And the rest of this week?" he asked, nudging her. "You look like you've been feeling pretty good."

"He's easy to be around," she said, watching him for a moment. "He's gone out of his way to figure out things I wanted to do that I never got to. It's been a breath of fresh air and..." she trailed off.

"You don't want it to end," he finished for her. "Nobody said it had to."

"You really think we can get away with this stuff back at Tena Castle under the watchful eyes of the queen?"

"If you're more subtle about all of this, yes," he said before pulling her to a stop. "If you're truly happy and want things to continue, then do not let anyone or anything get in your way, Ari. Not even the queen."

"I'm not afraid of many people, Danril," Ari said quietly as they walked along slowly. "But I am afraid of her. I am afraid of leading us both to our deaths."

"I know," he said. "And that fear means you're not just going to throw caution to the wind. But don't be too cautious. Don't ruin the best thing that's probably happened to both of you."

"You know that means I shouldn't ever open my mouth again," she said as they stopped at the door to her and Finn's room. He smacked the back of her head lightly and shook his head. "You know I'm destined to put my foot in my mouth. How many times did I get us in trouble with Lord Simeon just because I said something?"

"Fair point, so be smart. If you actually talk to the lad when you two have a problem, I don't think you can even destroy this." Danril ruffled her hair and pushed her toward the door. "Go get ready and Ari, just relax. The night isn't going to implode if you do." Ari entered the room, neither aware of just how wrong they were about to be.

****

While the trio prepared for the evening, in Thannid, the queen was sitting in her study, looking at a report from the captain of the secret police in regard to her son's activities in Tarka. Every last report included him being seen in town with her assassin who was supposed to be on some business for Shadow and Blade. Her attempts to speak to Simeon had resulted in a flurry of missives between the two with Simeon saying that Danril had asked for an extra hand in ensuring the prince's safety and that order business was none of her concern. The dismissal had irritated her endlessly, but the deceit angered her. The fact that her son, the one she'd been raising and grooming for years to be the final pawn in her ultimate move to take control of all the countries and be the supreme ruler, was running around and getting friendly, overly so, with this fucking whore of a commoner made her downright furious. Her father had instilled this love of power, this drive to be the only ruler of the lands and nobody was going to take her dream, not even Simeon's little bitch. Her thoughts were interrupted by a knock at the door. She looked up and glared at it before telling whoever dared to knock that they could enter.

"I do hope you'll forgive the interruption," the head of the police said.

"What?" she asked, clearly not pleased by his arrival.

"I have a new report from Darion," he said, placing it on her desk. "He reports that the prince is taking his common whore to the center of Tarka for the last night of their festival."

"I think it's beyond high time that she disappeared. Find your raiders from Trinda and have them head back there. Tell them they are to stir up trouble but not hurt anyone. I don't want any blood spilled but hers." Tatiana had a gleam in her eye that worried the captain.

"Milady?" he asked, confused as she grabbed her pen and wrote out something. "What's this?"

"A missive for Miss Penndra. Send it to Darion and have him deliver it to her. Tell your raiders to be ready in two days. They should try to ambush her when she arrives in the ghost town since she'll be exhausted."

"Even an exhausted Blade is a deadly one," he replied but took the missive from her all the same. "You do realize you invite war upon us if Lord Callwell finds out?"

"Then you best make sure Lord Callwell doesn't find out," Tatiana replied, her tone dismissing him. He nodded and left as quickly to make sure the message could get to Tarka as quickly as possible.

****

Drinks flowed freely and the music was lively in the middle of Tarka's town square. Laughter filled the air, cheers and yells replaced the music as another song ended. Her cheeks flushed, bringing color to her normally pale face. Finn couldn't stop staring at her. This was a completely different person in front of him, this woman whose laugh warmed his heart, whose smile made that same heart skip a beat. She was nothing like the cold-blooded killer that sewed his shoulder back together and he couldn't help but wonder what he would have to do to keep this version of her.

Another song ended and Ari let out a tired sigh. Finn took her hand and led her to one of the long tables where they sat. Or rather, Finn sat and pulled Ari into his lap. She put her head on his shoulder and watched as a new round of dancers filled the area, Danril among them. He could feel her smile as she watched her friend and mentor enjoy himself.

"He seems happy for a change," Finn remarked.

"Happiest I've seen him in four years," she replied, closing her eyes for a moment.

"Something happened four years ago to someone he was close to," he said, making a statement.

"Yes, but that's not a story I can tell," she replied. "And it's not a moment of time he likes to revisit." Her voice trailed off and her mood changed. Finn realized it was also a moment of time she didn't want to relive either. "But that's the past. He's moving forward in his own way."

"I suppose you are as well," he said, interlacing his fingers with hers. "Whoever that was clearly meant something to you as well." She nodded and took a deep breath, inhaling the scent of him. He smelled like a campfire mixed with pine and lavender. "Ari, about this week-" he started but she cut him off with a kiss.

"There's nothing to talk about," she said, her hand on his cheek. "Finn, these last few days have been everything I didn't know I needed. Thank you."

"Did I pass the test?" he asked, looking at her with wide blue eyes.

"And then some," she said, kissing him again. "Thank you."

"Keep that up and we're going to have to head back to the villa," he whispered when she pulled back. She smirked as she put her arms around his neck and was about to kiss him again but someone behind them cleared their throat. "Can I help you?" Finn asked, looking over Ari's shoulder. "Oh, it's you Darion."

"Pardon the interruption," he said, clearly not feeling bad he'd interrupted them, "but a message from her majesty arrived just a few moments ago for Miss Penndra."

"Fuck," Ari said, dropping her arms and standing up. "I knew something was going to happen eventually."

"What's happening?" Finn asked, also getting up.

"Orders," Ari said, reading the missive. "I need to leave for Trinda in the morning."

"You're dismissed Darion," Finn said darkly, putting his arm around Ari's waist. Darion nodded and left. "Do you want to go back to the villa?" Finn asked her quietly as she read the note again.

"Only if you want to," she said eventually, folding the note and sticking it in her pocket. "I don't want you to give up the night just because I'm riding for Trinda in the morning."

"Let's go back," he said, taking her hand. "I want to be selfish for this last night and spend it with you and you alone."

"I'd like that," she said as they left the square. She didn't say anything again until after they'd gotten back to the villa and curled up in their room in front of the fire. "Are you going to be ok while I'm gone?"

"I'm worried about you," he said, as he slowly ran his fingers up and down her arm. "Something doesn't feel right about this."

"Oh, it's just your mother's way of showing her disapproval," Ari said, nestling her head in his chest. "Just try not to worry too much."

"I don't think I can do that," he said, leaning over to kiss the top of her head, catching the scent of cedar and lilac. "I care too much. Can you promise me you'll be careful?"

"I will take every precaution," she said, her eyes growing heavy. "I can't plan for everything though." He let out a small grumble and she sighed. "If I had the gift of sight like some Fae, I'd know exactly what was waiting for me. The best I can do is rely on my training."

"I can't help but feel like you're walking into a trap darling." She snorted softly and shook her head.

"Even if I am, there's nothing much I can do about it. I either refuse on principle and she goes to war with the Shadow and Blade, or I walk in with my eyes open, spring her trap and fight my way out of it. It's nothing that hasn't happened before, and it's certainly likely to happen again." She looked up at him with a bemused expression. "You know I'm trained to handle any kind of threat to my life right?"

"I know," he said as he watched the fire while she settled back in against him. "Just be safe please."

"I will," she murmured as her eyes drifted shut.

"Sleep well, darling," he whispered as he wrapped his arms around her. He sat there, his thoughts racing as the flames danced, casting shadows all across the room. Eventually, he fell into an uneasy sleep on the couch with Ari, unable to shake the feeling something awful was about to happen.

Chapter 8

T HE MORNING OF HER departure came with the country's first frost. Their breath hung in the air as they stood outside the stables, saying one last goodbye before Ari rode north for Trinda. Finn was reluctant to let her go, and he could tell Ari didn't want to leave either.

"Promise me you'll be safe," he said again, his hands on her hips.

"Finn, I told you I will be as safe as I can," she said, her arms around his neck. "You really need to stop worrying. It's not like I've never been on a mission before."

"I know, but this is one my mother concocted, I'm very worried." He looked at her. "I still think it's a trap."

"Finn, I've been through far worse." She sighed. "I told you last night, I know it's a trap, but my hands are tied. I have to go."

"You shouldn't be so complacent," he admonished her. "This is your life at stake here."

"Finn, sweetie, I'm not being complacent. There are hundreds of unseen risks, I know. I'm just trying to tell you I've done this more times than I care to admit and that it will be ok."

"I'm not going to stop worrying just because you tell me to," he said as Danril came to join them. "Ride safe. Come back to Thannid soon."

"As soon as I can manage," she said, lifting on her toes to kiss him. "Don't mope around, ok?"

"I won't let him," Danril said. "You have a two-day ride ahead of you little one, best be going." She nodded, gave Finn one last hug, and then went to her horse. Danril stopped her before she mounted. "This could be a trap," he said in old Thenndin.

"I know," she replied in the same language. "But I have no proof, just a feeling."

"Lord Simeon should be made aware," he said as she mounted the horse.

"Then I leave it to you to do so, Master Danril," Ari replied. "Keep him safe. Tatiana has already proved she's not above causing him bodily harm."

"It's my job to little one," he replied. "Now go before the day gets away from you." Ari nodded and spurred the horse on, leaving a cloud of dust in her wake.

Finn watched the dust cloud settle and sighed, the pit in his stomach growing as he listened to the hoofbeats fade. Danril put an arm around his shoulder and squeezed.

"She'll be ok," Danril said. "She's tough, smart, and resourceful."

"I know. I just feel like something is about to go horribly wrong."

"Best not to dwell on it," Danril said as they went back in to finish their preparations to leave. "You'll drive yourself crazy otherwise."

Finn nodded and went back to his room, which felt cold and empty without Ari, and gathered his things before joining Danril in the carriage for the ride home.

It was nightfall when the carriage rolled back into Thannid, the sudden clacking of the wheels on the cobblestones jarring Finn from his nap. He sat up and rubbed his eyes, blinking in the darkness.

"Where are we?" he asked as he stretched. He looked around and his stomach sank when he realized it was just him and Danril in the coach.

"Thannid," he said as they came to a stop. "Are you ok?"

"Yeah. Dreams are just better than reality," he muttered as he grabbed his things and stepped out into the lit courtyard where Queen Tatiana was waiting. "The queen deigns to descend from her tower and greet a weary traveler," he said bitterly. "What do you want, mother?"

"That's really no way to greet your mother," she said, the carefully placed smile trying to falter.

"Oh, so we're just going to pretend nothing happened before I left?" he asked, crossing his arms.

"I at least thought a few days away would do away with this newfound animosity toward me," she said, lip curling into a sneer. "Clearly it has not."

"It's late and I'm tired, mother. I'm going to bed," he said, pushing past her. "I don't have time for your games or schemes."

She didn't stop him, letting him and Danril pass without a word. She supposed that a normal mother would've felt hurt at the exchange, but she felt nothing but indifference. In the grand scheme of her plans, it didn't matter if he liked her or not. By the time winter was over, she would be ruling all the countries, and her son and his emotions wouldn't be an issue.

Ari had made it to the first little village past the capital by the time night fell. She tumbled into the bed in the inn, exhausted, but unable to sleep. It had only taken a handful of nights for her to be used to sharing the bed with someone else, someone who made her feel safe and secure, who'd chased away the nightmares. The room felt colder without him there and she pulled the blankets tight around herself and willed sleep to come. By the time she did fall asleep, the sun was peeking over the horizon and the winter songbirds were singing their morning song. She got a few fitful hours of sleep before she was ready to finish the ride to Trinda.

Trinda had been the farming capital of Thendin, supplying the entire Faedom with much of its grain and other produce until the raid a month ago. Now, the village sat abandoned, it's people that hadn't succumbed to the raiders' blades fleeing to the nearby village of Farsten, the homes either shuddered up in the hopes that its owners would return or ravaged by the elements, windows broken by the debris whipped up by the winds, doors that had been left ajar wrenched from their hinges by the same winds. It made for the perfect place to lay low, plan your next move, or stalk your prey.

Within the borders of the now abandoned city, hid a group of raiders hired by the captain of the secret police, ready, watching for the one they'd been paid to target. The sun was setting as they continued to watch the road, looking for signs of a lone rider with golden blonde hair. The day dragged on, the sun doing little to warm them as they hid in the old, abandoned houses. As the afternoon sun faded, the youngest among them began to complain.

"Why are we waiting here, freezing our balls off?" he whined.

"Because we're getting paid handsomely to do away with this broad," said the leader. "Now quit yer bitchin and keep yer eyes on the road. Broad should be coming down the line any minute now." The youngest one shut up and turned his eyes back to the road, watching for the target.

While they watched the road, Danril was in a deep conversation with Simeon about the orders Ari had been given.

"Good gods, why?" Simeon asked, shaking his head. "In terms of the order, Ari is of little value."

"In terms of controlling her son though," Danril replied. "She has spies everywhere. If she knew-"

"Oh, she knows," Simeon inserted.

"Then removing Ari from the prince's life would remove her one and only obstacle for keeping him under her total control. Why she wants that, I haven't a clue."

"Neither do I but it's probably the only thing that would make sense," Simeon agreed. "I can send some Shadows out to Trinda, but it'll take them a day to get there."

"Ari can handle herself, but if it's not a one-on-one fight..."

"She'll manage. She must. Nobody can get to Trinda that fast." Danril nodded and stood.

"Thank you, Lord Simeon," he said as he left. Simeon nodded and waited for the door to shut before he waved his hand for the two spies lingering in the shadows.

"I need you both to ride for Trinda as soon as possible. A Blade's life depends on it."

"As you wish, Lord Simeon," the male said. "Are we to interfere if necessary?"

"Only if lives are at stake," he replied. "I feel the situation may be in hand when you arrive."

"Understood," he said quietly before he and his partner disappeared. Simeon went back to his papers, worried yet confident that the situation was as managed as he could make it.

The sun had long since set by the time Ari reached the borders of Trinda, exhausted and worn from the road. Knowing that there was likely a trap waiting for her and knowing she wasn't in shape to confront it tonight, she made an abandoned farmhouse her inn and collapsed on the bed, exhaustion taking her long before she could wish she was wrapped up in Finn's arms.

The sun was well overhead when Ari woke again, sore, stiff, hungry and lonesome. Some gentle stretching alleviated some of the stiffness and soreness.he dried meat from her pack cured the hunger but nothing could cure the lonely feeling in the pit of her stomach. It was annoying her that after just a few nights, she could feel like she was missing a small part of herself. She shook her head to clear her thoughts and finished her lackluster meal, thinking about the afternoon she'd spent with Finn eating steamed fruit buns. She gave her head one last shake and smacked her cheeks. Steamed buns would have to wait, she had to beat the queen at her own game.

The sun sank beneath the trees, Ari hid among the upper branches, watching for any sign of life. Her eyes scanned the road ahead of her and she smirked when she picked up four glimmered figures traveling down the road. It would be too easy for her to just pick them off one by one, but that wouldn't spring the trap. So instead, she took a couple of thin throwing knives and aimed at one of the shorter figures and let the knife fly.

The group, still searching for Ari, paused when one of them stumbled and then collapsed. Three sets of glimmer suddenly fell as they stopped to check on their fallen comrade. Before they could realize they'd been made, another knife came from the shadows, taking out a second member of the group. As the second member fell, the remaining two men drew their blades. They looked around, taking to the trees to avoid ending up like their fallen fellows.

"What the hell?" the leader barked at the older man, looking around, trying to find where the knives were coming from. "Find them!"

Ari quickly blended into the shadows and headed back toward the town, but before she could get too far, she got blindsided and knocked from the trees. She landed on the ground with a thud, feeling ribs crack in the process. Ignoring the pain, she got to her feet and pulled her remaining knives, ready to face the two of them. They materialized in front of her, knives in hand.

"Well would you look at this Critch," the leader said, sneering. "I think we found our mark."

"Wonder what a Blade did to get on the wrong side of the queen," Critch said as he looked at her. "We best be careful with this one Kydin."

"I'm not scared of a Blade," he said, as they began to circle around her. "Besides, this one doesn't even look that tough."

"That's the point," Critch replied. "She's not gonna look tough. Don't you know anything about them?"

"Nope, and I don't care to," he hissed, moving to strike her. She blocked the thrust, hiding a grimace as it jarred the broken ribs. "You have a death wish, girl?"

"No more than you do," she said, blocking another attempt to stab her before pivoting and planting her boot in his gut, knocking the wind out of him. "I'm just out here doing a job."

"Funny, so are we," Kydin said, as he tried to catch his breath. "You're from the Reudena region."

"What do you mean?" she asked, eyes narrowed.

"Your voice, you were born and raised in Reudena."

"No clue where I was born but I was raised in a shithole orphanage in Thannid," she said as they resumed circling her. "What's Reudena to you?"

"It was my home," Critch said. "Or it was before the queen's fucking army burn it to the fucking ground."

"That's nothing surprising," Ari said as she dodged Critch's next blow. "The queen's a fucking bitch."

"And yet you serve her," Kydin said, thrusting at Ari, who dodged.

"No, I serve Shadow and Blade. Why are you trying to kill me?"

"I got paid to," Critch said, lunging at her. Ari blocked, ducked, and with her free hand, drove her other blade into his gut.

"That's funny," she said as he staggered back before sinking to his knees, "so did I."

"Well, looks like a lifetime of wrongs has finally caught up," Critch said as he slumped over. A gurgle escaped his lips as he landed in the dirt and stopped moving. Kydin looked at Critch's body and then at her.

"I'd say if you surrendered, you could walk away from this, but we both know that's not the case."

"You're awfully cocky for a girl," Kydin replied. "Didn't anyone ever tell you cocky gets you killed?"

"Every damn day," she said. "Do not mistake my tone for cocky. I never go into a fight thinking I could win."

"You sound like something out of the fortune tellers' tents at the fairs," Kydin said with a snort. "Come at me and fight."

"You may have first move," she said, adjusting her daggers so they sat more comfortably and in a manner that allowed her more range of motion.

"I don't need your permission," he snapped, lunging.

The sounds of their blades meeting rang through the trees. Kydin immediately put Ari on the defensive, rushing at her, his one dagger moving as fast as two. With her injured ribs, Ari found it difficult to keep up and block on that side, resulting in several close calls. A seasoned fighter, Kydin was always looking for his opponent's weaknesses and after Ari nearly missed a block on her injured side, he grinned and laughed.

The laugh told Ari that he'd figured out she had been injured. She knew her best option was to run, but a glance at her opponent told her that she had no option but to stand and fight.

"Thinking of running?" he asked tauntingly. "That doesn't seem like a very sporting thing to do."

"I know when I'm beat," she said, figuring if she couldn't fight her way out, maybe she could talk her way out. "You've figured out I'm injured, the sporting thing to do is acknowledge you won and be on my way."

"I could, it's not like I wasn't already paid for this," he said, as he renewed his attack on her. "But where's the fun in that?"

Ari did what she could but with his knowledge of her injured side, she knew she was outmatched. He repeatedly slipped past her defenses, the tip of his blade biting into her skin. As he pulled away again, she studied him, before concluding that there was only one way to win this fight and fulfill her mission, but it was going to cost a lot of blood to do it. She sheathed one of her knives, tightened the grip on the other and looked at him. Her expression in the tree filtered moonlight had Kydin faltering in his next attack.

"Is something wrong?" she asked, her voice emotionless. "I thought you had a job to do."

"You Blades are insane," he said as she stepped forward again.

"What some call insanity, we call doing what's necessary," she said, taking another step. "I know who paid you, but I'm not willing to let her win."

"Crazy bitch," he said as she rushed toward him. "This is suicide."

"Maybe," she said as she got closer, "or maybe I live long enough to see you die."

"If you know who paid us, why are you doing this?" he asked, leveling his blade at her as she continued to close the distance between them. "You could just let me go."

"Where's the fun in that," she said as his blade bit into her skin and slid through like she was a piece of paper.

"Stupid," he said as he watched pain flood her eyes. He was about to continue on but something warm began trickling down his side. "So that was your game," he said quietly as they both pulled their blades back. "Sacrifice yourself to kill me."

"You already knew that and yet, you did nothing to stop me from taking your life," she said as she stumbled against a tree.

"When fate decides, you cannot fight," he said, as he collapsed. "Just like the families who knew that there was no saving Reudena."

"I know nothing of Reudena," she gasped, forcing herself to stay upright.

"Your parents... lived in a small cottage outside town. Many of us watched as the town burned, your parents included. Most assumed you'd died in the blaze."

"That little girl did," she said before stumbling out of the small grove and back toward the farmhouse.

She stumbled through the broken doorway, aware of the blood seeping through the wound but forced herself to get her pack. With shaky and bloodied hands, she dug through it and found her field kid before moving back into the moonlight. Steadying her hands, she moved her now ruined shirt out of her way and examined the stab wound in the pale light. It certainly could've been worse, the blood wasn't gushing out like she thought, but it was going to be tricky to sew with what blood was there. Carefully she threaded the needle and proceeded to sew the wound close, stopping every so often as her vision began to narrow. She'd reached the halfway point before the pain kicked in. Ari rarely screamed over anything, but she nearly did when the pain from both the broken ribs and the stab wound finally hit her. Her hands went from feeling normal to damp, making it hard to hold on to the needle.

"You don't have a choice," she said out loud through gritted teeth as she wiped her sweaty hands on her pants before resuming her stitching.

Every stitch was painful, every breath felt like fire in her chest, but she forced herself to close the wound, focusing on one stitch after the other. She tied up the last one, letting out a small sigh of relief and tried packing away her kit. However, with the immediate stress of patching herself up dealt with, Ari felt her limbs grow heavy and the room faded to black as she slumped over and passed out.

As the night gave way to the morning and then to afternoon, two hooded figures rode into town. Trained eyes surveyed the road, noting the two motionless bodies in the road but paying them little head. Gerid dismounted and moved the bodies out of the way as Cardine continued. She stopped short of riding into town as the whinny of a horse caught her attention and turned her horse toward the sound, coming to a stop at an abandoned farmhouse. As Cardine dismounted, she saw the trail of blood leading into the house. With a dagger in her hand, she slowly crept in, checking each room, until she entered one and found Ari lying on the floor. Cardine carefully knelt next to Ari and placed her fingers to the assassin's neck, checking for a pulse. The moment her finger touched Ari's skin; the girl's eyes fluttered open.

"The Gods have mercy," the woman said in Old Thenndin.

"No, they don't," she replied hoarsely, startling the woman further.

"You know the language?" The woman looked at her suspiciously. "Identify yourself."

"Ari Penndra, a Blade from Shadow and Blade," she said with a groan.

"Your password," the woman prompted her. Ari growled slightly but complied.

"Fire and Ice," she replied as she tried sitting up.

"I wouldn't do that," Cardine said, checking her over. "Multiple cuts, feels like broken ribs and a stitched-up wound. What on earth did you get into?"

"A fight," Ari replied with a hiss as Cardine pressed on the ribs. "Would you not?"

"Oh hush," Cardine said as she placed her hands on Ari's sides. "Take another nap or something."

Ari wasn't given a choice as the shock of her ribs snapping back into place had her eyes rolling back and she sunk back into a less than peaceful sleep.

After checking the remainder of the area, Gerid followed the sound of a horse whinnying. Simeon had been right about the situation being in hand. Finding Cardine healing a fifth injured party had shocked him, however.

"I assume you verified this one Cardine," he said, looking down.

"It's Fire," she said. "And it's just ribs I'm healing."

"You care too much Car," he said, looking down at her. "Matron could've done that easily."

"Matron isn't here and I'm not taking the risk of a broken rib puncturing anything on our way back."

"Fine. What can I do?" he asked, surveying the room, eyes landing on the field kit strewn in front of her. "Did she stitch herself up?"

"Apparently. Figure out what to do with her horse and pack this up." The man nodded. "I think we should hurry. If this is as Lord Simeon said, lingering here would not be wise."

"Agreed," Gerid said, scooping Ari's things into her pack and then standing. "I'll be back in a moment."

Cardine nodded and sank back on her heels. "You're really something else," she said to the unconscious Ari. "Tougher than I am."

"She's just a special breed of idiot. We all are," Gerid said as he came back in. "Her horse is ready."

"We should go," Cardine said. "Lord Simeon needs to be made aware of what happened and she needs a proper bed."

"Get on your horse," he said, kneeling to pick up Ari. Cardine went out and mounted, while Gerid carried the worn out assassin from the house. He handed her up to Cardine who made sure she had a secure grip on Ari before urging her horse off.

Gerid hoisted himself upon his, grabbed the reins to Ari's horse and took off after them, catching up soon as they raced across Thenndin's countryside to get home.

Chapter 9

THE DOOR TO HIS office slammed open, startling Simeon, who dropped his pen in surprise as he looked up at the intrusion. He composed himself and picked up the pen as Danril shut the door and came to sit in the chair in front of the desk. Simeon took a moment to scrutinize his face, noting the fear, rage, and worry, all emotions he hadn't seen on Danril's face in four years. He put the pen down gently and let out a deep breath before speaking.

"I see you got my message."

"What the fuck happened to her?" he asked, staring Simeon down.

"As Miss Penndra hasn't woken from her unconscious state, I have no idea," Simeon said. "It's likely that she sprung whatever was waiting for her in Trinda. Once she wakes, I will get her account and pair it with Gerid and Cardine's."

"I knew there was something off," Danril said, fuming.

"I'm sure she suspected as much as well. There's not much that could've been done though, Danril. She either had to tell the queen off or walk into the trap. Miss Penndra went with her eyes open and handled what she found as best she could. Cardine did say she kept muttering something on the ride back about Reudena."

"Reudena?" Danril looked confused. "Why Reudena?"

"Unknown. Cardine said Miss Penndra was too out of it to answer any questions, likely due to severe stress. I have the scholars digging into it. It's likely that whomever she encountered mentioned the city and its misfortune."

"She's been having that dream more and more lately too," Danril said, slumping in his chair. "She's started having it on missions as well, almost cost her the last one the queen sent her on."

"I can see about keeping her out of the field for some time. Those few days in Tarka seemed to improve her mood and spirits nicely."

"She actively enjoyed herself, experienced life. It was interesting to see." Danril fiddled with his sleeve.

"So I heard. The Shadows were full of interesting tales," Simeon said, the corners of his mouth turned up in a slight smile. "She needs to be careful going forward, however. The queen will not take kindly to this."

"The queen doesn't already. Why else would she send Ari on a mission that would nearly kill her?"

"For the sport of it, to control her son, take your pick Danril," Simeon said. "You've heard the rumors about her, and you know she's constantly butting heads with Shadow and Blade."

"In the grand scheme of things though, Ari isn't very important to the order. When we became Blades, we were told we were expendable, replaceable, and to be so was the path we walked. Every day could be our last."

"I know that, you know that, but the queen wouldn't care. She'd just see it as me having to spend time, resources and coin on finding a replacement."

"I suppose that does make sense, but could we even find a replacement at this point? All Thannid's orphanages have either consolidated or closed thanks to Queen Tatiana and those that remain don't usually want to collude with us."

"I am aware of this. Have you gone to see her yet?" Simeon asked, abruptly changing the subject.

"No, I came straight to your office first," Danril said, looking down at his knees..

"You should go see her. It would do you both some good, even if she's not awake yet."

"I'd just get in Marion's way," Danril said, shaking his head. "Plus, I have other duties to attend to."

"The prince would understand. You didn't see your face when you burst in. I thought you were going to break down and cry. It's been a while since I'd seen you show that much emotion. Go sit with her for a little bit."

Danril let out a slow breath and got up. "I really hate how well you know me," he said, pausing in the doorway.

"I've been your friend for at least fifteen years, Danril," Simeon said. "I know you about as well as you know yourself." He paused as Danril headed for the door before saying one last thing. "She's a lot like you, stubborn as fuck, strong willed, and feels everything to the core, if she let's herself."

"I am aware," he said, before leaving the office. "Very well aware." He made his way toward the infirmary and met by the mistress of the healing arts, who looked frazzled. "How is she, Marion?"

"The girl is too damn stubborn for her own good," she said looking up at him. "Stitched herself right up. Cardine had to heal some broken ribs so she could travel. She's been sleeping since they arrived early this morning."

"It's a day's ride to Trinda," he said, running a hand through his nearly black hair, "how'd they get back so fast?"

"I don't know but I'm not going to question it," Marion said, smacking his shoulder, "and neither should you."

"Ouch," he said jokingly, rubbing his shoulder as he looked in the direction Marion had come from.

"Oh, get over there and see her. She's near the window," Marion said, pointing toward the back wall. "She's going to be just fine too."

"Too stubborn to die," he said as he walked past the rows of empty beds before stopping next to hers. "You are just too stubborn, you know that?" he asked quietly as he sat next to the bed and took her hand in his. "Just next time, don't scare us like that." His chuckle sounded a little bit like a sob, and he had to wipe his face as a few tears snuck down his face. "You're my family, Ari. Don't leave me." There was no stopping the tears that fell after that.

Finn was aimlessly wandering the castle gardens, still wondering what had happened to make Danril take off in a dead sprint, almost flying out of the castle. There hadn't been any time for questions, so Finn had decided to get some fresh air, maybe put the worry that something had happened to Ari out of his mind. That plan failed spectacularly as he wandered through the calla lilies and heard his mother's voice over the near the hydrangeas. He ducked into an opening in the hedges that separated him from his mother and proceeded to listen.

"What do you mean they are all dead?" Tatiana hissed. "How?"

"Your intended target eliminated them all. She must've realized that she was walking into a trap."

"Of course she did," Tatiana snapped. "She's not stupid. I just didn't expect her to figure out that soon."

"She's clearly skilled," the captain said. "The oldest of them was touted as the leanest, meanest fighter. Trinda is proof of that."

"Yet he could not beat one small little girl," Tatiana said, and from his hiding spot, Finn could hear the sneer in her voice. "She did come back with a near fatal wound, but that's not what you promised me." Finn felt his stomach drop to his knees at those words. He suddenly realized why Danril had taken off and he bit the inside of his cheek to keep from letting out the sob.

"I understand, Your Majesty," the captain said, bowing his head. "Can I be of any other assistance in this matter?"

"No Grimmitt, you've bungled it enough as is. I'll see to any other future plans regarding that stupid whore's demise." From the bushes, Finn bristled and restrained himself from jumping out of the bushes to defend Ari. It wouldn't do him any good to anger his mother over the matter, not after the last time she'd gotten mad at him. He rubbed his shoulder and continued to listen.

"Of course, my lady," he said, disappearing. Tatiana let out a low growl as he left.

"Of course, the little bitch would survive," she muttered, pacing the path. "Simeon spares no expense on training his little pets. But I need to get rid of her. Her presence is causing problems with Finn. He's grown entirely too fond of the stupid whore, and he's beginning to question my authority over him. No matter, if I can't rid myself of her, I'll just try something different." She continued down the path, away from Finn.

Finn sat in his hedge, shaking, wondering what else she had planned and torn between a desire to know and a desire to run as far away as he could. However, worry for Ari overshadowed all his desires. He carefully extracted himself from the hedge and disguised himself with glimmer to leave the castle grounds. He needed to find Danril, and he needed to know what happened to Ari.

Danril was wandering the halls, partially to stretch, partially because he couldn't sit there any longer. His wandering took him into the courtyard where he encountered the two Shadows that had brought Ari back. When he approached them, they stood and dipped their heads in respect for the more senior member of the order.

"There's no need for that," he said, "if anything, I should be paying my respects to you."

"We only did what Lord Simeon asked of us," Gerid said, "your gratitude is not necessary, Master Craine."

"All the same, I appreciate it," he said, sitting on the fountain. "Many in your position would've left her."

"I don't think Cardine would've let me. She has a soft spot for people."

"Just because I can see the inherent good in them, doesn't mean it's a soft spot," she retorted, smacking Gerid's arm. "You could do to be less cynical of the world at large."

"I'll be cynical, you continue to be soft. It's worked this far," he said, nudging her shoulder. She rolled her eyes and smiled. "But seriously, Master Craine, please don't feel like you owe us. I feel like Lord Simeon would've had us back on the road had we left her."

"Very likely," Danril said with a small laugh. "You two look like you need more rest."

"Probably. We made a day's ride in half a day," Gerid said as Cardine yawned. "If you'd excuse us."

"By all means," Danril said as they stood to leave. "Rest well." The pair nodded and left, leaving Danril to sit alone by the fountain, listening to the gentle sounds of the water falling behind him. He probably would've drifted off, had he not caught sight of a familiar face passing by. "You look troubled, Finn," he said, just loud enough for the prince to hear.

"Hardly surprising given the conversation I just overheard my mother having with the captain of her secret police."

"You best come in before someone else sees through your disguise," Danril said, getting to his feet and coming to open the gate. "That must've been an unpleasant conversation to overhear."

"Uh huh, especially on the heels of you tearing out of the castle this morning," Finn said, mouth twisted in a frown. "Were you going to tell me?" Danril sat back down on the edge of the fountain and motioned for Finn to join him. The afternoon sun highlighted the tear stains on Danril's face. "How bad is it?"

"Oh, I suspect it could've been much worse, but she's fine. Still sleeping right now." Danril looked at Finn. "What did your mother say exactly?"

"Which part because there's the conversation she had with the captain and then her mini rant after the fact," Finn said dryly. "The latter is not very flattering in many respects."

"Best to have that conversation where prying eyes and open ears cannot follow," Danril said, standing and motioning for Finn to follow. Finn did so and they passed through the halls before walking into Danril's office and chamber. The area was surprisingly cozy, albeit a tad dusty. Danril pointed to the chair next to the desk and sat across from it. "What was the conversation with Grimmitt about?" he asked as Finn sat.

"About how the people she told him to hire to kill Ari failed. He seemed rather shocked by the news." Finn looked at Danril. "You're not shocked by this. And I highly doubt you'd be shocked if I told you in that conversation, they said Ari came back injured, severely so."

"Severely isn't a word I would use," he said. "Though from the looks of it, it was rather nasty."

"How nasty?" Finn asked.

"Bad enough. I'll take you to her in a minute. The second half of the conversation?" Danril prompted.

"Right. Mother decided to continue ranting, calling Ari a whore on multiple occasions, and going so far to say that I was growing too fond of her and that's why she needed to be out of the picture, something about her causing me to question mother's authority."

"You're in your what, twenty-ninth year?" Danril asked. Finn nodded in response. "It's well past time for that in my opinion, but if it took thinking with your -"

"That's more than we need to get into," Finn said, cutting him off. "I've been very unsatisfied with my life for a while. Ari was merely the catalyst for change."

"She does have that effect," Danril said. "Ari's responsible for a fair few changes in my life."

"Now, if only she saw this effect she had on everyone," Finn said. "I'm concerned about what else my mother has up her sleeve."

"Not much you can do about it," Danril said. "We'll just have to deal with things as they happen."

"It would feel a lot better if I didn't feel like I was trapped in the castle constantly." Finn leaned forward and looked at Danril. "What exactly happened to Ari?"

"I do not know, and I suspect we won't know until she wakes up. Come with me," he said, getting up. "I'll take you to her."

"Are you sure?" Finn asked as he also got up. "I wouldn't want to break any rules."

"I doubt Lord Callwell will take issue," Danril said as they left the office. "Besides, I think you need to see her and whether she's awake or not, she needs you there."

Finn nodded and they left the office. "She doesn't care that much," he said as they walked down the hall. "Not after just a few days."

"I've known her much longer than you, you don't see what I do. If you doubt her feelings for you, you're going to hurt her."

"I don't want to do that," Finn said, as they approached the infirmary door. "Are you sure about this?"

"I promise, she's very much alive," Danril said as they paused outside.

"It's not that I don't believe you, I just don't know if I want to see her like this." Finn fiddled with the cuff of his sleeve. "Vulnerable is just not something I associate with her."

"Vulnerable is not something Ari has associated herself with in twelve years. The fact that she finally relaxed around you, Finn, is proof enough that she trusts you." He pushed the door open. "And if you pull away or give her reason to doubt you, she'll withdraw from everyone, and I don't think we'd be able to get her back."

Finn sighed and nodded as they entered, and the Matron looked up and smiled at them.

"Ah, Danril, and oh, Prince Finnian, welcome to our humble halls," she said, curtseying a little. "What brings you here?"

"Came to see how Ari was doing," he said, dipping his head toward her. "She seems like she's in excellent hands here though."

"You flatter me," she said, with a light laugh. "She's over by the window, and she just woke up. Don't push her though." Marion looked at them with narrowed eyes. "Simeon was just here, talking to her about something. She seems troubled now."

"We won't stay too long then," Danril said. "Thank you, Marion."

"Go on now, go see the lass," she said, shooing them away.

Finn headed the direction Marion had shooed them toward, forcing himself not to run toward her. As he approached, she turned her head to see who was there and he could see a huge grin on her face.

"I've been worried about you," he said as he came to a stop next to her bed.

"I told you I'd come back," she said wearily as he sat next to her. "You didn't mope, did you?"

"Too busy with the stupid little shit my mother decided to shove on me to handle," he said, putting his hand over hers. "But I thought about you every chance I had."

"I missed you too," she said, closing her eyes for a second. "How long has it been since I left?"

"Three and a half days," Danril said.

"It feels like I just barely left yesterday." She let out a sigh and leaned her head towards Finn's shoulder. "Can you stay a bit?"

"For a little while, yes," he said. "At some point, I will have to return to the castle. Mother's been watching me like a hawk lately."

"For as long as you can then," she said as he moved to put his arm around her.

"What did Lord Simeon want?" Danril asked as he sat at the foot of the bed. "Matron said he'd been here."

"He said the scholars had searched every record, every scrap of paper that pertained to Reudena that they could find and found nothing about the town and its residents. I can either take the word of two goons hired to kill me, or I can just accept that I might never know the truth about where I came from."

"There are always the castle archives," Finn said as she sighed. "Knowing my mother I'm sure there's something in there."

"Maybe. Those same two men also told me Reudena was burned by the queen and her soldiers."

"What do you believe?" Danril asked as he looked up at Finn. "Do you believe the queen ordered the destruction of an entire town?"

"Danril, I just came back from her piss poor attempt to have me killed. Now's really not the time to ask me what I think."

"Fair point child," he said. "What are you going to do? Accept it or deny it?"

"I don't know yet. I think a part of me wanted to know why I kept having that dream while another part of me just wants to be done with it and just forget about it."

"What if I told you we had some answers?" came the voice of Simeon.

"I thought you said the scholars couldn't find anything," she said, looking up at him.

"They hadn't, but not all of them had reported back to me," he said, pulling up a chair. "He found your arrival records from the orphanage."

"Really? I was under the impression those burned along with the orphanage," she said, finding Finn's hand and interlacing her fingers with his. "What was in them?"

"Your arrival date, which is a few days after Reudena burned, as well as a general idea of where you were brought from. According to the records, a group of Thenndish soldiers brought you to the capital from the west." Simeon looked at her sadly. "That dream you've been having; it may have well been what happened to your parents."

"Did they truly witness the city burning and did nothing or did they take part?" Finn asked, putting his other arm around her. "I wouldn't put it past my mother to have ordered the city burned."

"Official records say Reudena was attacked by raiders from Dengard or Ringnad. The rumors have never been proven, just like they say that Trinda was attacked by Pertina and Stuttgad."

"That's a load of horse shit," Ari muttered, sinking against Finn.

"I can confirm that it is," Finn said, giving her a light squeeze. "I heard Mother and the captain of the police speaking about it in the garden."

"I'm sure Stuttgad would love that information, especially in light of what happened to one of their ministers." Simeon gave Ari a pointed look. Ari just shrugged, not saying anything. "Though the official story says that he was killed by a shark who's been arrested."

"Good, one less of them on the streets," Ari said thinly. "Did the minister have a family?"

"A wife and child. They've long since left the capital for a quieter part of the country." Ari let out a small sniff. "We should probably let you rest."

"Thank you for the information, Lord Simeon," Ari said as he got up to leave.

"Of course, child. A letter detailing that you are not to be sent on any missions for the next month will be sent to the queen. Whenever Marion deems you ready, you can return to the castle."

"If she feels up to it, she could return as soon as tonight," Marion said. "There's little else I can do for her."

"It's up to her," Simeon said. "I have other things I need to attend to. Have a pleasant evening everyone." He left abruptly, leaving the four of them there.

"Well, what do you want to do, child?" Danril asked.

"I don't know. I hadn't thought about it," she said, with a yawn. "Honestly, I thought I was going to be here for a while."

"If you come back to the castle, it's less likely I'd have to leave," Finn said, pressing his lips to the top of her head. "But it's only if you feel up to it."

"Tempting. My body feels like lead though. I doubt I'd be able to walk there."

"It's almost like someone would have to carry you back, how terrible," Finn said with a grin and a chuckle.

"Oh nonsense, you'd be able to take the carriage," Marion said. "If you want to return tonight, I'll make the arrangements for you."

"That would be nice Matron Criftview, thank you," Ari said.

"Very well. Danril, I think there's still a few clean changes of clothes in her room. You should grab her one."

"Of course, I'll be right back." He got up and headed out while Marion left to go make arrangements for them to get back to the castle, leaving Finn and Ari alone.

"Are you ok?" Finn asked quietly.

"I will be," she said. "But I don't think you're referring to my physical wellbeing, are you?"

"Smart girl," he said with a smile. "No, I'm checking on your mental state. You got a huge load dumped on you just now."

"It answered a question, nothing more," she replied as Danril came back. "Thank you," she said, taking the shirt and quickly changing as Marion returned.

"The carriage is ready for you all. I had your pack loaded for you, little one."

"Thank you Matron Criftview," Ari said as Finn got up and carefully helped her out of bed and out to the carriage.

They rode back in silence, the carriage arriving in the courtyard. Danril took Ari in to make sure she got settled before the queen could see her and then came back out to Finn.

"You're going to have to head back to where you were before you snuck out," Danril said quietly. "Your mother's on the warpath because she hasn't been able to find you."

"To the garden then," he whispered as they both glimmered and snuck past the searching guards. As they did, the order's carriage left as quickly as it arrived. Finn led Danril to where he'd been in the garden, releasing his glimmer as Danril moved a few feet away before releasing his own. Their timing was impeccable as Tatiana stormed down the path, looking for her son.

"What are you doing out here, Finnian?" she snapped. "I've had guards scouring the palace for you."

"Clearing my head, getting lost in my thoughts, dying of sheer boredom since you've confined me to the grounds as of late."

"I will not tolerate your flippant tone, young man. You know exactly why I'm keeping you behind the palace walls."

"You mean the reason you've convinced yourself of," he retorted. "We both know you're doing it to control me, make me do what you want." Finn stalked off. Danril inclined his head toward her and followed him.

"Finnian, *FINNIAN*," she called after him, but he didn't stop. She made to follow him, but suddenly a figure in a cloak appeared in front of her. "Make it quick," she snapped, recognizing the cloak. "I haven't the time for one of Simeon's little errand boys."

"A missive from Lord Simeon," the figure said, handing her the sealed letter.

"What does the windbag want now?" Tatiana snapped, taking the note and opening it. "Is he serious?" she asked, looking up in fury.

"To the point he will remove Miss Penndra from your service if you do not heed his instructions. She is badly injured and before she can return to her duties, she needs to heal. Lord Simeon sends his regards and sympathies in the matter, but he will not bend."

"Get out of my sight," Tatiana snapped, crumpling the note. The cloaked figure vanished as quickly as they had appeared. The moment they'd left, she lifted her palm with the crumpled note and reduced it to ashes. "You think you can tell me what to do, Simeon?" she hissed to the empty garden. "Nobody tells me what I can or cannot do in my Faedom." She blew the ashes from her palm and turned on her heel and left as the remains of the missive floated away on the breeze.

Chapter 10

A RI SPENT THE BETTER part of a week after the Trinda mission either in her room resting or in the library to avoid seeing or speaking to the queen, which the more the queen tried to find her, the angrier she grew when she couldn't track down the elusive assassin. The knowledge that the queen was growing more and more frustrated gave Ari something to smile about as she lounged in front of her fireplace, reading a book.

Her door opened and Finn entered, for the brief moment that the door was open, she could hear Queen Tatiana screaming about something down the hall. She put the book aside and sat up as Finn shut the door before coming to flop next to her on the couch.

"What's her deal now?" Ari asked as he kicked his boots off before he pulled her into his lap and stretched out across the couch. "And make yourself at home."

"Considering this is a room in my home, I'll do just that," he said, making sure she was comfortable. "Besides, it's not like you're complaining."

"Why would I when you make a very comfortable pillow?" she asked, settling against his chest. "We haven't had much time together lately."

"Mother keeps finding ways to make me miserable and next week is the annual meeting of the Faedoms so I've been handling meetings and preparing for that nonsense."

"Sounds awful," Ari said.

"It could be worse," he said. "At least I know you're hiding somewhere around the castle."

"Much to your mother's displeasure," she said, causing him to laugh.

"How much longer do you plan on hiding from her?" he asked, moving his hand to play with her ear.

"As long as I can," she said, twitching. "That tickles. Finn, stop it," she said, half protesting as he kept at it.

"Would you really deny me some fun after all I've been able to do for a week is sneak in and basically pass out?" He moved her hair and lightly kissed her neck. A small shudder ran down her spine, and he chuckled softly. "I should've brought some dinner with me."

"I could eat," she said. "But I really don't want to move right now."

"That's problematic," Finn said, "because I'm starting to get kinda hungry."

"We should probably go get food, otherwise we'll both end up on the wrong side of both Matron and Danril," she said, gently caressing his hand with her thumb.

"Can't have that now," he said, sitting up. "Why don't you wait here. I'll be back with some food in a bit."

"Don't take too long," she said, giving his hand a quick squeeze as he scooted her so he could get up.

"Quick as a bunny," he replied, kissing the top of her head. She smiled and laid back against the arm of the couch and grinned at him. "Quicker than that if I can manage," he added before grabbing his boots. Ari laughed and stretched, grimacing slightly as the movement pulled on the still healing stab wound while he pulled his boots on and disappeared.

True to his word, Finn wasn't gone long, but when he returned, he wasn't alone. Ari could hear angry voices outside her door, first Finn's, then Queen Tatiana's. Ari groaned and sat up and went to open the door. Before she could touch the handle, it flew open, catching her in the face. She flew backwards, landing on her ass, her hand pressed to her face.

"Fucking gods, what on earth are you two fighting about?" she said as they stepped in.

"Ari, are you ok?" Finn asked, setting the plate on the table near the door and kneeling next to her. "What happened?"

"One of you two idiots slammed a door right into my face," she snapped as Finn moved her hand to examine the injury. "Nothing's broken," she said as he started gently pressing on it.

"Are we done?" Tatiana asked, crossing her arms. "I have business here."

"What do you want, Your Majesty?" Ari asked as Finn helped her up and then picked up the plate from the table and carried it over to the sitting area.

"Your report, obviously," she spat. "It's well overdue."

"Hm, and considering I sustained a very life-threatening injury during this most recent errand of yours, I think that I should be able to give my report when I'm feeling up to it and not a moment sooner."

"Why you insolent little bitch," Tatiana hissed as she stepped toward Ari, hand raised to strike her. She probably would have but Finn appeared next to her and grabbed his mother's hand. "Let go of me at once," she snapped at her son. "This is no business of yours."

"You're making it my business by threatening her," he said quietly. "She's not your punching bag."

"Let go Finnian," she said, trying to pull her hand from his grasp.

"I will once I feel you're not about to continue taking your anger out on Ari," he said. Tatiana glared at him before relaxing. He released her hand and stepped back toward Ari.

"Were you able to complete the task I gave you in Trinda?" she asked, rubbing her wrist.

"Clearly," Ari said curtly. "Otherwise, I wouldn't be here."

"Good. Simeon has already informed me of your necessary month of rest. If you cannot return to duty by then, I will have no choice but to send you back to them."

"How terrible," Ari said dryly. "I'd have to go back to the order where I serve the calculated and planned whims of Lord Callwell and not the emotional whims of a madwoman."

"Take care with how you speak, child," Tatiana said. "One day, there won't be anyone to save you."

"What makes you think I need someone to save me?" Ari asked in a very quiet voice. Her tone caused Finn and Tatiana both to take a step back. "Is there anything else you need from me, Your Majesty?"

"Just be prepared to attend the annual celebration of the gathering of the Faedoms next week," Tatiana said, turning on her heel. "Finn, let's go."

"Why?" he asked, stepping next to Ari again. "I thought I'd made it perfectly clear I was going to be spending my time in my way."

"You have a duty to the people, to the Faedom," Tatiana spat, whirling back around. "Abandon these foolish notions at once."

"No. My duties are the parts you give me each day to play. I'm done with those. This is my time, and this is how I chose to spend it." He put his arm around Ari's waist and pulled her next to him. "I don't care if you don't like it. I'm not seeking your approval."

"How dare you be so insolent," she hissed. "She's nothing but trouble for you."

"And she is standing right here," Ari replied, "wishing you'd get out of my room."

"The room you're allowed to have because I decreed it so," Tatiana snapped. "I ought to ship you back to the order to break whatever spell you put my son under. It's all your fault he's become so stubborn."

"I don't think I had anything to do with it. Pretty sure you encouraged this stubbornness all on your own, Your Majesty," Ari retorted. "Now, if there's nothing else..." Ari let the sentence hang while Tatiana fumed before turning on her heel and storming out of the room. The door slammed and Ari sank against Finn. "That was exhausting, can we eat now?"

"I wish I had some place I could threaten to go," Finn said as they sat, "someplace that isn't full of her people."

"You should have one. Just for you," she said, wrapping her arms around him. "It would do you some good."

"It would require getting some coin together, which isn't hard, and some time to go look, which after I decided to take that trip to Tarka, is harder to come by." Ari gave him a light squeeze.

"Where would you want to go?" she asked as she let go and stretched her legs out in front of her, putting her head on his shoulder.

"Tarka or somewhere toward the south of Thenndin," he said, getting the plate. "The climate further south is more to my liking. Thannid gets far too cold for my liking."

"Even Tarka gets chilled," Ari said. "The frost had set in the morning I rode out for Trinda."

"Yes, but the snows are brief and mild." He bit into a sandwich. "I wouldn't mind a small place overlooking one of the few lakes around Tarka and Fradana."

"That does sound nice," she said, making short work of a couple sandwiches. "Why don't you start looking?"

A knock came at the door before he could answer, and Ari looked at it with a frown before she called for the person to come in. Danril entered, another plate in hand, and joined them in the sitting area. As he sat, he got a good look at Ari's face and pursed his lips in disappointment.

"I thought you weren't going to get on her bad side," he said as he got back up to examine the black eye. "This is nasty."

"That's not from my mother," Finn said, swallowing the last of his sandwich. "Well, not directly. She threw the door open and caught Ari in the face."

"I see," Danril said, channeling his magic and pressing his palm to her bruised face to heal the bruise. "And her current foul mood?"

"Probably my fault," Finn said, snagging one last sandwich before Ari ate them all. "I refused to follow her around."

"Can you at least try not to aggravate her?" Danril asked as he picked up the cracker from his own plate.

"I've lived under her thumb long enough," Finn said. "If it eventually means running from this life, so be it, but I'm done being her puppet."

"Run where?" Danril asked, not liking where this was heading.

"Wherever I fancy," he said. "Tarka, Fradana, anywhere south." He reached down to get another sandwich and was surprised when he found one.. "Anywhere that I can just live as myself, not as her puppet."

"And what brought this on?" Danril asked, looking at Ari suspiciously.

"You really think I had something to do with this?" she asked, raising a brow at him. "I'm not a fan of the queen but I'm not insane."

"It's all my idea," Finn said. "It's something I started thinking about after Mother threatened to send her back to the order."

"And you wanted an escape," Danril said, nodding. "It makes sense. But why south?"

"The climate, mostly and the lakes that are found around there. They're secluded and I'd be left alone, except for whatever company I chose," he said, putting his arm around Ari. "That is if she wants to come."

"That's got a lot of strings attached," Danril said. "While yes, she could apply for a sabbatical and yes it would most likely be granted but if something were to happen and Ari is needed, she'd be recalled and unable to say no."

"I could live with it," Ari said, curling her legs underneath her. Danril looked at her, brows raised in surprise. "What? Am I not allowed to decide that I want to live quietly for a while? Twelve years is a long time to do what we do without a break, Danril."

"What else is behind this decision, Ari?" he asked quietly. "It's been four years since I made my own decision about taking a sabbatical, you chose to continue on as a solo operative at that time. What's changed?"

"Knowing about the past," she said quietly. "It's not Simeon's fault but I need time to come to terms with it all."

"I understand that," Danril replied quietly. "Do you want me to take the request to Simeon for consideration?"

"Let me think about it," she said quietly. "I feel that if I tried right now, he'd just ask me to wait until things with the queen are resolved."

"Fair point," Danril said, standing and taking the plates. "Get some rest in the meantime and no rash decisions from either of you."

"It's not rash if it's something I feel strongly about," Finn muttered. Danril rolled his eyes as he left. "Well, it's not." Ari couldn't help but laugh as the door shut.

"He's only looking out for you," Ari said, moving her head to his shoulder. "He's doing the same for me."

"I know. But I'm serious about this." He turned to face her. "I'm serious about finding a place that few know about, and I hope you'd come with me."

"And I would love to come with you," she said, taking his hands. "But before we can do this Finn, we need to make sure your mother doesn't have anything else disastrous planned. She's tried to kill me and who knows what she could be planning for the annual gathering next week."

"I know," he said, leaning over to put his forehead to hers. "I'm so done with all this."

"Just hold on to your dream," she said before kissing him. "We can work to make it come true, eventually."

"I'd love that," he whispered. "Ari, you…" He trailed off, not sure if he wanted to say what was on his mind.

"What Finn?" she asked, but he shook his head. "Finn, tell me what you want to say."

"I don't want to spoil the moment. We haven't had time to ourselves since we parted in Tarka, and I don't want to make any assumptions about your feelings."

"Well, I think it's very safe to say I like you more than a little bit," she said, looking at him with a smile. "Speak what you want."

"I enjoy every moment I spend with you, to the point where I can't think of much else. While you were gone, I had the hardest time trying to fall asleep because you weren't there." Finn looked down. "I was selfishly asking the gods for you to return safely for my happiness, because you add light to my life Ari."

Ari recalled how she'd felt the night after leaving Tarka, how it'd taken her so long to fall asleep and that when she finally had, it hadn't been restful. She let go of one of his hands and cupped his chin, bringing his tear-filled sad eyes up to look at her. With her thumb, she wiped away a couple that had escaped and smiled at him.

"When I stopped for the night after leaving Tarka, I wasn't able to fall asleep because it was so lonely in the room without you. And when I finally did fall asleep, it wasn't restful. I care for you more than I realized then," she said quietly. "Which is why I'm willing to leave the capital with you, if that's what you want to do."

"Ari, you...I... what god did I please to have you come into my life?" he asked, putting his free hand to her cheek.

"I don't know. I think they're all cruel bastards the way they toy with people's lives," she said.

"You are much too cynical, darling," he said, pressing his lips to hers.

"And you're much too optimistic, *astori*," she said with a small chuckle.

"*Astori*?" he asked, looking confused. "Ari, I don't know that language."

"It's Old Thenndin, a language only used by Shadow and Blade now," she said, pinching the bridge of her nose, cursing herself for being so stupid.

"Ok, so what does it mean?" he asked.

"Darling. But you cannot tell anyone about this. Old Thenndin has been all but lost because of the Ophirs that have come before you. Because only those from the order still use it to communicate with one another, I could face serious consequences by using it with you."

"I won't tell a soul," he said, pulling her into his lap. "I rather like it." He kissed her again, a little deeper this time, and Ari tasted the need there. "Can we go to bed now?" She nodded, and he scooped her up, kissing her again, his need matching hers and he took her to bed where need, desire, passion and connection were to be found.

Ari had gone right to sleep after all that, her head resting right over his heart, but Finn was still awake, all kinds of thoughts racing around his mind. Her decision and willingness to give up her current life and leave Thannid with him stunned him, and though he knew he probably shouldn't, he was questioning why. Why would she give up her life as an assassin to follow him? He knew she cared about him, there had been something different about the way she felt and responded to his touch tonight, but when had that changed? Was she simply agreeing to go with him because she had nowhere else to go, no one else to turn to? His heartbeat quickened and Ari stirred and picked her head up to look at him through half lidded golden eyes.

"Your mind is very loud tonight," she whispered. "What's bothering you?"

"Troublesome thoughts," he said, smoothing her hair out of her face. "Nothing to concern yourself with."

"It's making you lose sleep. I'd say that's a concern of mine," she said, sitting up. "Now, tell me what's bothering you."

"Forgive me for this, but it just feels like this is all too good to be true. Did I really change your mind in Tarka? You're not just messing with me?" Ari's tired face flashed through several emotions before she was able to arrange her face into something calm and composed,

"And what, pray tell, brought this fucking bullshit on?" she asked, her voice cold as ice.

"I'm sorry if it's caused you pain, but I'm afraid this will turn out to be one giant joke orchestrated by my mother who's going to pull the rug out from under me and let me crash to the floor, shattering my heart and soul into a million pieces. I care about you too deeply for that to happen and I'm terrified that's where I'm heading, especially after you agreed to go with me so readily."

"You're scared," Ari said, letting the anger and irritation fade. "Finn, I understand that, but what do I honestly have to gain from being in cahoots with your mother? I get nothing from hurting you."

"Yes, I am scared. I'm absolutely terrified of having this dream come crashing down around me," he said.

"You know I wouldn't do that to you, right?" she said, laying back down on his chest.

"I know," he said, stroking her hair. "Ari, I didn't mean to insult you or cause you anger."

"Finn, I understand," she said sleepily. "Get some rest, ok?"

"I will," he said with a yawn. "Thank you, Ari."

"For what?" she murmured.

"For being so understanding," he said, as his eyes closed slightly.

"Fear makes the brain do weird things," she said, moving to stroke his cheek. "Just relax and know that I do care about you." His hand moved down to her back, coming to rest just at the small of it. "Are you going to sneak off in the morning?"

"Not unless I have to," he said, adjusting the blanket over them. "Just rest Ari, I'll be here for as long as you need me."

"You're too good," Ari muttered as she dozed off. "You deserve more than..." she never finished her sentence before she fell back asleep.

"It's not a matter of what I deserve," he whispered, knowing what she was about to say. "It's a matter of what I want." Finn kissed the top of her head as he let his eyes close. "And Ari, what I want is you."

Chapter 11

THE MEETING OF THE Faedoms dawned on a clear, bright day that brimmed with promise and good intentions, which was quite the change after a week of rain and dreary weather. Sun reflected off the morning frost in such a way that it bathed everything in a blinding light, which many took as a sign of good fortune for the upcoming discussions. There was only one who wasn't taking this as a good sign was Tatiana, who was less than thrilled that Thenndi's turn as the chosen host this year. Many of her schemes and plans would be so much easier to enact if she was not the host of the meetings this time. She watched as carriage after carriage rolled by, each coming to a stop in the courtyard. Footmen jumped down and carriage doors opened and the four kings of the other Faedoms emerged.

King Praslin Bertone of Pertina was the first to approach Tatiana. She watched, her silver eyes studying his every move, looking for foul intentions or anything else she could twist in her favor, and continue forward with her ultimate plans to rule all five Faedoms herself. She found nothing and tamped down her disappointment as he came to a stop in front of her.

"Queen Tatiana, it has been far too long since we've seen each other," he said warmly. His tone matched the warm red color of his hair while his green eyes sparkled like a child at the holiday festivals. Tatiana found him tiring but remained polite in her reply.

"A year is far too long indeed," she said with so much false sweetness that the party assembled behind her, which included Ari and Danril, grimaced. "I trust you remember my son, Finnian?"

"Prince Finnian, you look well," Praslin said, turning toward Finn, who was busy hiding his boredom at this fake show of welcoming. He knew his mother didn't want them here any more than she wanted him spending his nights and free time with Ari.

"Thank you, Your Majesty," he said, dipping his head in respect to the king. "Welcome to Thannid."

"Forgive me for being incredibly bold, but I am surprised to see that you're still unattached," Praslin said, causing Tatiana to bristle and Finn to laugh.

"Still waiting for the right woman, Your Majesty," he said. "Just haven't found her yet." It was a subtle movement, but Praslin watched the prince's eyes flick back to the line of people and the only woman in Tatiana's rear guard while Tatiana glowered.

"One day son," Praslin said as he headed toward the open castle doors, "one day."

Finn nodded and moved on to greet the next visiting royal while Praslin headed in, glancing at Ari as he passed. She acknowledged the king with a slight dip to her head, but otherwise kept her eyes forward. Danril watched the exchange and raised a brow, but didn't say anything until the remainder of the royals were in the castle, Tatiana and Finn included.

"What was that about, little one?" he asked as they entered the hall behind the guards.

"Your guess is as good as mine, Danril," she replied as they took up a place near the stairwell to see what was going on without being in the queen's way. "Unless it had to do with the conversation King Praslin was having with Finn."

"The boy isn't very subtle, given that he glanced back toward you when he was talking about finding the right woman," Danril whispered as Tatiana began to speak. Ari nodded but didn't say anything as the queen's welcome speech droned on.

"While you are here, please treat Tena Castle as your own home. Rooms have been prepared for you and your attendants. Should you need anything, do not hesitate to ask. We'll have our luncheon in the southern dining room in forty-five minutes. A servant will come to lead you to the luncheon hall so you do not get lost in the maze that is Tena Castle." Tatiana paused, forcing herself to smile at the crowd. "Until then, your time is your own. The meetings will not start until tomorrow proper, and we will have our usual welcome feast after sundown tonight."

The crowd dispersed, each party being led down various halls toward their rooms. Ari waited until the hall was completely empty before disappearing out to the garden while Danril blended into the crowd. Finn waited until his mother turned her back so he could off to the garden as well. He checked the usual spots only to find her in the gazebo, head in her hands, staring at the drooping hydrangeas.

"What's that look for?" he asked quietly as he sat next to her.

"What look?" she asked, turning to look at him.

"The one that says someone kicked your dog," he said, putting a hand on her knee. "Something's bothering you darling, what is it?"

"Just thinking," she said, turning back to the flowers.

"Ari, whatever this is between us, it doesn't work if we don't talk to each other. My mother didn't say anything so it must be something King Praslin said. Tell me what it is."

"It's stupid, and probably selfish of me, but seeing all the royalty reminded me that there's always the possibility that your mother could marry you off on a whim. I'm nothing more than a commoner, what right do I have to protest that?"

"I don't think I've ever seen you this scared," he said, putting his hands over hers and brushing away the tears that escaped. "Or be selfish, for that matter. If I didn't know how much you cared already, I'd know now." He gently kissed her forehead. "My mother won't marry me off to another royal, because that would mean she'd have to bargain with another royal. Stuttgad is out because my father was King Stannish's brother. She hates Praslin, thinks that Dresyn is too weak to hold the throne of Dengard, and Rusin would rather stab her than speak to her. Out of the four of them, Stannish is the only one who has a daughter anyway, and Stuttgad and Thenndin haven't been on speaking terms since my father died. I really don't think you have anything to worry about."

"And what if she decides that she'd rather see you marry a cousin than cavort around with me?"

"Ari, this isn't like you," he said, getting worried.

"It's exactly like me. If I'm going to get hurt, or lose you, I need to prepare," she said, biting off the words.

"You're not going to lose me," he said, recoiling at the harshness of her voice. "I just told you that."

"How can you guarantee it?" she snapped.

"Because my mother would see me dead before she married me off to another country and gave them any sort of power over Thenndin." Ari's response died in her throat at his words. "Don't you get it now?" he bit off, irritated. The area grew warm, and he got up to pace. "My mother just wants the power the throne gives her, and she wants to exert all the control she can over every last one of her subjects, me included. She despises you because she can't control you or the order you belong to, which is why she tried to kill you to bring me back under her thumb." He stopped and knelt in front of her. "I'm not going anywhere without you, even if I must run away with you in the middle of the night."

"That would go over so well," she said, cracking a little bit of a smile. "I'm sorry I snapped."

"Don't be. I like seeing your emotions. It reminds me you're alive and not a mindless Fae soldier like the ones that serve my mother."

"Did you know you give off heat when you get mad?" she asked as he sat next to her again, taking her hands in his.

"Only if I don't control it," he said. "I've set things on fire before by getting mad."

"And you want to run off to the middle of nowhere with me," she asked, raising a brow. "I can be a very aggravating person."

"I think I can manage," he said, pulling her over to kiss her before getting up. "I should get to lunch before my mother sends a guard after me. Meet me in the library later?"

"As long as you don't have meetings to attend," she said, getting up and giving him one last kiss.

"Ari," he said with a slight groan as she pulled away with a smirk. "I can't skip lunch right now. Mother would kill me."

"After lunch then we skip the library," she said with a light laugh. "I'll be waiting for you."

"My room," he whispered. He watched her go, flitting away as though she had her wings out to carry her away on the breeze, feeling like his heart was dancing away with her.

Ari slipped into Finn's room and flopped down on his bed; thankful she didn't have to be at some stuffy royal lunch right now. The door creaked open and someone who should've been at that royal luncheon crept in.

"I half expected to find you at lunch with the prince," came the voice of King Praslin.

"And incur further wrath from the queen?" Ari asked as the king took a seat near the fireplace. "I've bled enough lately, Your Majesty. What can I do for you?"

"You don't do small talk, do you?" he asked, looking over at her.

"King Praslin, I have no doubt you know who and what I am. Forgive me if I don't feel like beating around the bush."

"How blunt," he said with a bit of a laugh. "It's refreshing to speak to someone who doesn't bend over backwards to appease me."

"Sir, if I refuse to appease Queen Tatiana, do you really think I would appease any other royal?" Ari sat up and crossed her legs in front of her. "You followed me into the prince's room, so it's safe to assume you were spying on him in the garden. What do you want, Your Majesty?"

"My curiosity sated, if you feel like indulging me," he said, "and depending on where your loyalties lie."

"Those lie with the people of Thenndin," she said thinly. "Ask your question, King Praslin."

"How badly does the prince want the throne?" he asked. Ari kept her composure, but the question had not been the one she was expecting. "And would he be making you the queen consort?"

"Answering those questions would force me to betray the trust of a person I care deeply about. Do I strike you as a double agent, King Praslin?"

"No, you strike me as someone smart and shrewd, but not blind to what Tatiana is trying to do."

"Unless ordered to act, I do not interfere with what goes on in this castle," Ari said. "I don't have anything I can tell you, Your Majesty. If you want a feel for what goes on, ask the castle gossips. I'm sure they have some juicy tidbits for you."

"You're a stubborn one," Praslin said as he stood. "I hope the prince knows what he's getting into."

"Oh, he knows exactly what he's getting into," came Finn's voice from the doorway. "He doesn't mind."

"Your Highness," Praslin said, dipping his head toward the prince. "Forgive the intrusion. I was just on my way out."

"You missed a very entertaining lunch," Finn said as they crossed paths. "Mother took full advantage of your absence."

"I'm sure she did," Praslin said as he placed his hand on the doorknob. "I've seen Tatiana's wrath once before. Take care you don't fall victim to it." He closed the door behind him, leaving his words hanging behind, like some ominous warning. Ari snorted, alway very well aware of the queen's wrath, having been victim to it very recently.

Finn shook his head and sat down, sliding off his boots before he grabbed Ari and pulled her against him. "What was that all about?" he asked, nuzzling her neck.

"He was trying to get me to give him information about your claim on the throne," she said, shivering as his lips moved from her neck to her shoulder. "I told him if he wanted court gossip, there were far better sources."

"Smart," he said. "Now, I believe you and I had plans for after lunch," he said in her ear.

"Did we?" she asked, turning around to face him, a smirk on her face.

"Uh huh and you're not getting out of it," he said, hands on her hips.

"When did I say I wanted out of these plans?" she whispered as her lips met his. Finn smirked as he pulled her down with him. She let out a small gasp in shock as the world shifted before all thoughts simply faded and the only thing that mattered was the two of them in that moment.

Out in the gardens as the weather grew cold and the now overcast sky threatened snow, Tatiana was overseeing the final preparations for tomorrow night's welcoming ball. As she watched the butler direct a servant on where to place a sculpture, Grimmett, the captain of the police, came to stand next to her.

"Is everything in place for tomorrow night?" she asked quietly as the butler barked out orders.

"Several tried and tested rouges are ready and willing to hide here in the gardens and strike at the right moment."

"Excellent." She walked around the garden, Grimmett following almost like a little puppy. "And for the other matter we discussed?"

"Regarding?" he asked, confused. "We routinely discuss many other matters, Your Majesty."

"The matter we spoke of regarding the disposal of that common whore, you dumbass," she hissed as they continued along the path

"Oh, right. Managed to get you a three for one deal, Your Majesty. I got enough muscle to take out him, her and the other guy. Bonus is one of them holds a grudge against the girl and her buddy."

"Just how many people did you find?" she asked as they proceeded out of the garden and toward her private study.

"Ask around the slums and there seems to be no shortage of people who don't like Danril Craine or Ari Penndra, Your Majesty," Grimmett said as they entered and shut the door behind them.

"Interesting," she said as she sat at the desk. "This isn't a very subtle approach."

"I understand that but there are also enough rogues who wouldn't be opposed to taking out some other royals, if necessary, Your Majesty." Tatiana laughed and pointed to the chair across from her desk.

"Excellent thinking for a change, Grimmett," she said. "Though I'm sure Praslin and Dresyn are still at their fighting peak."

"Even so, there's at least a dozen of them ready to lie in wait for this," Grimmett said. "Even at their peak, I doubt Praslin and Dresyn are capable of handling more than a couple of dirty street fighters."

"Hm, yes, the combat style might be too much for them. I highly doubt your rouges are going to fight fair too."

"I'd be sorely disappointed in them if they did," Grimmett said, as he rose. "Is there anything else this evening milady?"

"This evening? No. Be sure to have these rouges in position for after dinner tomorrow night. The garden will be clear while we eat."

"Understood, milady," he said, bowing his head and leaving. He didn't get paid to think about the reasons behind her decisions, but tonight he couldn't help wondering why she would want to dispose of her own son. He shook his head, decided he didn't get paid enough to think things like that and went back to his business.

Unbeknownst to the queen and Grimmett, they hadn't been alone in the garden. Always watching and listening, Danril had picked up on their conversation and had followed them, listening to every word of the queen's plans to dispose of Finn, Ari, and himself. Once the pair had gone into the castle, he'd shook out his wings and taken flight, racing through the air to the order to speak with Simeon about what he'd just overheard.

The lord's door burst open, and Simeon sighed. He set his pen down and grabbed the whiskey from behind his desk as Danril sat across from him.

"One of these days you're going to break that door," he said, pouring two glasses of whiskey and passing one to Danril.

"Hardly likely," Danril said with a snort as he took the glass. "That door was there when we were both initiates, and our master was bursting into this office. If it can withstand the three of us, it'll surely outlast us."

Simeon snorted before taking a drink. "So, why have you burst into my office this time?"

"Tatiana has had Grimmett, the captain of the secret police, organize quite a few rouges from the slums to hide in the garden tomorrow night and attack during the welcome ball for the Faedom meeting."

"Do you know how many for certain?" Simeon asked, setting his glass down with a thunk.

"Not sure," Danril said. "That part of the conversation may have happened after they left the gardens."

"Were they at least careless enough to say who the targets were?"

"Myself, Ari, and the prince," Danril said. "From the sounds of it, Grimmett found Aermore too."

"Fucking hell," Simeon said, rubbing his brow. "Normally this wouldn't be a problem, but Aermore Drimdark? He wants nothing but your blood."

"Ari's too, after she bested him in a knife throwing contest about a month ago." Danril shook his head. "People have wanted Ari and I dead for some time, but why would Queen Tatiana want her own son dead?"

"Any number of reasons I suppose," Simeon said, picking his glass back up and making short work of the contents. "But the timing of this is what I find more intriguing. She's doing this the night the Faedom meeting truly kicks off. What's to stop her from blaming each of the other Faedoms from trying to kill her pet assassin, her son, and his bodyguard?"

"But what does it gain her?" Danril asked.

"Think about it Danril. She's a power-hungry mad woman who has a son in his twenty-ninth year and should've taken the throne by now. The fact that he hasn't should tell you that she won't give up the throne unless she's dead. She's been looking for reasons to go after the other countries. If Prince Finnian is killed while they're here, all she has to do is accuse any one of them of plotting against her. The meetings grind to a halt, everyone goes home, and she plans all out war."

"She's already been planning all out war," Danril said.

"We know that and so does half the castle, but she could do so openly now, using the attack on the prince as a rally point."

"That's if any of the royals survive this," Danril said. "With any number of assailants in wait and the chaotic scramble to get to safety, it's just a bloodbath waiting to happen."

"I will gather who I can and have them wait on the castle walls around the garden, but I can't promise many. You and Ari will have to do what you can to protect yourselves and the prince."

"Understood." Danril stood to go. "You know, this was supposed to be a quiet, easy mission, but I think I've done as much work in the last four years as I did while actively serving the order."

"I'd say you could always come back, but I don't feel your heart would be in it as it once was." Simeon got to his feet as well. "You were one of the best for the longest time, but there's too much blood on your hands and too much grief in your heart still. Once this business with the queen is over and things settle down, you should consider leaving Thannid."

"And leave the prince?" Danril shook his head. "I have duties to carry out."

"And some little birds have told me the prince is thinking of leaving Thannid, with yet another of my best assassins," Simeon said, shaking his head. "Prince Finnian would have Ari to look after him. You need to deal with that grief you pretend doesn't exist anymore." Danril scoffed as he pulled open the door. "Watch yourself tomorrow night Danril. I've lost too many friends to the sharp end of a blade already."

"Be that as it may, Blades are expendable, Simeon. There will always be another to take my place at the order," Danril hovered in the doorway for a moment before closing the door softly behind him.

"Yes, another Blade could take your place here, but no one can replace you in the heart," Simeon said quietly. He took a moment to compose himself before he summoned a page.

"Gather any Blades that may be in Thannid and in the building and assemble them in the meeting room."

"Yes sir," the page said before disappearing.

Simeon sighed and headed for the door, pausing only to grab the official-looking garment from the coat rack by the door. As he donned the robes the lord of the order should be wearing all the time, he couldn't help but feel as if they were heavier than normal, weighed down by his decisions. He composed himself and left his office and went to wait in the meeting room. Watching as people slowly trickled in. When no more entered, he sighed and spoke.

"Tomorrow night, an ambush has been set for the prince, Blade Penndra and Blade Craine."

"Penndra and Craine are more than capable of handling a few thugs on their own," someone spoke from the rear. Simeon glared at them with narrow eyes and cleared his throat.

"But they cannot protect five royals, four of which are visiting for the annual Faedom meeting. Should any one of them die on Thenndin soil, this country and its innocents will be at risk from the all out war that will follow. You have the right to say no, but I am asking, no rather, I'm begging, for you to aid them in keeping any blood from being shed other than the necessary rouge blood."

"Who's behind the plot?" asked a small voice from the front. Simeon looked down at the one called Copper.

"The queen. The information was brought to me by Blade Craine after he overheard her and Chief Grimmett speaking about it in the castle's gardens."

"Then I will assist," Copper said, her partner nodding beside her. The rest of the assembled group slowly agreed.

"The Welcome Ball usually kicks off at dusk, we'll need to be on the castle walls before then so we can be ready to intervene when necessary." He paused as the group made to leave. "It's long said that Blades were expendable, that there would always be another to take their place. But please act with caution, think of people who may care about you tomorrow night. You may be expendable to the order, but you are never expendable to those you care about. You are all dismissed."

He left the hall before anyone could ask him what prompted the sudden caution. He shed the robes and left the order, going home to his wife.

Blissfully unaware of what was in the works, Ari and Finn were sitting on his bed, watching the sunset through the bedroom window, picking at the plates of food Finn had managed to swipe from the kitchen. As she laughed at some joke he'd just cracked, Finn watched her and smiled at how her face grew softer when she laughed and at how tiny she looked in his sweater. He leaned over, placed a hand on the back of her neck and pulled her toward him so he could kiss her. She smiled at him as he leaned back and picked up a grape.

"What was that for?" she asked, grabbing a piece of cheese.

"Because I could," he said. "And because you look absolutely adorable right now."

"Absolutely adorable is not something you usually associate with a deadly assassin," she said with a half grin.

"If you're not careful with those half smiles and smirks, we're just going to end up right back in bed," he said with a half growl. Ari smirked in response. "I warned you," he said, moving the plates before pinning her to the bed. However, before they could get any further, the door opened and in walked Danril. "You probably should've knocked," Finn growled as he let Ari up.

""Something's not right," she said, looking at his face, twisted in worry and fear. "Danril, what's wrong?" Ari asked, getting up and going over to him. "You don't look well."

"There's danger brewing," he said, switching to old Thenndin as he sat on the couch.

"What do you mean?" she asked in the same language as she sat next to him.

"The queen is planning to have us attacked tomorrow night at the Welcome Ball."

"Not wholly surprising," Ari said. "She couldn't kill me in Trinda, so it makes sense she'd try again, and try for more targets. What aren't you telling me?"

"The rogues that are planning to attack include Aermore and other rogues from the slums. You know there are no shortage of people from Thannid's slums that would like us dead."

"I assume you've already been to see Lord Simeon," she said as Finn came over and sat next to her. Danril nodded. "And what did he say?"

"He would do what he could, but could not make promises." He looked glum at the thought.

"Then we make do where we can," she said, reaching over and taking his hand. "There have been worse odds for the two of us."

"But never where we've had innocents to protect," Danril said. "This whole situation is a disaster in the making."

"Danril, the kings all have guards, highly trained ones from the looks of them, and we'll be there to protect Finn. That's our priority." He nodded and let out a small sigh. "You know this means we can't sneak out this year."

"Don't remind me," he groaned, causing Ari to laugh. "Not that we're allowed in at the Rose anyway."

"The Gilded Lily is always nice," Ari replied. "But we'll be fine. We've both beaten worse odds."

"You're weirdly optimistic," he said, squeezing her hand before getting up.

"I'm just feeling good right now, that's all," she said. "You should probably go eat something."

"When did the tables turn on me?" he asked, shaking his head. "Good night you two," he called over his shoulder, switching back to the common language.

"G'night," Finn replied, looking at Ari curiously. The minute the door closed he spun her around to face him. "What was that all about?" Ari bit her lip wondering how much she should tell him. "Look, clearly it was something he didn't want me to hear, otherwise he wouldn't have spoken in a language only one of us understands. But you tossed my name around and I feel like I deserve to know."

"You're right, you do, and in the simplest terms possible, there's going to be an attempt on your life tomorrow night," she said. "Beyond that, you need to let Danril and I handle this."

"Why? I've trained with a sword and dagger. Do you think I can't handle myself?"

"I have no doubt you could in a fair fight, *astori* but these men, they won't fight fair."

"So teach me," he said, standing up. "If street fighting differs, teach me so I don't have to rely on everyone to save me."

"I can show you a few techniques, but you don't learn by instruction, you learn by being in the thick of it and figuring out that you either hit hard and hit first or it's your blood on the ground."

"Then try not to spill blood," he said, standing.

"Get changed," she said, getting up and grabbing her own clothes. "Care to make a little wager?"

"I win, you have to come to the welcome feast and ball with me," he said, causing her to pause as she pulled her shirt on.

"Pardon?" she asked, recovering enough to pull her shirt on.

"You heard me," he said, putting his hands on his hips.

"Very well," she said, "if I win, I get to pick what I want, when I want."

"Very well," he said. "Let's begin."

"You're probably going to regret this," she said as they moved to the open space in his room.

"I might," he said, mirroring her stance. "Or I may not. Just depends on how well you teach me." He smirked.

Ari rolled her eyes and proceeded with the lesson, and true to her word, made him regret asking. He hobbled over to the bed, groaning at how sore he was while Ari walked over and sat next to him.

"I win," she said, leaning over to kiss his forehead.

"So you do," he said, rubbing his ribs. "You pack a mean punch for someone so small."

"Just remember you asked me to do this," she said, kissing him again before getting up.

"Where are you going?" he called out with a groan as he tried to sit up.

"To draw you a bath to help with those sore muscles," she called from the bathroom. "And I'm claiming my winnings."

"Really?" he asked, as he slowly made his way to the bathroom. "This is what you want?"

"We got interrupted earlier," she said, as she added some scented oil to the water. "I'm finishing what got started."

"You're going to be the death of me," he said with another groan, as she laughed. "And this bath will help?"

"Tried and true method," she said. "Given to me by the guy that kicked my ass on a regular basis."

"Well then, I suppose I can't go wrong," he said as he undressed and sank into the tub. The warm water was very soothing, and he let out a small groan as he sank down to his neck before sitting up. Ari joined him a few moments later and settled next to him. "I know I lost, but would you still accompany me to the feast tomorrow night?"

"Of course, *astori,*" she said, turning around to kiss him softly.

"Thank you," he whispered, closing his eyes and letting the warmth sink into his bones. "You know that means you can't wear your leather pants, no matter how much I like you in them."

"I am aware," she grumbled as she leaned against his chest. "Worry about it tomorrow."

"Deal," he said, wrapping his arms around her, and that's where they stayed until the water turned cold and the evening sky lost the remainder of its vibrant hues.

Chapter 12

HE HAD INTENDED TO wake up early and ask her for another hand-to-hand lesson, but between nearly dozing in the tub and then Ari having a nightmare in the dead of night, they'd both ended up sleeping til nearly lunch. It was only a knock at the door that woke him. Disentangling himself from the still sleeping Ari, he grabbed his pants and the sweater she'd been wearing last night and opened the door to a very sheepish looking servant.

"S..S... Sorry to bother you, Your Highness, but your Queen Mother wishes to know if you're coming down for lunch since you missed breakfast."

"Highly unlikely," Finn said, rubbing his eyes against the bright light. "Have some lunch sent up please and tell my mother I will see her at the feast tonight."

"S...S... She said if you said that to tell you that if you plan to have her accompany you tonight, you are to make sure she dresses appropriately for royal company."

"I'll handle it appropriately," Finn said with a yawn. "Anything else?"

"No, Your Highness," the servant said, bowing before retreating. Finn sighed and shut the door. The snap of the door shutting woke Ari from her sleep. She sat up, hair everywhere, and looked around, blinking at how bright things were.

"I'm sorry I woke you," he said as he sat down and moved a strand of golden hair out of her face. "You look like you need more sleep."

"I'll be fine," she said with a yawn. "What time is it?"

"Around noontime," he said, getting up and grabbing her a sweater. "I'm having some food sent up."

"Oh good," she said, taking the sweater and pulling it on. "How are you feeling this afternoon?"

"You're the one who slept like shit and yet you're asking how I'm feeling?" Finn shook his head.

"I'm not the one who got their ass kicked last night," she said, getting up to deal with the tangled mess that was her hair.

"Good point. Whatever you put in that bath last night really did the trick. I still have some fun bruises, though."

"I have some salve that will clear those if you want," she said as she worked to detangle a knot from her hair. "I can go grab it for you. It's in my room."

"Maybe later," he said, going to help her as she struggled to get the hairbrush untangled. "Are you sure you don't need more rest?" he asked as he carefully worked the brush out of her hair and studied her reflection. "Ari, you look exhausted."

"I'll manage," she said with a yawn as he worked the knots out of her hair.

"You're taking it easy until dinner tonight," he said, putting the brush aside and kissing the top of her head.

"Hmm, I think I can manage that," she said, stretching. "Are we sure I can't wear my usual pants and tunics? It'd be so much easier to keep weapons on me."

"Yes," he said. "While it would probably be easier to fight should it come down to it, I have been informed that you need to be wearing something more appropriate for royal company."

"How disappointing," she said, leaning forward and resting her elbows. "I don't have anything that would work."

"Leave that to me," he said as a knock came at the door again. "I'll sneak out to the market with Danril while you rest up. Just no complaining about what I pick, ok?"

"Fine, but I have just one condition," she said as he went to the door and got the food that he'd asked for.

"What's that?" he asked, bringing over the two bowls of stew and handing her one.

"I need to be able to have my weapons on me. If what Danril told me last night comes to pass, I will need them."

"I'll keep it in mind," he said between bites. "Eat up." She picked up her spoon and did, eating quickly, so quickly that Finn raised a brow. "Clearly, we need to start making it down for dinner or lunch more often."

"We slept through breakfast, of course I'm hungry," she said, putting aside the empty bowl.

"Maybe then I shouldn't have let us sleep through breakfast," he said, finishing his bowl and putting it next to hers.

"And where would be the fun in that," she said, stretching. "Be careful in town."

"Of course, darling," he said, leaning over to kiss her. "Get some more rest. I should be back before sundown."

Ari nodded as he grabbed his boots and a jacket and left. She sat there for a few more minutes before grabbing her pants and deciding to grab a book from the library before going to her room to read. Content with her book, she settled in, but before she could even get through the first third, her eyes started to drift shut. Her grasp on the book loosened as she dozed off and she was completely asleep by the time the book slipped off her lap and onto the bed.

In town, Finn and Danril huddled in their coats against the first snowfall as they passed a few shops. People were racing to get out of the cold, wet snow. Danril noticed Finn was only half paying attention, his mind clearly not on the task at hand. After they passed the third dress shop with barely more than an appraising glance, Danril pulled him into a nearby tavern, ordered two mugs of spiced cider and sat him down at the table.

"What's bothering you?" Danril asked as soon as they had their mugs. "Did she tell you about what your mother had planned?"

"I'm worried, but not about that," Finn said, picking up his mug and taking a sip. "Ari had the nightmare again last night."

"Not ideal timing but she'll manage," Danril said, sipping his own cider. "She's been pushing that nightmare down for over twelve years. It's only gotten in her way once. You don't have anything to worry about."

"I can't help it," Finn replied, putting his mug down. "Because not only do I care about her, but it's also all our lives on the line tonight should something happen."

"It's all being handled. Your job is simply to enjoy yourself and pretend like you're not expecting anything to happen."

"That's possible?" Finn asked, going back to his cider and finishing it.

"Just watch Ari and follow her lead," Danril said. "Now, if you're done being wrapped up in your head, you came out here for a reason."

"Right. She had one condition, she needed to be able to keep her weapons on her."

"Of course she does," Danril said, rolling his eyes. "Which means she's going to hate whatever we pick. Might as well go for broke then, kid."

"Hmm, there was that dark red one two shops back that might work."

"The one with the slit?" Danril asked. Finn nodded. "I feel like you have other ideas in mind with that one, though."

"No reason it can be multi-purpose," Finn said with a shrug and smirk.

"I'm going to pretend this conversation didn't happen," Danril said, shaking his head and shuddering. "We should hurry if you want time to get ready."

Finn nodded and they left, stopping at the shop to purchase the dress. They started at it a moment before Danril spoke.

"She's going to hate it."

"She'll get over it," Finn said, motioning to the shopkeeper. "She owes me for the bruises she left last night anyway."

"Boy, there are just some things I don't want to know about her personal life," Danril said, smacking his shoulder.

"Har har har," Finn said before he explained what he needed from the shopkeeper. "I asked her for some hand-to-hand tips last night."

"That was a dumbass move," Danril said as the shopkeeper disappeared with the dress. "You're lucky all you got were bruises."

"I am aware. She packs a mean punch for someone so tiny."

"When you're the smallest and frailest initiate, you learn to hit hard and hit first or they hit you and they hit harder." Danril paused as the shopkeeper came back with the dress in a box and a smaller box on top. "The second box?" he asked as Finn handed over a small bag of coin for the parcels.

"Appropriate shoes to go with the dress. She's absolutely guaranteed to hate them." Finn thanked the shopkeeper and he and Danril left the shop. "I hope mother planned for the snow. The last I knew the ball was in the garden."

"Does she seem like the type to leave anything like that to chance?" Danril asked as they pulled their collars tight. Finn shook his head, and they headed back. Once in the castle, they went their separate ways to get ready for tonight's festivities.

Finn checked his room and was surprised to find that Ari wasn't there. He changed quickly, discarding the sweater and pulling on a tight fitting dark red tunic about the color of Ari's dress and black pants, completing the look with shiny black leather boots. After running a hand through his hair, he headed out to check the library and then finally headed to her room, where he found her curled up in a small ball on her bed. She whimpered slightly and hunched over even tighter. Finn carefully put a hand on her shoulder and tried to comfort her. However, the touch startled her awake and without thinking, she jolted up, moved his hand and had him pinned against the bed before she realized who was there.

"Easy darling," he said as she moved her knee from his chest. "I should probably be grateful that you didn't put your knee elsewhere."

"It would've been unfortunate for both of us," she said, moving so he could get up. "You look all fancy."

"Fancy party means fancy royal clothes," he said. "Did you sleep ok? You were whimpering when I came in."

"You caught me at the beginning of the nightmare," she said, rubbing her arms.

"Again?" he asked, pulling her into his arms and holding her against him tightly. "Maybe we should skip the party."

"We can't. It would rouse your mother's suspicions," Ari said, nuzzling against his chest, his embrace helping soothe the tremors from the nightmare. "I'll be fine, promise." She adjusted so she could give him a light kiss on his cheek. "I should probably get all dressed up since you are."

"Hm, yes," he said, tipping her chin so he could kiss her properly before letting go. "No arguing about the dress, ok. Options were limited since you insisted you had to be able to keep weapons on you."

"What do you mean?" she asked as he moved her off his lap and grabbed the larger of the two boxes.

"Just go see for yourself," he said, pushing the box at her. She took it and went behind the screen. He heard the box drop lid drop and then the box before she came back around holding the dress.

"What the hell is this thing?" she asked, holding up against her.

"The aforementioned dress," Finn said. "It's the only one I could find that would let you keep a weapon on you."

"Beyond that, there is no possible way this is the right size," she said, pulling on the fabric that made up the bodice.

"Why don't you just put it on and quit stalling? We're going to be late if you keep it up. And if we're going to be late, it may as well be for something fun, not your bitching." Ari stuck her tongue out at him and disappeared again, Finn crossed his arms and tapped his fingers impatiently as he waited for her to change. Various curses came from behind the screen as she worked herself into the dress. Eventually, she came back around, and Finn swallowed hard. "Good gods," he whispered.

"I look ridiculous," she said, pulling on the bodice to hopefully move the slit that nearly reached her hip. "It's almost impossible to hide a weapon on me."

"If we had time," he said, putting his hands on her waist, feeling the smooth fabric as it clung to her curves, "I'd help you out and back into it."

"It cannot look that good," she said, looking in the mirror. "I don't recognize myself. And where do I put a knife?"

"Try this," he said, pulling a blood red leather strap from his pocket, before leaning his head down to kiss the back of her neck. "It's probably not going to allow you to keep as many as you'd like but you could at least have one on you."

"One is better than none," she said, unable to fight the shudder that went down her spine. "Dinner, Finn. If nothing goes wrong, you can peel it off after the ball."

"I'm going to hold you to that," he whispered in her ear before letting go to get the box that contained the shoes.

"What are these?" she asked as he handed her the box.

"Shoes. I doubt your usual scarred leather boots would be welcome tonight."

He watched in amusement as Ari sneered at the shoes that were meant to be worn with the dress. He could hear her say something about impractical death traps as she slid them on, quickly buckling the thin strap around her ankle. After finding her a wrap that she could wear to ward off the chill, they headed down to the feast, arriving well after everyone had been seated and food had been served despite their best attempts to not be late.

"Finally, my son deigns to join us," Tatiana said, giving them a disgusted look. "Though his taste in consorts does leave something to be desired."

"To each their own, Queen Tatiana," said the king of Stuttgad. "Your son has fine taste. She's quite exquisite."

"Common born," Tatiana said bitterly, "raised in an orphanage. She's only here because I need the services she provides."

"She looks experienced," the king said, eyeing her, lingering on how the silken fabric clung to her breasts, which though not as big as some of the noble ladies in the room, stood out thanks to the dress. "Wouldn't mind seeing how experienced."

"Good luck prying her away from my son," Tatiana said dryly, "since he's formed some kind of attachment to that thing. I highly doubt he could be convinced to give her up, even for a night."

"Give her enough alcohol, I'm sure I could convince her do to most anything," he said, his eyes still on Ari. "She looks so soft and unspoiled." Tatiana snorted but didn't say anything.

"Mother, King Stannish," Finn said, bowing. Ari followed suit. "Please forgive our tardiness."

"Showing up with that exquisite beauty on your arm, apologizing for being late, I'm envious boy," Stannish said, throwing his head back and laughing. "I don't think an apology is necessary."

"Take your seat Finnian," Tatiana said, ignoring the king. "I trust this is not going to become a regular occurrence?"

"Does it matter if it does?" Finn asked, pulling out Ari's chair for her before he sat. "Or do I need to remind you that I am an adult, capable of deciding when or if I want to come down for dinner."

"You'll not speak to me in that tone," she hissed. "I am your mother."

"Only because you gave birth to me," he said as a servant brought plates for him and Ari. "But that's all. Now, this isn't the place for our family squabbles," he said as Danril appeared. "Good evening Danril."

"Prince Finnian, Miss Ari," he said, dipping his head toward them before taking his seat next to Ari. He slipped her a sheathed blade under the table, and she affixed it to the leather band Finn had given her. "Quite a productive day was it not?"

"You two clearly had a more productive day than I did," Ari said, as their plates were served. "I confess I spent much of my day in bed."

"There's nothing wrong with that," Finn said, reaching over and squeezing her hand. "Resting when the body needs to is just as important."

"Well, that would definitely explain your tardiness," King Stannish said with another laugh. Finn felt Ari stiffen next to him. She was clearly uncomfortable around him, and with the comments he was making, Finn couldn't blame her.

"I believe you're making my consort uncomfortable with your insinuations, King Stannish," Finn said quietly. "I would appreciate it if you would stop."

"Speaking up for the common blood whore," Stannish said, "how admirable."

"I would watch how you speak," Finn said, putting his hand on Ari's leg to keep her in her chair. He could feel her quaking with anger under his hand. "Visiting royalty or not, I won't stop her if you push too far."

"Won't stop her from what?" King Stannis asked. Before either Finn or Ari could answer, Danril spoke up.

"Best not to ask questions that yield unpleasant answers, sire," he said, his voice quiet yet hard enough to be heard over the din of the hall. Stannis gave him a curious look but dropped the subject. The rest of dinner passed without incident, the plates cleared away and the guests were led out to the gardens for the remainder of the evening's festivities.

Ari barely recognized the gardens when they walked out. They'd been transformed into what some would call a wonderland. Twinkling lights adorned the trees and bushes bathing the garden in a soft glow. A magical barrier over the area set aside for the desserts and dancing kept the falling snow at bay. It was hard to believe that lying in wait somewhere out there were any number of rogues from the slums hired to kill the three of them. But for all the wonder the scene before her caused, Ari still couldn't keep the scowl off her face.

"You may want to stop scowling," he said in her ear. "It's a little off putting."

"Good," she grumbled. "Maybe then the hungry bastards around here will quit staring at me like they want to devour me. It's unnerving."

"I take the blame for that," he said as she adjusted her wrap for the third time to cover herself. "But just remember you are far more capable than the average Fae woman at defending herself from them. And I will stand by you if you do need to defend yourself."

"Hopefully it won't come to that," she said as he laced his fingers with hers. "You know you're getting dirty looks left and right."

"Do I seem bothered?" he asked, as the musicians filed in. "They're just jealous because I have the most beautiful woman in the kingdom on my arm tonight."

Ari didn't say anything, as she reached for her glass, thinking there were far more beautiful women in attendance tonight. As the gentle sounds of a slow string waltz filled the air, people began to file out to the floor and began to dance in time to the music. Ari would've been more than content to just watch them, but Finn was on his feet moments later, dragging her out onto the floor.

"Finn, I really don't dance," she protested as he pulled her onto the floor and then against him.

"Oh, I know that's a load of bullshit," he said as he began to lead her around the dance floor.

"Fine, I don't do this stuffy dancing stuff," she retorted. "Finn, what are you doing?"

"Showing off who clearly has the most beautiful woman tonight," he said as they moved around the floor in time to the music. "Plus, I don't think you'd rather be alone, with the eyes of several hungry royals and nobles on you. Plus, what if some other noblewoman or royal consort here tried to steal me from you?"

"I'm more concerned about anyone that would try to stab you right now," Ari said dryly, as she followed Finn's lead. "Now, if people weren't waiting out there to kill us, I would probably be ready to stab someone for trying to take you."

"You really don't trust anyone, do you," he said as she shook her head. "I don't suppose I can blame you, life hasn't exactly been the kindest to you."

"I don't expect anyone to swoop in and make it better either," she said, looking right at him after a brief glance around the room. What I've experienced, felt, done in my life has shaped who I am. I don't plan on changing that just because a rich royal takes an interest in me."

"Well good," he said, deciding that he'd resisted long enough and leaned down to kiss her. "Because I like the woman in my arms for who she is, right now."

"You are much too bold for a royal," she said quietly, but there was a hint of a smile on her face. "Kissing a commoner like me."

"I have other things I'd like to do to this commoner," he said in her ear. "Don't tempt me to leave early."

"If there weren't a handful of people waiting to kill us," she whispered. He smiled as the song came to an end. He led her back to their seats, only this time he pulled her into his lap. "Either you really want to anger your mother, or you really truly do not care about the differences in our backgrounds," she said looking out at the crowd. "Many of these people look as though they either want me dead or..." she stopped and pulled the wrap around her tighter before shoving the emotions down where they wouldn't cause problems. They sat there, watching the ball for a while, until Danril joined them.

"You're causing quite a stir," he said, slipping into Ari's seat. "Anything strike you as odd little one?"

"You mean aside from the stares that make it hard to focus," she said as Finn's arms tightened around her. "No, nothing."

"That dress does leave little to many of their imaginations," he said, "though the color does suit you."

"King Stannish from Stuttgad continually finds himself looking in my direction," she said, looking around again. "The last time I caught his eye, the man actually licked his lips."

"Stannish has always been quite the lech if I remember correctly," Finn said with a scowl. "Not sure I'd trust my uncle alone with anyone."

"Don't go starting anything," Danril warned, "Lord Simeon was able to find volunteers to aid us but starting a fight with another royal, especially over a commoner, would not end well for anyone."

"If it were any other time..." Finn said, as the music changed. "We should probably dance again."

"Ah, yes," Danril said, as lines formed. "Go and have fun little one." Ari looked at him suspiciously before joining the lines.

The glimmered figures in the bushes were becoming clearer and clearer. Ari's eyes flicked back to Danril's and he nodded. She put a hand on Finn's arm to warn him as they took their places among the dancers. He nodded but kept the smile on his face, though he suddenly felt nervous.

Ari wanted to swear as they proceeded with some line dance that was clearly meant for simple nobles who couldn't master advanced steps. The figures kept creeping closer to the dancers, which allowed Ari to finally see through their glimmer. The nearest one to her was Aermore. She could see his stupid grin, the murderous glint in his eye, and all she wanted to do was wipe that stupid look off his face. As they circled around again, all the hidden rogues dropped their glimmers and rushed the floor, Aermore running straight for Ari and Finn. Danril appeared in front of him, blades in hand.

"I don't think so, Aermore," he hissed, mimicking the man's movements. The burly man growled as he continued to try to get around Danril. "Not once in twelve years have I let you near her and I won't start today."

"I'm getting paid handsomely to finally get my hands on that blonde brat of yours, Craine. Your usual tricks won't work." Aermore sneered and lunged with his dagger. Danril countered, and the two of them continually traded blows.

The royals nearby screamed as the rouges appeared, causing a mad dash for the entry-way to the castle while the guards that accompanied the royals drew swords and rushed toward the attackers. Ari pulled her blade from the sheath and fended off the nearest attacker to her. The area was nothing short of chaotic, even more so when eventually the Blades hidden on the castle wall swooped in from above to aid Ari and Danril in their fight to protect the prince and the other royals, many whose guards had already sustained all manner of injuries.

While Danril was still fighting off Aermore, Finn was fending off his own attackers, holding his own, as was Ari, but with only two weeks of rest after patching herself up in Trinda, the fighting was beginning to take its toll on her body. She made short work of three of the four rogues that had just rushed her but the fourth was proving more challenging. Minutes into their fight, she'd lost the upper hand and was now fending off blow after blow as he drove her back. Eventually, he'd pushed her back far enough that her foot slipped in a puddle of spilled wine, and she fell to the ground, her knife flying out of her hand and skittering across the floor. She struggled to her feet, ignoring the pain in her ankle and facing him.

"The infamous Ari Penndra ain't so scary when she's not armed to the teeth," he said with a sneer.

"I don't need to be armed to the teeth," she hissed, taking advantage of a semi-relaxed stance as he gloated. Had she been taller, or broader, and not in the infernal death traps for shoes, she probably would've been able to knock her attacker off his feet. Instead, as she slammed into him, he stepped back to maintain his balance and wrapped a hand around her throat. "You fucker," she choked out.

"Yeah, you ain't so scary," he said again as he put more pressure on her throat.

Danril's fight with Aermore was quickly turning into a draw with the two of them trading blow after blow that the other would always block. Aermore's next blow would've hit Danril but it never landed. As Aermore tumbled to the ground, suddenly unconscious, Danril looked up and found himself staring into the face of the one they referred to as Sun. A snarl crossed Danril's face as he stared at Sun.

"We can settle our differences later, Fire's in trouble," Sun said before he turned and went to subdue another rogue while Danril took off across the garden toward Ari.

There were several disadvantages to being short, Ari thought as she dangled off the ground but the worst one at this moment was the fact that she had no leverage to push the assassin off as she hung there, his hand keeping consistent pressure on her throat. The second disadvantage she found was that her opponent had much longer arms so even with the slit in her skirt allowing her to kick freely, she couldn't reach him to get a good solid kick in. She struggled, clawing at the hand that caused black spots to appear in her vision while he laughed, thinking that it was hilarious that this tiny girl, this top-notch assassin could be defeated so easily. Her desperate attempts to free herself slowed as the pressure on her throat tightened. She felt her arms go limp and vaguely thought that she'd tried but failed as the blackness almost completely took over. The pressure suddenly and she was vaguely aware of landing on the ground while someone took over her fight.

"Aww, the wee lil girl needs her big bad protector to come save her," the rogue taunted, wiping his bloody lip as Danril put himself between the attacker and Ari.

"She doesn't need me to save her," he said, as he lunged, feinting before he put his blade between the man's ribs. The rogue sputtered and staggered back. "But I won't hesitate to defend her when she finds herself outmatched."

Ari's vision was just beginning to clear when Danril knelt next to her and carefully sat her up.

"Can you stand?" Danril asked as he wiped his bloody blade on a pant leg while the attacker lay on the floor in a pool of his own blood. Ari looked up and nodded, carefully getting to her feet, refusing to let the pain in her ankle stop her. "Don't push it too much," he said, putting an arm around her to support her.

"Where's Finn?" she asked, hoarsely. Danril quickly scanned the crowd and pointed toward the table where he took out another rogue with an impressive right cross. "He learns fast," she whispered.

"How many lessons did you give him?" he asked as they carefully made their way over to him.

"Just the one," she said. Danril let out something between a sigh and a low whistle, which is how Ari knew he was impressed.

Finn looked up as they approached, a grin on his face but worry in his eyes at the sight of Ari limping. A flicker behind Finn had her breaking free of Danril's grasp and running toward him despite the pain in her ankle. She crashed into Finn knocking him to the side as a long red line opened on his arm. She faced the final attacker down unarmed, her usually warm golden eyes full of steel as they stared into his dark brown ones.

"Give up," he hissed as he pushed her back.

She tried to right herself only to step on the injured ankle and she collapsed. She tried to get back up, but the attacker kicked her right in the ribs. Everyone nearby heard the cracking of ribs and Ari fell back down, not moving. "Take another step boyo and you join her on the floor," the man said to Finn as he started toward Ari. "Good boy. Now I got paid handsomely to mess up your pretty face and your pretty girl here, it'd be a shame to waste someone's hard earned coin."

Finn clutched his arm as the rogue approached, knife ready. However, he never made it within striking distance as Danril appeared behind him and with one swift movement, put his blade between the man's ribs and pulled it out quickly. The would-be assassin gasped and gurgled before collapsing into a puddle of his own blood. Finn blinked rapidly as Danril wiped the blade on his coat sleeve and put it back in his sheath.

"Is it over?" Finn asked, clutching his bloody arm.

"I believe so. We should get out of here and to the order," Danril said, carefully helping Ari up. "Matron needs to look at you two and I need to speak to Simeon."

"Bandage his arm," Ari said through gritted teeth. "It's bleeding badly."

"There's no time," Finn said, "we should go before anyone else tries to attack."

"Agreed," Danril said as he scooped up Ari, who yelped in both pain and shock.

"What are you doing?" she managed eventually.

"You can't fly, let alone walk back to the order," he said, shaking his icy blue wings out. "So yes, I'm carrying you. Finn let's go." Finn shook his own wings out, and in the glow of the lights in the garden, Ari noticed they were black with red edges. Just as they took to the snowy sky, Queen Tatiana came running into the carnage after them.

"Finnian," she called as he flew off. "FINNIAN." When he didn't come back, she sniffed and smirked, pleased that the wheels of her plan had been set in motion. Even with the sheer amount of dead or wounded rogues in her garden and the order's interference, Finn sustained a nasty injury and was forced to flee the castle, all as she had intended. She arranged her face into a distressed look and went back inside. It was time for her to put on a show.

Chapter 13

TATIANA STRODE BACK INTO the castle, pausing outside the meeting hall to arrange her face in a distraught look, one that she hoped would sell the emotion since she was the furthest thing from distraught having orchestrated the whole plot. Behind the distraught look, she hid her pleasure at how things had turned out. She'd gotten everyone on edge, and though she hadn't expected Shadow and Blade to interfere, a matter she fully intended to investigate, she had enough to accuse the four kings waiting for her in that meeting room of plotting something as Finn had gotten injured in the scuffle. Forcing herself to sniffle and pinching her cheeks repeatedly to force tears into her eyes, she pushed the door back open and proceeded to put on her best show of emotion since her husband had died.

"Queen Tatiana, what happened?" King Praslin asked as the rest of the royals gathered around. "Is everything all right? Was anyone hurt?"

"I believe it will be," she said as one of the forced tears rolled down her face. "But someone that I allowed into my home-" She paused here to sob dramatically before she continued, "-someone brought evil men intent on causing me and mine harm." She looked around at them and sniffled. "My son could have been killed because someone decided to allow these men access to the grounds."

The gathered royals began shouting over one another in response to her accusations. It was Praslin who spoke up, his voice sharp enough to cut through the cacophony of counter accusations and quiet everyone.

"And what proof do you have, Queen Tatiana, that it was one of us?" he asked calmly but Tatiana could hear the simmering anger in his voice. "All of us faced the same dangers as your son, but when he was in the most danger, you didn't bother to pull him to safety with you."

"It was the heat of the moment" she spat, causing many to recoil. "I thought that his bodyguard and that stupid little whore of his would make sure he was safe. I clearly underestimated them."

"Twenty or so men rushed at them," Praslin shot back, "the prince is your son, you could have, should have, taken responsibility for him and made sure he was pulled to safety. Unless of course you had reason to leave him in the thick of that."

"How dare you accuse me of wanting my own son, my only heir to the crown, dead," she said, furious.

"Then show us the proof that any of us had a hand in this attack," Praslin snapped. "I'd love to see it, and I'm sure the rest of them would as well." The other three kings nodded in agreement.

Tatiana bristled. She had no proof. That hadn't been the point of this. She'd been trying to turn them on each other, sowing the seeds of distrust so that she could topple their reigns and assume control of their countries, making her the all-powerful leader. Instead, she was scrambling, trying to figure out how to make this turn back in her favor. Before she could come up with something, the king from Rignand spoke up.

"Things happen in the heat of the moment Praslin; we cannot blame Tatiana or accuse her of wanting her son dead just because he had to fight his way out of a sticky situation. Who's to say you didn't orchestrate this whole thing just to destabilize her country?"

"You're all fools," King Praslin snapped, "I wouldn't not be so stupid as to force the entirety of the nobility and the ruling class to suffer something so terrible." He turned and glared at Tatiana. "You however..."

"You accuse me," she said in a shrill voice. "Me, in my own home, when it was my child who was attacked by these vicious thugs?"

"And pray tell me Tatiana Ophir, what happened to Oberin Castmere, Stannish's brother? Do we need to speak on the rumors that still surround his death, twenty-nine years later?"

"Praslin, Tatiana," King Dresyn said, "that's enough. We've all suffered a terrible shock tonight. Perhaps we should adjourn, rest if we can and revisit this topic in the morning."

The other three kings nodded, leaving Tatiana forced to concede to them. She nodded and everyone dispersed, leaving the queen to make her way back to her chambers. The sun had long since faded as she stepped out onto her balcony and into the gentle late-night snow. She let it drift down on her, her mind replaying a long-lost moment, possibly the only moment she truly enjoyed with Oberin before she'd plunged the knife into his gut and let him bleed out into the snow. She didn't regret what she'd done, she wouldn't regret trying to rid herself of her stubborn, tradition-bucking son, and she sure wasn't going to regret disposing of the snot-nosed assassin Simeon had saddled her with. With a disgruntled sigh, she headed back into her chamber ready for bed and to figure out how she could salvage her plan to bring four countries to heel and under her rule.

While the queen plotted, Danril and Finn walked through the wide stone and steel gates, stepping out of a moment of terror and into a haven. Those that had been at the castle fighting paused as they came over the gate. Some dipped their heads, others nodded, acknowledging the hell they'd just been through. Those in the courtyard had the same tired or pained expressions, except for one person, a petite brunette who came sprinting across the courtyard when she spotted Danril.

"Dani, what happened to you all?" she asked. "You all looked like you got attacked by some wild creature."

"The same rogues that everyone else was fighting Tissa," Danril said, nose crinkled at being called Dani. "Where's Simeon?"

"In his study, like usual," she said, "dealing with the aftermath of all of this. Are you looking for Marion?"

"That's my first stop. Ari took a hell of a beat down."

"Oh, you poor thing," Tissa said. "You've gone through hell lately."

"You want me to take her so you can go speak to Lord Simeon?" Finn asked.

"Can you manage with just one arm?" Danril asked.

"I'll be fine. Go, this needs to be addressed. Especially before my mother can regroup and try again."

"Nothing can touch you within these walls," Tissa said as Danril carefully maneuvered Ari into Finn's good arm. "Now come, let's get you both to Marion. That's a nasty looking cut on your arm."

"Would've been worse had Ari not shoved me out of the way. Only the tip of an assassin's knife caught my arm instead."

"Barely saw the glimmer in time," Ari said, clearly in pain.

"You shouldn't talk," Tissa said as they approached the infirmary. "You're in pretty bad shape."

"Thanks for noticing," Ari said as she opened the door. Marion was already waiting for them along with three of her aides.

"Miss Penndra, what happened to taking it easy?" Marion asked as Finn set her on a bed gently.

"Talk to whomever hired the jackasses at the party," Ari said, wishing she could just curl up in a ball and let the pain take her away.

"Bandage up that arm and then help me put this child right," she said to the aides. "How bad is it?"

"Bumps, bruises, broken ribs, and my ankle," she said as Marion started checking her over, wincing as she checked every limb, and whimpering when she messed with a particularly nasty bump on her arm.

"Broken arm, sprained ankle, nasty bruising on your throat too," Marion said with a click of her tongue. "You should've made Danril do the fighting."

"He was busy fighting Aermore," Ari said, wincing as ribs popped back into place.

"Ugh, that waste of space," she said, crinkling her nose in disgust. "Who won?"

"I have no idea. Four of the thugs ganged up on me at once. Three went down easily, fourth is responsible for the ankle and the throat. I'm assuming Danril managed to take care of Aermore because he dealt with the asshole who had me by the throat."

"It's going to hurt but there's no last damage to it," Marion said, running her hands over Ari's throat. "I hear the prince did a fair bit of fighting on his own."

"He had to," Ari said, voice dropping to a whisper with how much her throat hurt. "Danril and I were far too busy to make sure he was ok." Marion watched the girl's face twist from the pain, but it wasn't just physical pain.

"That fact bothers you," Marion said as she moved on to Ari's ankle. "Why?"

"Just put me back together please," Ari said as tendons and bones went back together. "I'm still piecing together how I feel."

"Why are you acting like you're not allowed to have feelings, Ari?" Marion asked as the light around them faded, "If you weren't, Danril wouldn't treat you like his little sister,

Simeon wouldn't be married to Tissa, Simeon and Danril wouldn't be as close as brothers, and neither of them would consider me to be like their family."

"I'm an orphan who's trained to kill people, usually on the whim of the queen. He's the son of that queen.Finn's royalty and I'm just nobody. He tells me he doesn't care but what happens when he must marry for political reasons?"

"Tatiana wouldn't allow him to step foot out of the castle dearie," Marion said. "For years, nobody even knew the prince existed. We only found out about him when he snuck out and the castle guards had to chase him down." Ari snorted softly. "She doesn't want anything that will compromise her rule, which would be him marrying a neighboring royal, which the only one he could marry is also his cousin, and I doubt Stuttgad is in a hurry to marry someone off to the Ophir's again."

"What do you mean?" Ari asked, looking over at Finn as the aides kept working on the bandage.

"Finn's father was the brother of King Stannish of Stuttgad. The same year Finn was born, Oberin Castmere was found dead in the snow, stabbed in the gut."

"That's what he meant when he said he never knew his father," Ari said. "That's horrible."

"He's also grown up with the rumors that his mother was the one who stabbed Oberin. Anyone who's ever spent any time with the queen doesn't doubt the claims."

"No wonder Finn doesn't want to carry on that legacy," Ari said quietly.

"So you two have already had that talk?" Ari nodded. "What brought that on?"

"Danril was concerned I was going to have another episode after I came back from Stuttgad a little over a month ago."

"He never said anything to me about it," she said, narrowing her eyes at Ari.

"Because there wasn't anything to say on the matter. I wasn't sleeping due to that stupid recurring nightmare."

"If you're sure," Marion said, still squinting at her. Ari nodded emphatically. "I want you in here tomorrow morning for a full once over to make sure. You know it's a possibility, however slim, that you could have another, and it would be fatal."

"I know Matron," Ari said. "Can I go now?"

"Yes, limp yourself to bed and rest up. I'll make sure Simeon takes you out of commission with the queen again."

"Thank you, Matron," Ari said, easing herself off the bed.

"And take him with you. You both had a trying night," she called after Ari, pushing Finn toward her. "Get some rest, actual rest you two," she called after them before going to write a note for Simeon.

He stumbled slightly but recovered enough to stand beside her as they walked down out of the infirmary. As they walked on, she reached out and found his hand, feeling more at ease when his fingers intertwined with hers.

"Something wrong?" he asked quietly as they walked on.

"Not really, I'm just glad you're ok."

"Are you really in danger of having another of those episodes?" he asked as she came to a stop outside a very plain-looking door. "And why would another almost certainly be fatal?"

"Because I'm not at the order constantly enough for her to monitor it. Danril is on sabbatical watching you and the only other person who shares the rare blood I have is Lord Simeon," she said as she opened the door. The motion stirred up a cloud of dust that sent her into a coughing fit. "Open the window," she said, trying to catch her breath. "You'd think at least one person would've been in to dust the room in the last four years."

"We'll freeze," he said looking at her and then at the bed. "Those aren't very warm blankets."

"I'd take freezing over wheezing," she said, still coughing as he opened the window to a gust of cold air. "But back to the conversation at hand, I take a great risk going on solo missions. Should something happen and trigger an episode, I could bleed out and die."

"Ari," he said, grabbing her hand before she could get away and change the subject. "Why do you take the risk?"

"Because I don't know anything else, because the only sabbatical I would've gotten would've been teaching new initiates and I have no patience for that."

"You had plenty of patience teaching me those moves that I guarantee saved my life tonight," he said. "I don't want you to make a rash decision or anything, but please, consider taking a sabbatical. I used to worry about you just going out there and not coming back because you got killed. Now, if you go out, I'm going to worry you're going to get killed, or that something triggered this episode."

Ari was about to say something about how it wasn't likely she'd ever have one but as she turned and looked at his face and saw the worry, fear, and sadness, she let the words die in her throat and just moved closer to hug him. The moment her arms wrapped around him, he felt a surge of emotion and the adrenaline that had carried him from the excitement of the ball to now disappeared and he began to shake as he held her.

"Finn, can we sit?" she asked, feeling her ankle trying to give out on her. "I don't think my ankle can take standing much longer, even though Matron healed it."

"Right, sorry," he said, sniffling. "I don't know what came over me." A knock came at the door followed by the sounds of footsteps retreating. He let go of Ari, who went to the door, and went and sat on her bed. She came back and tossed a small bundle at him. "What's this?"

"Clothing by the looks of it," she said as she limped over to her wardrobe. "You are a little bloody looking."

"Hmm, isn't really much privacy to change," he said looking around. She looked over her shoulder and raised a brow.

"Afraid to change in front of me now?" she asked, pulling out some plain looking pants and a shirt. "You've had no problem undressing in front of me before. In fact, I can think of several occasions where we've made short work of each other's clothing."

"That's different," he said as she started working the dress off. "Here I feel like I'm going to get caught."

"I guarantee that you'll have more privacy here," she said as the dress finally slid off. Finn swallowed hard but any thoughts he had were quickly shoved away when he saw all the bruises and red splotches from her fights to keep the rogues from winning. "In the castle, your mother has spies everywhere."

"This is true," he said, giving up and pulling off his ruined shirt. "Are you sure you're going to be ok?"

"My injuries?" she asked, as she pulled on the soft familiar shirt.

"Yes," he said as he pulled the shirt on and discarded his trousers while Ari worked into hers. "They look nasty, especially the ones around your throat."

"They're just bruises, *astori*," she said, "They'll heal."

"You probably shouldn't use that word around here," he said, pulling the borrowed pants. "I don't want you to get in trouble."

"Shit, you're right," she said, sitting on the bed. "It's just more intimate than calling you Finn. I like it."

"I like it too, and that you consider us intimate enough to trust me with it, but I'm not going to be the one that gets you in trouble," he said as he sat next to her.

"You wouldn't be getting me in trouble unless you told somebody I used it outside of Shadow and Blade business," she said, taking his hand. "The fault would be mine and mine alone for using it carelessly around the other order members."

"All your secrets are safe with me, darling," he said as he pulled her tight against his chest. "Even that one."

"Thank you," she said, yawning. "We should get some sleep." She tilted her head up and moved so she could kiss him. "The next few days are going to be very trying."

He yawned and nodded and closed his eyes in the faint glow of the lamps. "I suppose I'm just going to have to peel that dress off you another time."

"Maybe we'll just skip the dress," she whispered. He grunted softly as he drifted off, a smile on his face while Ari laid her head on his chest and immediately fell asleep.

Over in Simeon's study, Danril stood looking at the bookshelf, the smell of ink and old parchment filling his nose while Simeon sat at his desk and rubbed his temples. He wondered if that scent had always been there under the overtones of the hardwood and polish while he examined titles that he'd long since memorized after the first time he'd been in the office.

"All the rogues are either in a Thannid prison or on their way to the local doctor to give them back to their loved ones for burial. Aermore Drimdark is unfortunately one of the ones in a cell."

"I'll deal with Aermore some other time," Danril said, still bitter that he hadn't been the one to take him down. "We can't thank you and the others enough for being willing to step in tonight, Simeon."

"Had we not, we'd be holding funeral rites for you, Ari, and the prince," Simeon said, rubbing his temples. "That wasn't feasible for the two of you alone. There were a good twenty at least."

"I couldn't keep track, Aermore had me tied up for far too long."

"The man's had it out for you for almost ten years, I'm not surprised," Simeon said as Tissa entered. "Ah, Tissa darlin, everyone all cared for?"

"As best as possible," Tissa said.

"How's Ari?" Danril asked, rubbing his face.

"Patched up and in her room. Poor things look exhausted," she said, going to sit on her husband's lap. "I don't blame them though. Ari especially has had a rough go lately."

"I should've been faster," Danril said with a sigh of disappointment in himself. "She wasn't fighting at full strength, not after just a couple weeks after being stabbed like that."

"She didn't have much of a choice," Simeon said. "You're still angry with yourself."

"Because I got held up and I couldn't help her. Not until Sun knocked Aermore out."

"And what's irritating you more, the fact that Sun had to help you, or the fact that the second person ever to get under your skin was in a situation where she nearly died, and you could get there fast enough."

"Both," he growled. "Sun's always been a condescending asshole toward me, and toward Ari, and I would rather have taken the blow Aermore was going to land than ever except help from him. I've beaten Aermore more times than either of us can count but tonight, it was different. He matched me, blow for fucking blow."

"You're not the only one to say some of the rogues were far more powerful than normal," Simeon said, pointing to the chair. "Sit down. You look like you're about to collapse."

"Dani, beating yourself up isn't going to help anyone," Tissa said as Danril sat.

"I was supposed to be watching for danger Tissa," he said bitterly. "Instead, I was watching a girl who I think of as a little sister and the prince who genuinely cares about her having a good time."

"Enough Danril," Simeon said. "You did nothing wrong. There were more threats than either of you could reasonably handle. The fact is, you're all alive, even if she's pretty beat up. How severe were her injuries?"

"Broken ribs, a badly sprained ankle, fractured forearm, numerous bruises, including around her throat," Tissa said, handing him a handwritten report from Marion. "Marion took care of the breaks but is letting the bruises heal naturally. She also requests that you extend Ari's leave for another two weeks."

"Tis, my love," Simeon said, kissing her cheek, "what would I do without you?"

"Drown in papers, dearest," she said, patting his cheek. "It, however, is getting late, and I suspect that Danril probably wants to rid himself of those bloody clothes."

"I hadn't thought about it," he said, looking down at his now ruined shirt and pants. "But changing would probably be helpful."

"As would a good night's sleep," Tissa said, getting up and pulling Simeon out of his chair. "Whatever happens next cannot be helped nor planned for because you have no information."

"We should make the next move," Simeon said, fighting off a yawn.

"No. Let her continue thinking she's winning," Tissa said. "Soon enough, she'll make a mistake, and you'll have your chance."

"My wise one," Simeon said, taking her hand. He paused and looked at Danril. "Stop beating yourself up. We'll see you at breakfast."

"We'll see old friend," Danril said, with a chuckle. They parted and Danril went to his room, changed, and was asleep as his head touched the pillow.

Chapter 14

IN THE WEEKS FOLLOWING the rouges attacking the Welcome Ball for the Faedom meetings, things ended with their usual vitriol between Tatiana and Praslin, while Stannish continued to make every attempt he could to track down Ari, who'd spent the remainder of the meetings at the order with Finn. The bruising faded, cuts healed, some faded into scars, and life seemed to go back to its normal routine. Finn and Ari eventually returned to the castle with Danril, only to be greeted by the queen upon their arrival.

"I was starting to wonder if you were even going to come back," she said as Finn stepped out of the carriage that had brought the three of them back.

"Trust me mother, the thought crossed my mind," Finn said darkly, holding his hand out for Ari as she climbed down. "However, it's too damn cold and too deep in places to try getting somewhere that isn't here."

"How are you feeling?" she asked.

"Just fine," he said, having to bite his tongue to keep from saying anything else. "I'm going to my room."

"Are you both joining us for dinner?" she asked as they passed.

"We'll see," he said curtly. Tatiana sighed and as they passed by, her mouth twisted into a frown as Finn laced his hand with Ari's.

Ari didn't say anything until the door to his room shut behind her. "If you're trying to not make it obvious that you know she set you up to die, you need to tone down the anger and hostility."

"Why?" he snapped, dropping the bag he'd brought back with him on the floor with a thud. "Why shouldn't I let her know I know?"

"Why are you snapping at me?" she asked, hands on her hips. "We've told you that we need her to think we're blissfully ignorant so she continues as she planned. You should take a few minutes to cool off. I'm going to my room."

"Ari," he called but it was too late. She shut the door with a snap, leaving alone feeling irritated and foolish. With a sigh, he flopped on the couch, grabbed a pillow and let out a muffled yell just as the door opened.

"Did you stick your fucking foot in your mouth or something?" Danril asked as he shut the door.

"In a manner of speaking," he said, not moving the pillow. "I snapped at her when I shouldn't have."

"Way to go," Danril said with a shake of his head. "Are you going to apologize?"

"Eventually. I go see her right now though, I'm likely to just get hit." Finn finally moved the pillow and sat up.

"Probably. She looked like she was about to cry, which isn't like her. She obviously likes you much more than she's let on to anyone." Finn groaned and fell back, putting the pillow over his face again. "Give her the evening to calm down. Are you coming down for dinner or do you want me to tell the cook to have yours sent up?"

"Send it up. I don't want to be around my mother right now. I'd probably say something stupid to her too."

"Probably a smart choice," Danril said, turning to go. "I'll make sure Ari eats tonight." His only response was another groan from the couch.

After telling the cook to send food up for the prince, Danril took a couple plates to Ari's room and knocked on the door. She pulled the door open and much to his surprise, he could see she'd been crying.

"Well, this is a shock," he said as he came in, closing the door with his foot as she had already gone back to her bed. "Never thought I'd see the day where Ari Penndra was crying over someone."

"Keep talking and I'm going to hit you," she said with a sniffle. "What do you want?"

"I'm making sure you eat," he said, setting the plates down on the table by the couch. "Are you going to mope and make me drag you over here or are you going to come eat willingly?"

"Fuck you," she grumbled as she got off the bed and plopped on the couch. "Why am I so upset over this?"

"Because you really care about him. I don't know exactly what he did, and frankly I don't want to because you two are adults and can work your own shit out, but for what it's worth, he's feeling just as bad as you are right now."

"Feelings are stupid," she muttered picking at the food on her plate.

"The full moon rises soon," he said, changing the subject. "It'd be good for you to get out there." Ari nodded, taking her first actual bite of the food. "And you need to make it a point to talk to Finn. Either tonight or tomorrow, I don't care. But you need to be at your best, Ari. We don't know when the queen will make her next move."

"I'll talk to him after I eat," she grumbled, stabbing a bite from the plate harder than intended.

"Just remember that you've done and said stupid shit too," he said. "Take it easy on him Ari. He's under just as much stress, if not more than we are."

"I know," she said with a sigh before she made short work of her plate. "Are we meeting in our usual spot at the usual time?"

"Yes," he said as she got up. "Bring Finn if you want." Ari nodded and left, heading over to Finn's room. She knocked on the door and then opened it when there was no answer. "Finn?" she called as she stepped in.

"Ari?" he said, his voice muffled. "I didn't think you'd come back this evening yet."

"I had a small chat with Danril. I didn't stop to think how stressful coming back here had to be for you."

Finn sat up and looked over at her. "Yes, it's stressful being under the same roof as a woman who tried to kill me but, Ari, darling, that doesn't mean I take it out on you. I'm sorry." He got up, went over to her and put his hands on her cheeks. "I hurt you, and I shouldn't have."

"I took it to heart, and I shouldn't have," she said, but Finn shook his head.

"No, you didn't do a damn thing wrong," he said. "Don't start apologizing for anything."

"I felt hurt but I'm not mad, don't feel like you need to keep apologizing," she said, rising on her toes to kiss him.

The kiss turned from sweet and soft to ravenous and passionate in moments. He'd just barely picked her up when a knock came at the door. Finn growled slightly as he put Ari down and went to go answer the door.

"Yes?" he asked, not amused to find one of his mother's handmaidens outside his door.

"Beggin your pardon for the interruption," she said timidly.

"What can I do for you?" he asked as Ari appeared to see who was there. Her own heart sank as she realized who was there.

"Beggin pardon again," the handmaid said, "but the queen wishes to speak with Miss Penndra."

"Oh goodie, a summons," Ari said dryly. "I'll be right there."

"I'm sorry miss, but the queen ordered me to escort you personally to her meeting room." The handmaid looked uncomfortable.

"Very well, wait outside the door," Ari said. The maid nodded and Ari pushed the door shut "Summons likely mean I will be gone for a while. Stay close to Danril ok, *astori*?"

"Of course," he said, placing his hand against her cheek. "Be on guard, darling. It's cold, the snow is deep in places, all things that could be used to make you disappear."

"I know. Hopefully I won't be gone for too long," she said, before rising back on her toes to kiss him hard and deep. "Hold on to that feeling until I get back, ok?"

"That's not playing fair Ari," he said in a low voice as he picked her back up and kissed her with the same intensity. "We're even," he said. "You have to come back now."

"As soon as I possibly can," she whispered before he put her back down. He watched her leave, afraid and as he heard their footsteps recede, he left to find Danril.

Ari followed the handmaid down the hall and into the queen's meeting room. It was little more than a sitting room with a small table and a small fireplace. Queen Tatiana sat at the table, looking at some papers in front of her. A small sheet sat on the table and Ari suppressed a sigh. There was no doubt that she was going to have to brave the snow, ice, and cold to end more lives.

"That will be all, Inda," Tatiana said as the handmaid quickly bowed and left the room. "You could take a seat, you know."

"That would imply that I would enjoy spending time in your company, let alone have something to speak on other than you giving me orders to eliminate someone," Ari said, placing her hands behind her back. "And as much as I love our little talks when they happen, for both our sakes it would probably be best to keep this brief as possible."

Tatiana sniffed but didn't say anything as she pushed the paper toward Ari. "The Pertina ministers found to have been colluding with Stuttgad to attack our borders. See to them."

"Yes, Your Majesty," Ari said, taking the list. To avoid any further conversation, she turned and left sighing at the names on the list. However, as she looked over the list, one name gave her pause. "That's not right," she said quietly to herself as she pushed the door to her room open.

"What's not right little one?" Danril asked from next to her door.

"The newest list," she said, unfazed to find him waiting in her room even though she'd figured he'd left when she went to speak to Finn. "Nothing really happens in this castle without you hearing about it, does it."

"Finn told me you'd gotten a summons. He's very worried about it."

"He's right to be," Ari said, shoving the list at him while she went to gather the necessary things to leave. "I don't know what she's playing at, especially after a very public fallout with the King of Pertina."

"She has to know the other three Faedoms will point the finger at her, especially after they fought in the center of town nearly two weeks ago," Danril said. "I don't like this; it reeks of another trap."

"I know it does. But I don't have a choice. At least I'm going into it with my eyes open," she said. "Tell Finn I will be gone longer than I expect.."

"Why not go to the order?" Danril asked. "Bring your concerns to Lord Simeon?"

"If they're unfounded, I've wasted his time, and the queen no longer trusts me. Which wouldn't be a big loss...." Ari let the sentence trail off as she bent over her writing table, scrawling out something on a piece of paper.

Until Finn gets caught repeatedly sneaking out," Danril finished. "But walking into a trap doesn't help either of you. If you're not going to go to Simeon, I will."

"And what good is that going to do, Danril?" Ari asked, whirling around with the paper in her hand and looking at him. "We don't know the truth about anything,"

"And you owe it to one person in particular to know the truth," he said, slamming his hand on the table. "He cares about you deeply. You'd break him by not coming back."

"You think I don't know that?" Ari snapped. "You think I want to hurt him like that?"

"Then you should go to Simeon about this." Danril looked at her. "Why are you being so damn stubborn?"

"I never said I wouldn't tell him," Ari said, giving Danril a letter. "But I don't think going to him directly is in my best interest. The queen's going to be watching my movements carefully." Ari had switched to old Thendin at this point, "I can't give her a reason to distrust me right now."

"Very well," Danril said, taking the note. "Please be careful."

"When am I not?" she asked, slinging her bag over her shoulder.

"You came back last time unconscious with a stab wound you'd stitched up yourself." he called as she pulled the door open. "Exercise extra caution Ari."

"Extra caution then," she said as she pulled her coat from the rack. "Keep him safe."

"Of course, little one," Danril said as she pulled the door shut and left. As soon as she did, the Shadow in the room dropped her glimmer and looked at Danril.

"I can speak with Lord Simeon about having her stopped," Cardine said as Danril handed her the note. "Pertinan officials can be waiting for her."

"Let Simeon make the call," he said with a sigh. "She'll ride hard and fast so go swifty." Cardine nodded and disappeared again. Danril went to the window and watched the snow fall, "Don't be too mad little one," he said quietly. "It's the only way to save you."

Ari swiftly rode for the Pertinan border. The cold winds whipped by her as she pushed past piles of snow and through villages and towns. Her vision was obscured by the blowing snow but still she pressed on, eventually reaching the border. She slowed her horse to a walk and shivered as the wind bit through her large outer jacket as she passed through the checkpoint unhindered. As she made her way to the closest border town in Pertina, she noticed the whole country seemed on edge. People didn't look one another in the eye on the road, no pleasant greetings were exchanged, and even the town was eerily quiet as she rode in and inquired about a room for the night. The exchange between her and the innkeeper was terse and to the point, which Ari wouldn't have minded but added to the rest of the experiences, it had her paying even more attention to her surroundings.

After a warm meal, a lukewarm bath and a shot of whiskey to ward off the chill, Ari crawled into bed and listened to the wind howl and rattle the window. The fire did little to keep her warm as she huddled under the blankets, wishing she was curled up in bed with Finn. Eventually the sounds faded into the background, and she drifted off into a fitful sleep.

As she slept, soldiers for the king of Pertina entered the inn, startling the patrons. Many who were dealing in illicit goods made a hasty exit, though the soldiers seemed to mind little. They had one purpose for their visit to the border town of Serthi. The captain of the guard stood at the base of the stairs, looking up with trepidation. The missive they'd received from Lord Callwell said that the woman they were to apprehend was as dangerous as they came. Each of his men was wearing their thickest plate armor and chainmail and while it would take away the element of surprise, it ensured that nobody would be going home in a shroud.

He motioned to three men, top notch soldiers, to follow him up the stairs to the room where she slept. They were as quiet as possible, a feat with the heavy armor, and slowly pushed the door to Ari's room open and crept in. Had one of them not creaked a floorboard, Ari likely wouldn't have known they were there. Instead, the creak startled her awake and she was out of bed, daggers in hand, staring at them, a mix of irritation and resignation on her face.

"Put down your weapons, Miss Penndra," ordered the captain. "We have orders to bring you before the king, forcibly if necessary."

"And what does the king want with a Thenndin like myself?" she asked, staring at the men. "And how does a single traveler rate men in plate armor with chainmail underneath?"

"The fact that you can tell all that just by looking at us Miss Penndra tells me you are not an ordinary traveler." He rested his hand on the hilt of his sword. "I have no doubt you could best the four of us, however, we have the building surrounded. It's in your best interest not to fight or flee."

Ari looked around the room, weighed her odds and slowly lowered her hands. "Fine," she said, softly. "No need to start a problem. Let's go see the king."

The captain nodded and they gathered her things before escorting her out of the inn. The ride to the capital of Petrina was cold, Ari colder than most since she was in her thinner bed clothes. A cold wind whipped around them fiercely as they climbed the pass that led to Prinda, Pertina's capital, and by the time they passed through the gates, Ari was close to losing feeling in her hands and legs. She rubbed her hands together and then rubbed a hand on her legs, trying to get the blood to flow. By the time they escorted her into the castle, she was shivering and trying to keep her teeth from chattering. The sun was barely peeking through the windows as the guards led Ari to a sparsely furnished room and shoved into a chair. The door shut, leaving Ari in with the chill.

By the time anyone bothered to come back, Ari was freezing and furious. Her teeth chattered, her whole body was shivering, and she could barely move as they escorted her to the throne room. When she entered, Praslin took one look at her and snapped out some orders. He hadn't finished speaking when servants rushed off to gather several things

"Miss Penndra, my sincerest apologies," he said as he descended from the throne. "Nobody bothered to tell me you were here until after breakfast. Let's go into the sitting room and get you warm."

"I can't expect much better given where I came from," Ari said as her teeth clattered together. "Or who's employ I currently spend my time in."

"Miss Ari Penndra, Blade in service to the oldest order of Thenndin, Shadow and Blade. It was you who told me I likely knew who you were and what you did."

"I said likely, and you did not correct me or deny my statement as true," Ari said. "So whether or not it is factual depends on how you came by that information, Your Majesty." She stopped speaking as they entered a brightly lit room with a roaring fire.

"If I told you the information came from Lord Simeon Callwell himself," he said, gesturing to the couch for her to sit.

"Then you would not be mistaken," she said. "Though there's little else I could tell you."

"I don't need specifics. I had you brought here because I need you to understand that everything that Tatiana Ophir has had you do, the acts she's asked you to commit, were all lies woven to serve her needs." He paused and scrutinized her face as a blanket and a warm drink were brought in for her. "I get the impression this fact does not shock you."

"I've been serving at Tena Castle due to a brokered deal between Lord Simeon and Queen Tatiana four years ago. I'd be a naive fool to not realize that she has asked horrors of me that did not serve her own needs."

"You are much wiser than she made you out to be," King Praslin said as she sipped the tea. "I cannot say I am surprised however. Simeon Callwell does not seem the type to suffer fools or train them."

"I would've thought our conversation at Tena Castle would've told you that," she remarked dryly. "I assume you have much more to tell me than something I already knew, Your Majesty?" Ari leaned forward to set the teacup on the table. "I highly doubt you had your best soldiers collect me from Serthi in the dead of night for this brief of a chat."

"You can be quite infuriating," he said, raising a brow.

"Queen Tatiana shares that sentiment," she said.

"And your court manners are lacking."

"You already knew this when you decided to follow me into Prince Finnian's room," she said dryly. "I spend little time among those of the court. Queen Tatiana prefers that she only know of my existence, not see proof of it." Ari adjusted the blanket as she finally began to feel the chill leaving her body. "But my question still stands, Your Majesty. What is it you wish to speak of that is more than a mere warning?"

"Indeed. Tell me Miss Penndra, what do you know of her plans for Thenndin and the continent."

"I know she planned to kill me the last time I came this far north," Ari said warily. "And that it was her idea to have her son attacked and either killed or seriously injured."

"And how is the prince?"

"Escaped with a minor injury. He's fully recovered." Ari resumed sipping her tea. "I'm not a spy for Thenndin, Your Majesty," she said. "There was no training in the arts of sleight of hand and misdirection for me. They trained me to be a killer, an assassin. I stalk my prey, learn about them, and then I attack when the conditions are right."

"Hm," Praslin said, looking at her with searching green eyes. His gaze unnerved her but not in the same way Stannish's had during the ball. "So tell me, because I'm sure you've already thought about it, if you were to carry out Tatiana's orders to kill me, how would you do it?"

"Are you sure you wish to hear this?" she asked, setting the teacup down. He nodded, motioning for her to go on. "Very well. I have limited options here, and very few escape options given the guard outside the door. A teacup makes a sharp cutting implement, but the shattering would draw the guard's attention and put you on your guard. I would probably have to knock you unconscious and smother you, which is far too much work and too much risk. Better to study, watch, learn your habits, find the point that can be exploited and then strike."

"Is that what happened to the minister in Stuttgad?" he asked, looking at her face, looking for any sign of confirmation. She started back, expression blank and he let out a small sigh of exasperation. "Oh come now. It was common knowledge that Ernst Henrich was so far in debt that he'd been threatened with death multiple times. I even heard a rumor that the shark he owed the debt to was threatened with a gruesome death should anything happen to Ernst's wife and child."

"You seem to have all the answers," she said, leaning forward, resting her elbows on her knees. "So, indulge me one more question if you please, what are you hoping to gain from me?"

"The knowledge of where your loyalties lie," he said. "But it's very difficult to tell."

"Then you should've just asked me outright," she said. "Though I did answer that question for you when you were in Thannid."

"You really don't hold loyalty to the crown, fascinating. So, if the other four Faedoms were to attack you wouldn't be compelled to help the Crown?"

"Shadow and Blade's duty is to the people first," she said, straightening up, causing the blanket to fall from her shoulder.. "Innocents do not pay for the mistakes of others. Those who live in Thenndin should not suffer a terrible fate simply because of Tatiana Ophir. We would not fight for or beside the queen, we would fight for the citizens, the discarded, forgotten, those that live in poverty so severe that even a copper coin makes them feel like they got a swing in their luck. Those are the people the spies and the assassins would fight for against both sides."

"Fascinating," he said again. "Truly fascinating. An organization only loyal to itself. How has Tatiana not squashed it?"

"Centuries of tradition," she said thinly as her stomach rumbled.

"Ah, well in that case, we should speak more over an early lunch," he said, rising and offering her his hand. "For I do have much to discuss surrounding events to come."

Ari took the hand and remained silent as she stood and followed him out of the room and down towards the dining hall. Events to come had her stomach rolling with emotions, many of which she needed to tamp down to keep from overreacting. She was a Blade, an assassin, and she was on a mission, even if the scope of it had changed. Though she may not have been a spy, Ari knew she had to learn more. Her life, and the lives of many others, depended on it.

Chapter 15

THERE WAS LITTLE TO say over lunch. Ari hadn't eaten since the night before when she arrived in Serthi so she was much more focused on the plate in front of her. Praslin watched her with interest. As soon as the plates were cleared and the tea and cakes were served, he poured them each a cup and then spoke again.

"What do you know of Tatiana's reign?" he asked, as he sat the cup back on the saucer.

"From personal observation or the history of it?" she asked. "Because if you want the latter, I feel a scholar may be of more use to you in that regard than an assassin." Praslin's mouth twitched in a half smile before he sighed.

"Your general knowledge of her reign will do," he said, but there was a small trace of laughter in his voice.

"Very well. From where I grew up in the slums of Thannid, the queen's name is spoken like a curse. Many had stories they told of her soldiers raiding villages, or burning farms, or something like that. I never put much stock in them because those stories always came from the drunks at the tavern but more recently, I'd believe it, especially after I met some who claimed to be survivors from the Reudena attacks. They told me that the queen ordered the destruction of that village. If they were to be believed, I was also a victim of that raid."

"And do you believe that?"

"The timing lines up but nobody can tell me for sure," Ari said with a shrug. "My memories are only of the shitty fucking orphanage in Thannid, the worst one in the slums. I had no love for the queen because the man who ran the orphanage would always blame her when we had so little to go around but praise her when he experienced a change in fortune, not that the children of the orphanage ever saw this change. Many of them died from the lack of supplies. I'll skip over what I encountered when I was summoned to his office one afternoon."

"Charming fellow," Praslin said with a grimace. "What if I were to tell you those stories were true? That Tatiana's soldiers were given orders to raid and burn villages."

"After what I've experienced at her hands myself, seeing what she's willing to do to her own flesh and blood, I'm not surprised, Your Majesty. She has a cruel streak, striking out at people who anger her. She even threw a letter opener at Prince Finn, striking him in the shoulder as he decided to leave the castle for a few days."

"Her temper is indeed legendary, which makes it all the less surprising that nobody has tried to remove her from power," Praslin said as he picked up his tea. "But after the summit, which yielded no fruitful discussions thanks to Tatiana, the other rulers and I met to decide what to do with her. Her reign is causing her people nothing but pain and suffering, even the nobles are feeling the strain thanks to the higher prices she's imposed on her goods leaving Thenndin."

"And what did you decide?" she asked, putting her hands around her teacup to steady them. "And why are you telling me?"

"Because at this point, Miss Penndra, you are my messenger. You'll take everything I say back to Lord Callwell or I could have you arrested. Crossing Pertina's border under false pretenses does come with a six month stay in the capital's jail."

"It's not false pretenses if I had no intention of carrying out my orders" Ari grumbled. "But fine, it's an acceptable exchange. I have people who do wish me to return. I don't need someone causing a problem."

"Ah yes, the prince," Praslin said with a shake of his head. "He's made quite a stir among the royals with his choice in women." Ari snorted. "Though few could blame him. You did look quite stunning in that dress."

"Love and duty are not always in agreement, Your Majesty," Ari said, not sure what to do with the compliment she'd just been paid. Her face reflected as much because Praslin laughed.

"Most people would thank someone when given a compliment," he said, his eyes still sparkling with amusement. "Not all of us are grubby leches like Stannish."

"Forgive me, I've spent twelve years of my life blending into the shadows. Being noticed is not something I'm used to," she said as she picked up her tea.

"Something you may have to get used to if you continue to consort with the prince," he said. "If we're successful with what we want to attempt, he will very well become the next ruler of Thenndin." Ari bit her tongue to counter his remarks, something that wasn't lost on Praslin. "Do you have information I don't have on this matter?"

"No, Your Majesty," she said.

"Hmmm" he said, taking another sip of his tea. "But back to the matter at hand. Rustin, Dresyn, Stannish and I want to see Tatiana removed from the throne and we're planning to do just that. However, we do not want to bring death or destruction to those that live on the borders of our countries."

"So how do you plan to manage that?" Ari looked confused. "If you send soldiers, she will just send hers and the countryside will become a war zone. Innocents will get hurt."

"Not if we, with some assistance, clear the countryside," Praslin said, looking at her. "Of course, we would need Shadow and Blade's help."

"Where would these people go? You cannot just clear the countryside and expect Tatiana not to notice."

"Stuttgad, Dengard, Ringnad and Pertina have begun preparations to safely house the citizens until our mission is complete. Once a new ruler is installed, whether that be the prince or someone else, we'll work with them to rebuild what was destroyed and let those people return home."

"How charitable," Ari said dryly. "What do you expect Shadow and Blade to do?"

"Simple. We need you to get to these people, explain war is coming and help them cross the border."

"You say simple, but King Praslin, have you ever been to some of these small villages on the border? The ones that just barely manage to eke out a living from the meager land they've been able to get? They've fought hard, they've bled on that land, and only an act from the gods themselves would remove them from that land."

"But the threat of coming war-" Praslin started but Ari cut him off.

"Would not be enough to move them. Look at Thenndin's history, look at Reudena and Trinda. Those people didn't leave until they were absolutely forced to," she said. "The same would happen along any of the other borders. And even if you did manage to evacuate some of them, there would be those stubborn enough that they would die before they give up the homes they've built."

"What do we do then?" Praslin asked. Ari would have responded, however, the door burst open, and a page entered, clearly out of breath. Both Praslin and Ari got to their feet as the poor lad stumbled over, a paper in his hand. "What is it lad?" Praslin pointed to an empty chair and the page sat, his hand shaking on the note. Ari took it from him and read it while the kid recovered.

"It's a message from King Dresyn," Ari said. "Tatiana decided to act. Her forces moved toward the border of Thenndin and Dengard last night." She looked up. "Dresyn is requesting aid from Stuttgad, Ringnad, and Pertina."

"Have Rusin and Stannish sent aid?" Praslin asked. Ari shrugged but just then another message entered with two more missives. "Ah, notes from both. Stannish and Rusin are sending soldiers and so will we. Send word to the soldiers. It appears the queen may have already begun her plan, Miss Penndra. How do you propose we handle this?"

"I need to go back and speak to Lord Callwell," she said as the pages left to deliver the king's message. "If she has snapped and launched an attack, those from the slums and those on Dengard's border are in danger of becoming her cannon fodder."

"It may be too late for that," he said.

"Maybe, but that doesn't mean I give up. I need to report to Lord Simeon. We may be able to stop the loss of life internally."

"Ride swift," Praslin said as he nodded to the remaining page who ran and returned with her things. "Nobody will hesitate to cut down the queen on the field."

"I wish you all the luck with that, King Praslin," she said, as she took her things and headed for the stables.

She rode at a terrifying pace for Thannid, her wings flaring out behind her to aid the horse's speed. Even with her aiding the horse, it still took her most of the day to reach Thannid. As the sun set, she burst through the gates of the order, exhausted. She knew she would not be able to rest, not when things were so dire, not with her mind full of anger and worry. Nobody got in her way as she strode down the halls before barging into Simeon's office.

"I see you've picked up that obnoxious habit from Danril," he said as she came in. "Care for a drink?"

"How long has she been planning this?" Ari asked, breathless and on the verge of collapsing.

"Sit," he said, pointing to the chair. "I really don't need you collapsing in my office." Ari harrumphed but sat. "As for how long this has been in the works, I do not know. She surprised even her most dedicated soldiers by moving them out to Dengard last night."

"Why Dengard?" Ari asked, as Simeon pushed a drink toward her. "It's always been the more neutral of the four."

"Our best guess is she sees Dresyn's neutrality as weakness," he said, sipping his whiskey. "Which will backfire on her. Dengard's military might is the greatest of the five Faedoms. Once they muster, it's game over for her."

"Pertina, Stuttgad and Ringnad are already mobilizing to aid Dengard," she said wearily. "Tatiana doesn't stand a chance out there."

"No, the soldiers she's conscripted don't stand a chance," Simeon corrected. "Tatiana Ophir is a dangerous woman especially when cornered. The four kings are sorely mistaken if they think they can best her on the field."

"What are we to do?" Ari asked, finally taking a sip of her drink. "Is the order going to sit back and watch as she burns the country and tries to take over the surrounding lands?"

"No child," he said. "Every Shadow and every Blade is out by Dengard doing what they can to either get the people out of harm's way or working with Dresyn to beat Thenndin's soldiers back across the border. Both tasks are not easy and require more resources than we have access to. But the order has sat by for too long."

"Forgive my boldness, but sir, why are you still here?" she asked, putting aside the empty glass. "Shouldn't you be out with the rest of the order?"

"Someone had to be here when you arrived," he said. "Go get some dinner and then get some rest. We're leaving at first light for the border." Ari nodded and stood. "Before you go," he said, pulling a letter out of his desk. "This was left for you."

Ari took the letter and left his office. She didn't open it until well after dinner and as she read through it, a strange feeling tore through her. She could recognize the rage, she'd experienced it often enough to recognize the old friend, but today, it had brought something she didn't recognize with it. Numb with rage and dread, she read the letter again, letting the words turn over in her head.

My dear darling Ari, she read, *if you're holding this letter then you got back sometime after Mother dragged me off to the Dengard border for a crazy war that has no business being fought. When you see him, tell Danril thank you for trying to help me even though everything ended up being in vain. Just know I'm trying to be safe out here and that I will be seeing you again, darling. Don't do anything crazy, for my sake. I'll be back in Thannid before you know it. Be well, yours forever, Finn,*

Ari wanted to scream, cry, and throw something as she held the letter in shaking hands. How did this happen? Why would Tatiana drag him to the front lines? Was this just another ploy to try and kill him so she could use his death to her advantage? Ari slumped against her pillow, burying her face in it as she fought back tears, only for them to fall as she got a whiff of his scent still on the pillow. She hugged it to her chest and eventually fell asleep, tears still falling.

They rode with haste, the urgency not leaving any room to speak. Ari's face was pale, her mouth set in a hard line as she and Simeon raced through the country toward the Dengard border. They made the makeshift camp by sunset, both riders and horses exhausted from the push to make it. As she dismounted her horse, Danril came running up.

"I wasn't expecting you," he said, giving Ari a hug, which was out of character for him, but she appreciated it all the same, given the contents of the note that still weighed heavy on her. "Little one, I'm sorry. I tried to get him away before the queen could drag him off. She was faster than I."

"There's little that can be done about it now. Why did she take him?" Ari dully.

"I wish I knew," he said as he released her. Nobody in the castle could tell me. Or if they knew, they were all too terrified to say anything."

"No matter. It's nothing good knowing her," she said. "Have the reinforcements from the other countries arrived?"

"No. The recent scouting reports say they're at least another day to two days away, unless they ride like the wind. Dengard can hold Thenndin back, but resources grow thin. Dresyn is due to arrive in the morning to rally his men."

"And what of us?" she asked, looking around. "What are we to do?"

"For now, we watch," Simeon said, coming to join them. "And we rest. You've ridden hard in the last couple days child, you're half dead on your feet."

"Mess tent is over here," Danril said, leading the way. "How did things go in Pertina?"

"I wasn't really given any good options, it was become Praslin's errand boy or spend six months in a Pertinan cell," Ari said dryly. "Not that it mattered after Tatiana forced everyone's hand. The kings were already banding together to launch an attack from every side. They just needed us to clear the countryside of civilians. They'd really thought long and hard about this."

The conversation ceased as they entered the tent and got their food. Their little group was silent as they poked at their food, Ari barely eating at all. As she pushed a potato around in yet another circle, Danril finally had enough.

"Is the moping helping anything?" he asked quietly.

"No, I suppose not," she said, looking up. "Why?"

"Then eat the damn food. If you need to throw yourself in the fray, are you going to be able to like this? Do you think you're of use to him and to us if you're distracted and half starved because you decided to mope like a child?" Ari wanted to say something, but while her face cycled through anger, fear, hurt, irritation and eventually defeat, the little voice in the back of her head told her that he was right. "Feel what you do Ari, but don't let it interfere with what is to come." Simeon nodded in agreement and the rest of the meal passed in silence.

****

Dawn broke over the country and many of the order's assassins, the ones trained to fight, took to the sky to survey the field. Ari looked down below and let out a sad sigh at the destruction. She had to work to push the dream of death and fire from her mind as the scene below brought back memories of it. She looked at the scores of troops below, the sun highlighting the sheer number of tents below. Dengard's blue and gold moon and stars blew in the strong breeze while the red and silver flames of Thenndin's flag rippled like a flame that the crest of the Ophir family bore. A trumpet sounded, summoning the soldiers to assemble as the sun grew level with the tent tops. As they circled and observed, Ari felt like she was being watched. Tugging on Danril's sleeve, she quickly covered herself in glimmer, hoping he would follow suit.

Danril picked up on her hint and quickly shielded himself from any prying eyes, passing along the message to the rest of the assembled scouts. One by one they disappeared from view and collectively returned to their camp.

****

The pair of eyes that had spotted the scouting party had been none other than Tatiana herself. She'd figured Simeon would be hiding out, looking to see what side he wanted to throw his lot behind. It was nothing more than an act, the fool wanted her gone from the throne. With a snort of disdain, she turned and went back into her tent, where her son was sitting, less than thrilled to have been dragged along. Eventually she resorted to binding his hands before he stopped trying to slip away. The rest of the march she'd been treated to his stoney glare, which he gave her now as she let her hand slip off the tent flap.

"You could try not scowling," she said looking at him.

"You could just let me go," he replied, holding out his bound hands. "I don't know what use I am to you here, but I guarantee you it's not worth it."

"Depends on how you define worth, boy," she said with a shrug. "Because to me, what I have planned for what's left of your short pathetic life will make it worth it to me." With a laugh, she turned and left again, leaving him to sit there alone, wondering what she meant.

****

It was late in the day when she returned, a dusty bloody mess, her silver eyes gleaming with a touch of madness. She didn't say a word to him as she dumped the bloody armor and went to change. He'd heard the battle from in the tent, the awful clang of steel on steel, the squelch of that same steel meeting flesh and blood. All combined, it was enough to make him sick. He wondered briefly how Ari had been able to handle that for the years she'd served as an assassin. Eventually she rejoined him as someone brought them dinner. Finn's stomach turned at the thought of food, but his mother had no such compunctions.

"How can you eat after what you've done today?" he asked, horrified. Even Ari had a hard time eating after a mission he noticed.

"The things out there bother me so little," she said. "Your grandfather, my father, was never blessed with a son so I did all the things he would normally do with a son, hunt and dress game, discuss matters of the state and even how to deal with criminals," she said, picking apart a piece of bread. "He was often shocked at my ideas. Shocked but pleased nonetheless."

"Surprising given that he was supposedly responsible for the largest massacre to ever occur in Thenndin," Finn said dryly. "He must be so proud that his daughter went down the same depraved path he did."

"I'd like to think so," she said, spearing a tomato. "And he's only responsible for the worst recorded massacre dear."

"What do you mean?" he asked, looking at her blankly. Part of him knew that she was probably talking about Reudena, or maybe even Trinda, but part of him wanted to go back to not knowing anything about his depraved mother.

"Have you ever wondered why there used to be so many orphanages in Thannid?" she asked, motioning for him to eat. "Or why the slums are as big as they are?" He shook his head. "No?"

"My curiosity was somewhat tempered by the fact you forced me to stay in the castle for so long." He raised a brow. "What are you trying to tell me mother?"

"That many of the towns and villages and the people that inhabit the slums are there because they simply had no other place to go. Crops burned, houses turned to ash, families torn apart. Didn't you ever wonder what happened to your precious little Ari to make her so destitute, living in the most rundown of Thannid's orphanages?"

"They searched for the answer after she came back from Trinda, when you tried to have her killed but the best anyone came up with was that she was given to that hellhole a few days after Reudena."

"I was there the night your sweet little Ari and the whole of Reudena met misfortune. It came in the form of her being violently ripped away from her parents and the family's house burned. Much of that stupid little village within the Prestile Forest burned that night. All because they refused to pay the extra taxes needed so I could put my plans of bringing war to these countries."

"Why wage war? Why not approach them peacefully and ask for what was taken?"

"Because my darling boy," she said with fake sweetness, "nothing was ever taken from me. I just crave more than what I have. I want to rule the entire land. And I just need one more sacrifice to achieve that."

"One more sacrifice?" Finn felt his stomach drop to his knees and a cold pit formed. "What do you mean?"

"Yes, but for now, you shouldn't worry about it. Just put it from your mind." She reached over and patted his cheek. In two nights, all will be revealed my son." She finished her dinner and got up, heading out into the cool night air.

A little way from the camp, she looked up, stared at the moon, which would be at its fullest in two nights, and smiled wickedly. If all went to plan, the moon's bright light would highlight blood red snow, and she would finally be able to obtain what she'd dreamed of since she was a child.

She shook out her silvery wings and took to the sky, laughing maniacally as she surveyed the camps below. Dengard's numbers held steady, and the latest reports from her scouts told her that Pertina, Stuttgad and Ringnad's forces would be arriving tonight, if they hadn't already. Another laugh escaped as she soared over the tents below. The combined military might of the four countries would've scared most rulers in her position, but she didn't care. Even without the ancient ritual of sacrifice under the full moon, she was still one of the most powerful Fae's to ever grace the throne of Thenndin. Her might was enough to counter the difference, of that she was sure.

But there was still the problem of Shadow and Blade. Simeon's stupid pets, and an organization countless Ophir's had tried and failed to remove from the capital, all because of a decree made by the first ruler of Thenndin. She'd hoped she'd would've been able to corrupt the one she'd procured from him those four years ago but to no avail. She'd been as stubborn as they came, head strong and about as willing to put up with anyone's shit as she was, making it impossible to break the girl. That all would change in the next two nights. Both her bastard son's and the common whore's blood would grace the ground and she would make sure of it.

Chapter 16

ARI WAS DEAD ASLEEP when someone shook her awake. Startled, she reached for her daggers but realized they were missing as she bolted upright, trying to figure out who was in the tent with her.

"You don't think I'm dumb enough to try and wake you before making sure you couldn't stab me, do you?" asked Danril as he dumped her weapons back in her lap.

"You're lucky I didn't decide to hit you instead," she grumbled as she stretched. "To what do I owe such a rude awakening in the middle of the night?"

"The Shadows are back after scouting. One of them overheard some disturbing information from the queen's tent."

"How disturbing?" Ari asked as she pulled on her boots.

"Disturbing enough if he's asking for a late-night meeting," Danril said looking at her impatiently. "Are you ready now?"

"So pushy," she grumbled as she secured her sheaths so they sat in the small of her back before exiting the tent.

Everyone was gathered in the mess tent, everyone's face looked just as tired as Ari's. As she and Danril took their places at the table, she studied Simeon's face. Under the exhaustion, fear and worry was something she'd never seen on the lord councilor's face. She had to squint at him to realize there was fury under all the other emotions. Ari knew that he had the calmest disposition, which had earned him the title of Lord Councilor while she was still an initiate training with Danril, so what would cause him to become so angry? She got her answer when he began to speak.

"In two nights, the moon will be at its peak and full," he began. "One of our scouts in Tatiana's camp overheard her talking to her son about a final sacrifice that would be performed during the full moon. You all know that the Fae for centuries has drawn power from the moon and its rays, it's why you all are encouraged to perform the age-old ritual. However, based on what was overheard, Tatiana plans to use this ritual to make herself ultimately powerful to beat the combined forces of Dengard, Ringnad, Stuttgad and Pertina."

"What's the sacrifice?" Ari asked, looking at him.

"It's unclear. But it's safe to assume that it involves her son, to which I will tell you to be cautious Miss Penndra. A wrong move will play right into her hands."

"What do you suggest?" Ari asked, mouth a thin line. "I won't just sit around and wait for her to put a knife to his throat."

"Nobody said you had to, but you are not going to rush into camp blindly to rescue him." Simeon looked at her as if he dared her to defy him. Ari kept silent and Simeon continued. "We will continue to try to gather as much information as we can, but we should all be warned that we may have to enter blindly."

"And face off against the queen?" asked someone and Ari recognized the voice of the Blade known as Frost. "When she's her strongest? Lord Simeon, begging your pardon, but that's insanity."

"What's worse? Taking her on when she's strongest or letting her commit a massacre of the surrounding countries?" he asked, looking at Frost with a steely glare. "Would you condemn hundreds of thousands to die because you don't want to take on Tatiana when we're all at our strongest?"

"N... n....n....no sir," he said, shrinking back as Simeon glared at him.

"Then we proceed as we can. We watch the field, study her moves, and see if we can find a way to prevent this sacrifice from happening. Now, go get some rest. Sentries swap out. Miss Penndra, Danril, hang back a moment please."

Ari and Danril waited as the mess tent emptied of the gathered Shadows and Blades. When it was just the three of them, Simeon took a seat and pointed to the chairs for Ari and Danril.

"You'll want to sit for this," he said. Ari raised a brow but decided not to argue. Danril sat next to her, and they looked at Simeon with matching puzzled expressions. "There was more in the Shadow's report that I thought the two of you should hear."

"All due respect, Lord Simeon," Ari said with a yawn. "It's the dead of night and I'm due to be on sentry duty with Danril. Could you please just get on with it?"

"Danril, I know I instructed you to teach her, but did you have to pass on your bluntness as well?" Simeon asked, looking at his old friend.

"That was already there when you told me to train her," he said with a slight chuckle. "I may have honed it a little bit."

"To a godsdamned point," he grumbled, rubbing his eyes. "Before Tatiana spoke of the sacrifice, she was taunting the prince with the knowledge that she was responsible for Reudena."

"Which we all figured was the case," Ari said with another yawn.

"The night she burned Reudena, she had you forcibly ripped from your parents, and the cottage they lived in was burned with them in it."

"I guess that means Finn was right after all," she said quietly. "The nightmare I keep having is from my past." Ari didn't know what or how she felt about the news.

"It would appear so. I'm sorry to have to give you this information," Simeon said.

"Thank you for doing so," Ari said, "if there's nothing else, Danril and I should be relieving Frost and Sunshine of sentry duty."

"Of course," he said, waving them off.

Ari and Danril took up their positions on the cliffside in the tree line that overlooked the road in and out of the valley. The slivers of moonlight that made it through the pine branches highlighted Ari's face. Because she knew they were alone, she wasn't making much of an effort to hide them. Danril moved a little closer to her and put an arm around her shoulder, giving her a little squeeze.

"Worrying will only distract you," Danril said after a few moments of silence. "What's eating at you more? The sacrifice or the news that the queen personally destroyed your family?"

"The sacrifice," she said, looking up at the cold clear sky and in the moonlight, he saw a tear snake down her cheek. "It feels like I'm going to lose a piece of myself if something happens to him."

"That's what happens when you care deeply about someone," Danril said, giving her another little squeeze. "Though I'd dare say what's between you two is more like love than anything else."

"Is not," she said indignantly. "I really care about him, that's all."

"Uh huh, you're protesting too much, little one," he said, laughing quietly. "Some things never change with you." She elbowed him lightly. "I'm sure if anyone asked him directly if he loved you, you know he'd say yes in a heartbeat. He cares about you more than anything."

"Too much, I think," she said, trying to blink away some tears. "He already wants to give up his claim to the throne and live a quiet life somewhere in the south, just the two of us."

"What's wrong with that?" Danril asked. "Jenna and I had talked about living in the countryside before she passed. We even picked out a little cottage that had room enough for you."

"Me? Why would you want me there?" she asked. "I was nothing but a pain in everyone's ass, especially yours."

"Because Jenna knew how much I needed you around, little one, and how much you needed me. Face it Ari, we're family."

"What would you do if we did go south?" she asked, turning her eyes to the road.

"Find a place nearby. I've seen you two when you're around each other. I'd be too afraid of walking in on something I don't need to see my little sister doing." Ari let out a small chuckle. "For what it's worth Ari, if you two are serious about this plan, you should do it. Life can be so short and fleeting to not seize a moment."

"I know," she said, taking a deep breath, wincing as the cold night air stung her lungs. "When this is over, I don't want to shed any more blood, mine or anyone else's."

"What brought this on?" he asked, looking at her curiously. Ari scanned the surroundings, looking at the tents below, watching for movement. "Ari, that's not something you drop in casual conversation and shut up. Something brought this about, I'm curious as to why."

"Couple reasons really," she said, tilting her head to the side as she studied a speck on the path below. "One, I don't want to cause Finn any more undue stress. He'd worry every time I'd left on a mission, especially since there's always the chance I could spontaneously have another episode."

"Another reason I'd be moving south if you go," he said. "But Finn already worries to no end, has for four years."

"What a dummy," she said, shaking her head, squinting at the road again. "But I don't want him to spend every moment wondering if I'm coming back through the door or if this will be the mission that does me in. I care about him too much to put him through that constantly."

"It's a valid point. So what's the other reason?" he asked, turning his gaze toward what she was looking at.

"The Stuttgad minister's wife. Her scream still haunts my dreams, so much so that it's what I hear in my dreams when the fire burns down what was my parent's cottage. I'm tired of death."

"I'm sorry Ari," he said quietly. "What do you plan to do about Reudena?"

"Accept that it happened and move on. I didn't know those people and if what the bandit from the north said is true, most people think I died in that fire. Might as well let that ghost stay a ghost," she said quietly, squinting at the speck. "Why does that keep moving?"

"I do not know," he said, watching it. "Whoever they are, they aren't trying to hide, which makes it very unlikely it's someone from Tatiana's camp."

"Well shall we go greet them?" she asked, shaking out her wings.

"Might as well," he said, following suit. They took to the sky, and stealthily landed in front of and behind the would-be intruder. He was startled when Danril appeared and turned to run, only to find Ari standing behind him. "That's definitely not Thenndin armour."

"Nope, that's Pertinan," Ari said. "Don't I know you?"

"Miss Penndra, I wasn't expecting to see you so soon," he said, sputtering. "King Praslin has a missive for Lord Callwell."

"Right, Pertina's captain of the guard, the asshole who left me freezing in a room for four hours," she said, skewering him with a glare. "I assume Praslin wants it hand delivered?"

"Those were his explicit instructions, yes," he said.

"Very well. What's your name?" Danril asked as he motioned for the guard to follow.

"Tinton, sir," he said as they headed for the order's camp. "Why do you ask?"

"In case I need to inform King Praslin of your untimely demise. It appears my partner is still pretty hurt about the treatment she received in Pertina."

"She'd crossed the border under false pretenses," he said haughtily. "She's lucky she got the treatment she did. I would've thrown her in a cell personally."

"You would've been dead before you hit the floor had you tried," Ari growled.

Tinton couldn't tell if the cold night air or the way she delivered those words as if they were fact that caused the shiver to run down his spine. He was spared from saying anything when she conjured a small bit of gold light. Next to him, Danril did the same, but only the light he held in his palm was silver. Two more balls of light appeared, one orange, one green before two more figures materialized in front of him. A scowled formed on Danril's face when he realized that the duo known as Sun and Grass were on duty as well.

"What'd the cat drag in?" Sun in old Thenndin, studying Tinton. "He's not from Thenndin."

"Pertinan," Ari replied in the same language. "He's here to see the Lord Councilor."

"What does he want with Lord Simeon?" Grass asked.

"He was sent by King Praslin," Danril said, shutting them both up. "Let us pass."

"How do I know you're not trying to bring a Thenndin spy through, Ice?" Sun asked in a haughty voice. Nobody had time to blink as Danril moved with intense speed and pinned the orange light wielder to a nearby tree. "This isn't helping your case, Ice."

"You know what would help either Sun?" he hissed. "Me snapping your damn neck because you're a fucking prick. You know better than most that the two of us have shed more blood for this order than the rest of you combined."

"Danril, let Embry go," came Simeon's tired voice. "Are you two ever going to get along?"

"Probably not," he said, letting go of the man.

"What's going on?" Simeon asked. "Who's this?"

"Captain Tinton, Pertinan Royal Guard, sent by King Praslin," Ari said, "he comes bearing a message from Praslin for you."

"Tell Praslin that the next time he wants to deliver a message, that it needs to be done in a less conspicuous fashion. Sneaking through the night is just going to get someone killed." Simeon held his hand out for the message.

"Yes sir," Tinton said, handing over the missive. "I will pass along your wisdom."

Simeon sighed and broke the seal on the message as Tinton left. "Praslin you idiot," he muttered. "Alert everyone. We'll be on the field at first light," he said. "Pertina is forcing our hand."

"What do you mean sir?" Ari asked as he turned and headed back toward his tent.

"The four kings have decided they are going to attack Tatiana head on tomorrow at dawn. We have less time than we need now to formulate how we're going to prevent her from making her sacrifice now. Once they launch their attack, she may choose to move her plans up."

"So now what?" Ari asked, stuffing her hands in her coat to hide the shaking.

"Rest while you can and survey the field carefully tomorrow. If you see an opening to find the prince, take it."

Ari nodded and went back to her watch. She and Danril stood there silently until the sun came up, its rays creeping between the tents. She watched it with dull, tired eyes, her mind miles away from where she really was. Eventually they were joined by the rest of the Blades, and they all took to the skies to watch the battle below.

Praslin, Dreysen, Rusin and Stannish rode with their troops toward the Thenndin camp, none of them surprised to see Tatiana's soldiers ready and waiting for them. She stood in front of her soldiers, a small figure but commanding all the same. They pulled their horses to a stop, dismounted and sent them to the rear. The troops assembled to put an end to Tatiana's reign of terror before it could start was an imposing one, but Tatiana did not look bothered by their might in the slightest. If they could've seen her face, they would've seen the devil may care grin and the utter excitement the coming battle brought her. Instead, they were fixated on the troops in front of them, the number, how terrified they looked, and they quickly put their heads together to formulate a last-minute strategy.

"Combined we have the bigger army," Rusin said, "but the soldiers don't worry me. Tatiana does."

"She's just a blowhard like her father before her," Stannish said, "I say we charge her head on and take her head."

"If you want your blood on the field Stannish, by all means, have at that plan," Praslin said. "We need to be smart about this. The Ophir line has always been full of powerful fire users, and she is no exception."

"So what are you suggesting Praslin?" Dresyn asked, exasperated. "Because from where I'm standing, our soldiers are nothing but field fodder for Tatiana."

"Have anyone that can construct a barrier do so. We can at least buy some time to slow her down and reduce the casualties. If we can weaken her, wear her down, we will have our chance to strike her down."

"It's the best plan we've got," Dresyn said with a resigned sigh. Rusin and Stannish nodded though Stannish still looked like he'd much rather run right at the mad queen instead of this waiting game. Dresyn went to relay the orders while the remaining three turned and faced the queen. As Dresyn returned and joined them, a cold pit of dread formed in their stomachs at was coming.

Tatiana watched them plan, watched them shoot glances across the field at her and her troops and shook her head, tapping her foot impatiently. She had grown bored waiting for them to make their plans and was about to attack first when the four of them finally broke their little huddle and took up their positions and drew their swords. A swell of magic covered the field, but she paid it little mind. Whatever weak magic they were playing with, it meant nothing with what she was about to rain down on them.

Her evil grin grew wider as she raised her arm in the air, hand open, palm facing the sky, while both armies drew their swords or prepared their magic. Nobody moved a muscle as eyes on both sides of the field were fixed on Tatiana as they all waited with bated breath to see what her first move would be.

As she drew on the magic, she looked over her shoulder to make sure her son was watching. Their eyes locked, hers were full of mayhem and madness, his were full of horror and pleading, asking her silently to not do it. She turned away and looked up at the sky as she summoned a flame that glowed white and silver, the hottest flame she could muster.

Finn was stuck on a horse, hands tied to the pommel of the saddle as she prepared to release her white-hot flames. He felt sick to his stomach, knowing that the moment she let that flame go, there would be hundreds of thousands of dead on the field. He lowered his gaze, not able to watch, knowing that it was going to be hard enough just hearing the sounds and tried again to burn away the ropes holding him captive. His efforts resulted in him burning his wrists. Cursing, he tried to get the horse to turn and run but it was no use. Like him, the horse was tethered in place. Resigning himself to witnessing an untold amount of horror, he closed his eyes and sent a small prayer to whatever gods were listening for his safety and everyone else's.

"Are you still willing to stand against me?" she called out to the four rulers on the other side of the field. "Or do you wish to surrender your lands, your crowns, and your armies to me and live?"

"You will have to pry our lands, titles and armies from our cold dead hands, Tatiana Ophir," Stannish called. "A would-be tyrant like yourself will never win."

"Stannish, you'll live to regret those words," she said as the flame in her hand grew more intense. "Have you decided to choose death then?"

"I will gladly die to protect my lands and people," he roared. "You will never get your hands on Stuttgad's crown."

"Then death you shall receive" she said, releasing the flames.

"Hold your lines," roared Praslin as the flames rained down on them. "Reinforce your barriers and prepare to charge the Thenndin line."

Tatiana scowled as her flames did more than fizzle across the barriers the mages from the other side had conjured up. She fired more bursts of flame, growing more and more outraged as they harmlessly landed on the erected barriers. With a scream of fury, she ordered her soldiers to attack.

"Shield's ready," yelled Dresyn as the Thenndin line rushed forward. "Spears out!" HOLD STEADY!"

Steel met steel as the two sides met. The four kings fought through rows and rows of soldiers to try and get to Tatiana while she pushed through her own lines to get toward them. The close quarter fighting meant that she was no longer able to launch her large-scale attack and had to reign in her power for close combat and defense. Flames flashed cutting down swaths of soldiers, bolts of what looked like lightning flew from the side of the kings, taking out rows of Thenndin soldiers, but neither Tatiana nor the kings could make it through the throngs to clash.

High above the field Simeon and the order watched as the two sides clashed below. There was no good opening to strike at Tatiana, not with her flames shooting every which direction and the sheer mass of soldiers from the opposing side rushing toward her every chance they got. The order flew above the field watching, waiting for the opportunity to swoop in and decisively end the battle.

The opportunity never came, however. The battle dragged on, countless men on both sides fell, and still nobody was able to get close to Tatiana. At midday however, Ari got a glimpse of Finn floundering on the field, doing his best to avoid the swords and spears from all sides. The horse he was on reared several times, and she watched as he grabbed whatever he could to keep himself on the horse. She hovered above as Danril joined her to see why she'd stopped.

"What...oh," Danril said, as he figured out what she was looking at.

"He's going to get killed down there," she said as they watched him dodge yet another spear.

"I don't see how we can get him out of there," Danril said, squinting at the field. "It's almost like she wants him to die so she can use that to her advantage."

"Simeon said something about a sacrifice and the full moon, you don't suppose the ancient ritual can be corrupted by false grief, could it?"

"Anything's possible when it comes to the depravity of Tatiana Ophir," he said, watching as Finn dodged more swords and spears. "I'll go find Simeon, see what he wants us to do. This is just cruel watching him like that." Ari nodded as Danril disappeared.

Her heart hurt watching him down there, but she knew she could not, should not act on her emotions, even though every fiber of her being screamed at her to go pull him off that horse and take him out of the battle. Danril and Simeon appeared beside her a few moments later and joined her in watching the scene below.

"This seems weirdly cruel, even for her," Simeon remarked. "Can we get down there safely and extract him?"

"We might be able to, though we do run the risk of Tatiana interfering," Danril said, watching carefully. "Ari what do you think?"

"If two of us are able to clear the area around him, the third should be able to pick him up off the horse and fly him out of there." She looked again. "If we can't get him out, we at least need to make him able to defend himself."

"Can you two provide just enough cover for me to do so?" Simeon asked. They nodded and all quickly descended.

She may have been nearly three quarters across the battlefield, but Tatiana had keen eyes and what some would describe as a sixth sense. So when Ari, Simeon and Danril swooped in from above to try and help Finn, she blasted her way across the field to put a stop to their interference.

"I knew you'd try something Simeon," she snarled as she conjured flames in her palms. "Step away from him."

"Danril, you cut him free," Simeon said, sheathing his blade as he turned to face Tatiana. "How depraved can you be? Leaving your own son defenseless."

"If he was truly worthy of the Ophir name, he'd have burned those ropes off and gotten himself somewhere safe."

"That would've required someone who gave a damn to help me learn how to control the flames," Finn spat as the ropes fell off and Danril got a good look at the burns.

"They look superficial. We can get some salve on them in a bit. Let's go," Danril said. Finn tried but hours on the horse had left his legs weak and jelly-like, making it impossible for him to stand and take off. Under normal circumstances, Danril would've hauled him out of there but the combination of the prince's deadweight and the fighting made it impossible for them to flee.

"I don't think so," Tatiana snarled, shooting flames in their direction. Her flames were quickly doused by Simeon's burst of water magic. "I wouldn't try that again, Simeon." She turned her attention back to the Lord Counciler and looked at him with narrowed eyes. "Doing so will result in your death."

"You're not the only powerful one on this field, Tatiana," he said, ropes of water swirling around his arms. The two faced off, water against flames. Finn repeatedly tried to get his bearings but time after time, he was only able to stand for a few moments before collapsing.

"Danril, you need to go," Finn said as the fighting intensified around them between Thenndin's soldiers and the four armies.

"Not without you. She'll have my ass if I leave you alone in this madness."

"I'm deadweight right now. Just go. Get her out of here and go. I'll try to get out of here on my own."

While they were arguing, Ari had been watching the queen and Simeon's fight, studying their movements, watching for an opening to attack. She knew she'd have to be fast, any opening the queen left would be short lived at best. The moment she spotted it, she adjusted her wings and rushed the queen. Had it been any other person, the blow probably would've completely incapacitated them when her blade struck their back. However, this wasn't just anyone, and Ari, who had only ever been on the receiving end of the harsh slaps the queen was fond of, finally got a taste of how ruthless Tatiana could be. Not only did the queen dodge the blow to her back from Ari's blade, but she also countered and drove her hand into Ari's stomach, launching the woman backwards a good ten feet. There was no time to react as she flew into a group of soldiers, knocking them over. She felt multiple bones break as she hit the steel plates making up armor and then the ground.

"Time to move boy," Danril said, launching himself up in the air to avoid a burst of flame from Tatiana's hand. Finn rolled aside to avoid getting burnt and pushed to his feet unsteadily.

"You do it child and I will roast your precious little darling," Tatiana said, pointing her flames at Ari, who was struggling to her feet.

"Go," Ari said as she got to her knees and stared down Tatiana. "Run." Finn saw the flames reflected in Ari's eyes, the unflinching stare in the face of death. He swallowed and staggered forward a little. "Do it. Save yourself."

"No, I can't," he said, his voice catching. "I can't do that to you." He turned to his mother. "Fine. I'll stay. Just please, don't hurt her."

"Finn, you fucking dummy, no," Ari said, one arm wrapped around her midsection as she finally made it to her feet. "Don't. Get away from here."

"I can't," he said, going over to her. "You're too important to me."

"You're important to me too," she whispered as he put a hand to her cheek. "So please, don't do this. Run, live. Do it for me."

"I'm sorry darling," he whispered as he brushed his lips over hers. "Go get yourself taken care of."

"That's enough," Tatiana said, pointing the flames at them as she looked at Simeon and Danril. "You two can either get her out of here or I can roast them both, the choice is yours." She tapped her foot impatiently, making the flames stronger. "I'm waiting."

"We'll withdraw for now," Simeon said eventually after he'd considered all possibilities. He motioned with his head for Danril to get Ari before turning his gaze back to the queen. "But we will return to end this Tatiana, you have my word on that."

"If you can't stop me now, you cannot possibly hope to stop me in the future," she said, pulling her son away from Ari. "Though I guess it will be interesting to see you try. Now. Get off my field."

"Can you fly?" Danril asked Ari. She hovered and nearly collapsed. "Don't push it. Let's get you to Matron."

The three of them disappeared, leaving the battlefield behind. Ari risked a glance over her shoulder and caught the look on Finn's face, the sadness and the fear as well as the tears that streamed down his face. She felt her chest grow tight as he became little more than a speck in the distance, her own tears trailing down her face. Danril did his best to comfort her as they left the death and destruction behind, but he couldn't help but wonder if they really did have a chance of beating the queen before it was too late.

Chapter 17

S IMEON PACED AROUND HIS tent the next day, trying to find a solution to stopping the queen's plan. He'd gone back out after making sure Ari and Danril had reached the first aid tent and watched the remains of the battle as night fell. The four armies, even after suffering great losses, had managed to keep Thenndin and Tatiana at bay but he knew that would not last long, not with what he knew was coming. The four kings, though weary and bloody, had called the battle a victory, but Simeon was hesitant to agree. If it was indeed a victory, it was a hollow one because tonight was the full moon, and the order had one last chance to stop her while they were also at their full strength. But no matter how much he planned, looked at the maps, and brainstormed, he had no good solution, no good way to bring her down before she could go through with her moonlight sacrifice. The tent flap opened, letting in the sounds of the battle and he turned, ready to scold someone for interrupting, but the lecture died on his tongue when he realized his wife had come in.

"Tissa, what brings you in?" he asked, face softening.

"You missed both breakfast and lunch," she said, handing him a wrapped pie and a water skin. "Why are you so troubled?"

"Because if none of us can stop Tatiana, the whole country is doomed," he said, gratefully taking the food and drink before kissing her cheek. "If she's allowed to go through with her plan, those who stand in her way face a horrible death. Thenndin is already on the brink of total poverty among its citizens as is. That will increase tenfold if she gains control of the other four countries."

"I have faith in you," Tissa said, rising on her toes to kiss his cheek. "I also have faith in the one who's powers have not yet come into fruition."

"You mean Ari?" Tissa nodded. "She's past the age of fruition my dear. That should've happened in her twenty-first year. She's now in her twenty-sixth year and can't do more than use glimmer. Marion hopes that she doesn't either."

"Why not?" Tissa asked as she sat on the corner of his desk.

"Because it could trigger a fatal episode." He shook his head before pressing his forehead to hers. "If that happens, I will lose Danril for good. And the prince would be absolutely beside himself. As much as I would love to see her become who she's meant to be, it could be the one thing that kills her."

"Diamonds form under immense pressure, Simeon," Tissa said, wrapping her arms around his neck. "Ari is a strong girl. She's survived horrible things that should've killed most people. Those bones she broke yesterday? She should've been unconscious when you brought her back. You don't call her Fire for nothing."

"You know that's an ironic nickname right dear?" he asked, wrapping his arms around her waist. "Danril's is at least a little more accurate in that he can conjure the ice. She's called fire solely for the temper she now keeps under wraps."

"And for the spark that keeps that soul of hers from fading into darkness," she said, letting go to pat his cheek. "Ari could easily be the light we need to rally the troops and win this war."

"We need more than a light to beat Tatiana's fire," Simeon said. "But because you have faith, I too will try to have some, my pet."

"I should go. Come back safely, my heart," she said, kissing him before leaving him with his thoughts.

As the sun began to set, every fighter the order had, both assassin and spy, assembled in front of Simeon in the middle of the camp, every face that he saw had a similar look of determination. A glance around would've told anyone that even though there was a good chance of death, none of them were afraid of it. Death was an everyday part of life for anyone at the order and for many it was something they were prepared to welcome with open arms.

"Brothers, sisters," Simeon began in Old Thenndin, "comrades in arms. Tonight is the night we embark on our most dangerous mission yet. For too many years we sat idly by, letting Tatiana and her father put their needs above that of the people of Thannid and Thenndin. Our inaction has brought us to the moment we now face, putting an end to the reign and life of Tatiana Ophir before she can become more powerful than we can imagine."

He paused for a moment and looked at the faces again before speaking. "I allowed centuries of tradition to override my good sense when I realized that something was wrong, and it is because of my inability to act that I now must ask you to put your lives on the line for our freedoms and our country." He waited here for people to dissent, to ask for leave from the coming battle that he was prepared to freely give. But it never came. The faith that his brothers and sister had in him filled him with a renewed hope and he pressed on with his speech.

"But I have faith in us. Faith in centuries of traditions that we've upheld. Faith in the traditions of our ancestors, traditions that the queen has forced many to abandon so she can remain all powerful. It is because of these traditions that we've kept alive, that we will be the ones to take down the queen." A roar of triumphant agreement came from the crowd. Simeon waited for a moment for it to subside before he pressed on.

"We have all we need in front of us. Our commitment to our people, our magic, our blades and our oath. We will fight to the last man standing and we will be victorious. The country depends on our resolve not wavering, our blades being as sharp as our skill, and our magic as true as the heart beating in our chest. Now fly, fly for victory, fly for our freedom. Fly to fight and be victorious!"

Another roar of triumph as they launched themselves in the air, a multitude of wings and colors flying through the sky. Anyone watching below would've marveled at the sight, the streaks of magic that flew off the wings looking like shooting stars and butterflies as they flew toward the rising moon.

Tatiana had perched herself upon a cliff with Finn, who'd finally resigned himself to his fate. He looked at the flat slab before him and then at her before he sat on top of it and looked up at the rising moon. As his mother prepared everything for her ritual, he watched it, wishing that he could experience this moment, his last moments, with Ari. He wanted to feel her head against his shoulder, her fingers interlaced in his. The thought of not getting to see her just one more time had a tear snaking down his cheek as he whispered a four-word sentence under his breath as his mother made the final preparations.

"Don't cry," she said, motioning for him to lay down. "You're doing this for a good cause."

"I'm doing it for your cause and because I couldn't live with myself if something happened to Ari," he spat, laying against the cold stone.

"Yes, my cause, the one that will make me the most powerful in the land. You should be proud that you can do something useful for me for a change."

"People are more than whether or not they can be useful to you," he muttered, closing his eyes so he didn't have to see her face.

She rolled her eyes and shook her head, deciding there was no use arguing with him. The boy was just as stubborn as his father, with his looks to boot. Tatiana hadn't felt anything the night she plunged the dagger into Oberin's chest, the same night she learned she was going to have his child. The snow had been on the ground then too, the blood staining it a deep red. She remembered being fascinated with the way the blood pooled and froze in the cold winter air. As she raised the dagger she was going to plunge into her son's heart, she wondered if his blood would pool and freeze in the same manner. As she began to lower the dagger in a slow, ritualistic manner, it was blown from her hands by a gust of wind so strong it knocked her backwards.

"That's well enough, Tatiana," came Simeon's voice as the entire order materialized from thin air. Finn looked up and had to squint at the sheer amount of light that came off their wings. "You won't be completing this ritual tonight or ever."

"How dare you use the power of the moon and stars against me?" she snarled, getting to her feet, another dagger in her hand. "I am Tatiana Ophir, ruler of these lands, the most holy and powerful. Only I hold the power to command the ancient ways."

"Those ways have been passed down in the order since before your forefathers took control of the lands," Simeon said as he landed in front of her. "The ancient ways belong to any who wish to practice them."

"How dare you," she snapped. "How dare you insinuate that the common riffraff be able to comprehend and use these amazing forces."

"Look above Tatiana," he roared, gesturing to the order who was slowly descending to surround her, "the common riffraff already use and comprehend. Why do you think you've never been able to control us?"

"That ends tonight," she said, lunging at Simeon with blade and flame.

Simeon moved with speed that even exceeded her imagination and blocked both. Once she had launched the first attack, the rest of the order joined, blade and magic flying toward the queen with impossible speed.

As the fight raged on, assaulting Tatiana from all sides, she found herself continually trading blows with Simeon, his water dousing her flames, her blade meeting his again and again.

"You all have no hope of winning," she snarled as he blocked yet another of her attempts to stab him in the side. "Give up this ridiculous charade and submit to my rule."

"We only need a little hope," he replied as water met flame and steam rose around them. "If the spark remains, we will fight to the bloody bitter end to keep you from carrying out this ridiculous plan."

"You all choose death over submission," she said, steel crashing against steel again.

"We choose death over the rule of a tyrant," he replied as they found themselves face to face.

"Then so be it," she said, dropping her knife. Blade and flame switched faster than Simeon could prepare for. The ropes of water that swirled around his arm took care of the flames that she sent toward his face but there was nothing to stop the blade she drove into his gut.

"Ari," Danril called in a commanding tone, "attend to the Lord Counciler. Those who can fight, with me. Those injured have your injuries seen to. Fire will determine if you need to go back to camp." A cheer went up, but it lacked the same convictions they had when the fight started. "If you're not fighting for the country, fight for your Lord Councilor." The fighting resumed, Danril leading the charge while Ari knelt next to Simeon with her field kit to examine the wound.

"Why are you wasting energy on me?" he asked. "There are others that need you more."

"Shadow and Blade needs your leadership," she said as she looked at the wound. "And I can patch this, but you'll need to see Matron sooner rather than later."

"Miss Penndra, you really should..." he trailed off as she skewered him with a glare and began to stitch the wound up. She worked quickly, closing the wound and bandaging it.

"Don't move," she said, moving on to assess the wounds of the others. "You four, can you fly?" she asked the worst of the injured. They nodded. "Good. You need to help the Lord Counciler back to Matron as fast as possible." More nods. "Then get moving."

Ari watched as they managed to support Lord Simeon and took off for the camp. She turned her attention back to the battle in front of her and went over to Danril, who was panting heavily.

"How goes it?" she asked.

"Not well. Lord Simeon?"

"On his way back to Matron," she said, watching the scene play out. Eventually her eyes settled on the slab where Finn was still laying. "Has anyone been able to get over there?"

"Nobody's tried, they've all been too busy keeping the queen at bay. You should go, he needs someone to remind him that he can still fight." She nodded and flitted off, landing near his feet. He barely moved his head as she kicked his boot.

"Why are you still laying here?" she asked. "Get up and show her that you won't give in without a fight."

"I'm not strong like that, like you," he said, eyes still closed. "I can't face death and not flinch."

"You think I could at first?" she said, squatting. "Finn, open your eyes and look at me."

He sighed and opened his eyes, looking up at a golden glowing Ari. "You're glowing. I must be dreaming."

"Is that all this is? A dream?" she asked, kneeling down and taking his hand. "Does any of this feel real?"

"I don't know what is and what isn't real," he muttered. "It's by far the strangest dream I've ever had though."

"It's no dream, *astori,*" she said. "All this is real."

"Then why are you glowing?" he asked, dully.

"It's the moonlight's effect on all Fae," she said, putting a hand to his cheek. "Forgive me for this." She moved the hand and smacked him hard with it. He bolted up and looked up at her, as she'd gone into the sky a few feet as he'd gotten up. "Do you believe me it's not a dream now?"

"If it is, it's a nightmare," he muttered, getting to his feet. "What's going on?"

"We're here to stop Tatiana," she said, coming back down to stand next to him. "You're not dead, she never started the ritual."

"Are you sure my subconscious isn't trying to protect me from the truth?" he asked.

"I can either slap you again or you can look around you and see for yourself. Many of my brothers and sisters have fallen, Lord Simeon was struck down. Danril fights to keep our spirits up while taking on the queen. We need another strong fighter out there with us," she said, taking his hands. "This is reality, Finnian." For some reason, using his full name finally snapped him out of it and he stood.

"Tell me what I need to do," he said, letting his own wings out. Ari took a step back as they unfurled, giant red and black wings that glowed like dying embers.

"Help us defeat her," she said, pointing at his mother. "The entire continent will not know peace unless we're able to stop her."

Finn nodded and grabbed her, pulling her close to him and crushing his lips to hers. "Don't die on me," he whispered as he let go.

Ari nodded, unable to speak as she watched him take to the sky. She joined him soon after, doing what she could to support everyone with what little magic she had.

Tatiana was still going strong, and though some of her movements had slowed, she was still able to defend herself to a degree that prevented them from landing a decisive blow. But when a blast of ruby flame came flying at her, she was barely able to dodge, and the flame singed her arm. She knew that flame, and she turned in the direction it came from, and looked at her son as he hovered overhead.

"You'd dare raise a hand to attack your mother?" she asked, as she fought off an attack that was intended to bring her down while she was distracted.

"You've stabbed me with a letter opener, tried to have me killed and were willing to sacrifice my life to obtain unholy amounts of power. And that's all recent. You've mocked me, put me down, and kept me away from the rest of the world. You are my mother by blood, but you never loved me. I was a tool, a means to an end for you, and for all I know, your duty as a royal."

"Tread carefully my son," she said in a warning. "Continuing down this path will not end well for you."

"Everything around you never ends well for me," he cried, conjuring another flame and launching it at her. "I told you I was done needing you to step in, done making my decisions for me. I am a grown man-" He stopped abruptly as he felt a searing pain in his gut. He looked down and looked down at the bright red splotch forming on his tunic and the dagger hilt sticking out before looking at his mother.

"I warned you," she said as the whole field went silent for a moment.

The silence had Ari looking over and realizing what happened. She shoved the jar of salve at the person she was treating and raced across the field as fast as her wings would let her as he slowly drifted toward the ground. Ari reached him just as his feet touched the ground and his knees buckled, and caught his head and positioned it in her lap so he laid comfortably.

"I'm sorry," he whispered as tears ran down her face. "I shouldn't have goaded her."

"Just shut up," she said, brushing a strand of his black hair away from his eyes. "Danril, I need my field kit," she yelled through tears

"There's not going to be time for that," he said with another cough. "Ari, make me a promise."

"You just stop talking," she said, looking up for Danril. "Where the fuck is my kit?" Her voice was frantic.

"Ari, look at me," he said, with a cough. "Don't withdraw from life. Promise me that, please?"

"Just stay with me," she said, choking on a sob. "I need you in my life,"

"I wish I could," he said, reaching up weakly to brush his fingers over her cheek. "Be strong darling." His eyes fluttered closed as his hand dropped to his side limply. Only the sound of his ragged breathing indicated he was still alive, though just barely.

"Finn, Finn, *FINN,*" she screamed, shaking his shoulder. When he didn't wake, the sobs she'd been choking back tore from her chest and throat, bringing an abrupt halt to the battle. Everyone still standing from the order could feel the despair and heartbreak in Ari's cries as they echoed around them. Only Tatiana seemed unfazed by the emotions swirling around.

As she held him, willing him to stay alive, she felt an odd sensation welling up inside her. Her skin felt full of pins and needles, her head feeling like it was about to explode. She cracked her eyes open and noticed that her entire body was a bright beacon of golden light, and it spread across the field. Those who'd been injured, or were too exhausted to fight, suddenly were healed or found the strength to keep going as Ari's light touched them. She looked down at Finn, and gasped as she noticed his color returning and his breathing growing more even. She carefully eased him off her lap and stood as Danril landed next to her.

"Took you long enough," he said, bumping her shoulder. "Bout time you came into your own, Firelight."

"Keep him safe for me?" she asked, rolling her shoulders and looking at the queen. "I have a score I need to settle."

"You sure about this, little one?" he asked.

"Never surer," she replied, drawing her twin daggers from behind her back and twirling them in her palms. Danril nodded and decided not to argue as she strode across the field with purpose.

Tatiana watched the girl as she approached, the golden light almost blindingly bright. Though she had trouble adjusting to the bright lights, she was ready with both blade and flame, eager to teach this cocky bitch a lesson or two about true strength. But all the preparedness in the world was not enough when Ari's hand, fist wrapped around the hilt of her dagger, appeared from what felt like nowhere and hit Tatiana square in the jaw. The flame went out and Tatiana staggered back, dazed from the blow.

"That's payback for all the times you've struck me, and I wasn't able to defend myself," Ari hissed. Tatiana had barely straightened up when Ari delivered a kick to the queen's knee, sending an unpleasant crunching sound echoing around the field. "That's for all the lies, all the bullshit you've ever fed me."

"And who bought into those lies," Tatiana said through gritted teeth. "What kind of person does that make you?" Ari's fist slammed into her side, breaking her ribs.

"That's for the family you stole from me," she snapped, before striking her again on the other side, breaking more ribs.

Tatiana coughed, sputtered and for the first time, let out a small cry of pain. The mood shifted around the field, the hope that had left with Simeon slowly returning as Ari faced off with the queen. "You could at least fight fair," she said through gritted teeth.

"Look around you, Tatiana," Ari said, gesturing to the field. "Look at the fallen bodies of my brethren and tell me you fought fairly. Who are you to demand that I give you what you could not, no, what you refused to give us."

"Then have mercy on me, please," she said, resorting to begging, dropping to her knees. "Let me live out my life in a cell."

"Would you have allowed those that opposed you to live their lives in a cell?" Ari asked, hands at her sides. Tatiana remained silent. "Then why should I let you?"

"Because you're not as cold as I am," Tatiana said, struggling back to her feet, eyes locked on Ari. "You may kill indiscriminately, but only when ordered to."

"Danril," Ari called over her shoulder. "Were we not instructed to end the reign and the life of the Queen?"

"Yes, I believe those were the exact words of Lord Simeon's speech," he said, coming over.

"So if we use her logic here, that I kill only when ordered, I have orders from the Lord Counciler himself to kill her."

"It could be interpreted that way," Danril said, looking at her. "Though you have to ask yourself, would you be killing her because you have orders or are you doing it for revenge?" Ari paused. "That pause is your answer, little one. You had to think about it. You know why you'd be doing it. There's been enough blood shed on this field today."

"Restrain her and take her back to the capital," Ari said. "Danril is right. Too much blood has already been shed tonight."

She turned her back to the queen, who seized the opportunity to attack. Twin flames formed in her hands as she lunged toward Ari. The sudden burst of heat alerted Ari to the attack, allowing her to fly up to avoid the flames, land behind the queen, and plunge both daggers into the woman's sides. Tatiana gasped as the blades pierced her sides and cried out in pain when Ari pulled them out.

"I thought... too much blood... shed," she gasped as she sank to the ground.

"That was before you tried to kill me," Ari said, wiping the blood off the blades in the snow. "At least this time, you tried to do it yourself, even if you still couldn't look me in the face."

Tatiana tried to speak but was unable to as Ari sheathed her blades and walked away. Everyone around her began to assist the wounded and gather those that had fallen to honor their death. As she felt the last of her life slowly slip away, she cast her eyes down to where the blood was pooling and watched it gather and freeze around her. With this as her last sight, she eventually slipped unconscious before passing, the blood still gathering and freezing beneath her.

Finn was back on his feet by the time Ari returned. She ran the last few feet toward him, launching herself into his arms. He caught her, staggering back only slightly, and held her tight.

"Looks like you were able to fix me up after all," he said as she buried her head against his neck.

"The hell I went through thinking I would lose you," she said, voice thick with tears and muffled by his shoulder. "It nearly broke me." She moved her head so she was looking at him, her gold eyes level with his deep blue ones. "Finn..." she stopped, unsure if she wanted to say the words.

"I love you, Ari," he said, knowing what she was about to say. "You're the golden light I cannot imagine my life without."

"I love you too," she said, smiling through the tears. "I've been doing a lot of thinking and I'm going to take the sabbatical. We can-" She stopped talking abruptly when his mouth crashed into hers.

"Time enough later to plan the future," he said eventually as Danril came over. "Is everything ok?"

"Maybe. Ari, you need to go see Matron." Finn looked between the two of them confused.

"I know," she said, still resting against Finn. "But I thought she said if I ever came into my powers, the episode would be instantly fatal."

"I'm not taking any chances and neither should you," he said harshly.

"I... I know," she said, looking up at Finn. "Come with me?"

"I should deal with the troops and the other kings," he said, looking down at her.

"The Shadows are already spreading the news of her defeat and death," Danril said.

"Oh, she's dead?" Finn asked, completely unsurprised. "Good riddance I suppose." He looked back at Ari. "Let's get you checked out then." He kissed her forehead and let go so they could take to the sky.

Outside the matron's tent, both Finn and Danril were pacing, both worried that Ari was just moments away from being taken from them. Eventually, the tent flap opened, and Matron walked out. She stretched in the fading moonlight and let out a sigh.

"Marion, anything?" Danril asked, impatient for the news about Ari. Finn looked up from the tracks he'd been making and stared intently.

"Since the episode didn't trigger during her awakening or during the subsequent fight, it's likely she won't have one. She still needs to be careful to avoid triggering one in general, but it's safe to say it's very unlikely she'll have one because of this." She laughed when the two of them visibly relaxed. "Go on, get in there then. It's good to have another healer among the ranks, even if she's planning on leaving for a spell." Marion headed for the mess tent while Finn looked at Danril with a raised brow.

"She's serious about this?" he asked before they went in.

"She finally found something worth living for outside Shadow and Blade. You'd be a fool if you didn't let her," Danril said as he lifted the tent flap. "The girl risked literal death for you. Break her and I might break you."

"I won't break her," Finn said as he went in, Danril behind him. "I'd sooner die than do that."

"Nobody's dying, not today," Ari said from the far side of the tent where she was still changing.

"Thank the heavens for that," Finn said. "Don't take this wrong, but I expected to see more of this tent full. My mother was a powerful fire wielder."

"We had our field medic out with us," Simeon said, from one of the occupied beds. "Without her, I think we would've had more wounded for Marion to deal with."

"You're supposed to be resting," Tissa said from next to him as Ari emerged. "I can't thank you enough." Tissa got up and ran over to give Ari a hug.

"Lady Tissa, I didn't do anything that I wouldn't have done for anyone else on that field," Ari said, not sure what to do.

"You made sure my husband lived, that means more to me than you'll know," she said, tears forming.

"No, I think I understand, Lady Tissa," Ari said, finally putting her arms around the woman and looking at Finn. "I think I understand."

Epilogue

THE WARM SPRING SUN reflected off the lake and warmed Finn's shoulders as he sat on the dock that overlooked the crystal blue waters that made up the back half of the home he now shared with Ari. She hadn't been the only one to walk away from her previous life, he too had given up everything in pursuit of the quiet life he now lived just north of Tarka.

It hadn't been an easy transition or seamless for that matter, he thought as the afternoon breeze came up and ruffled his hair. The other four royals from the surrounding countries had been very resistant to the idea of him abdicating, almost to the point of threats to get him to rule in his mother's stead. The final conversation with them replayed constantly as he sat there looking across the water.

"What do you mean you're going to abdicate?" Rusin had asked, the words all but exploding from his mouth. Everyone but Danril, Finn and Ari had shirked away from the outburst.

"I don't see how much plainer I can make it, King Rusin," Finn had said, slowly getting to his feet to stare down the much older royal. "You've been told repeatedly that I have no interest in the crown or the headaches and heartaches that go with it. I wish to live in peace away from all this."

"Who would rule in your stead?" Dresyn had asked, always trying to keep the peace.

"I don't know and quite frankly King Dresyn, I don't care. The name Ophir is despised across all of Thenndin. I don't need my rule tainted by the legacy of all the Ophir's that came before me. I'm sorry, but I won't take the throne."

"Your father'd be ashamed of you boy," Stannish said, getting to his feet.

"Well thanks to my mother, I never got to know him," Finn shot back, slamming his hands on the table. "You want Thenndin, you can have it Stannish. You can all fight over it for all I fucking care. I will not take the crown."

"Fighting amongst ourselves would serve no one," Praslin said, also getting to his feet. "Perhaps the prince is right. New blood would be needed for Thenndin to move forward peacefully with our countries."

"And how do you suggest we do that?" Stannish asked, crossing his arms.

"A new monarch could be found amongst the nobles. In the meantime, we can have a ruling council guide the country." Praslin said, motioning for Stannish to sit. "Perhaps we wouldn't need a monarch."

"You all do as you see fit," Finn said, pushing the chair back. "The country is not my responsibility."

"You insolent stupid child," Stannish said, reaching out to grab him. That had turned out to be a mistake because Ari had moved faster than any of them could blink and had Stannish's arm behind his back, almost twisted to the point of breaking.

"I'd keep your grubby hands off him," she hissed as he squirmed, trying to get away from her. "He's made his decision. Belittling him in a manner like Tatiana did will not change his mind."

"She's right, Stannish," Dresyn said. "We can't force the boy to pick up the crown any more than we can force you to stop being a slimy bastard."

"Breaking his arm isn't going to help anything, Ari darling," Finn said, exhausted with the whole ordeal. "Just leave him to his own devices."

"Fine," she said, letting go. "We need to finish packing anyway." He smiled at her tiredly and held out his hand for her. She took it and together they left, leaving four kings scrambling to figure out who would rule Thenndin.

He was still sitting on the dock when Ari came down an hour later, plates of food in hand and sat next to him. When he didn't acknowledge she was there, she elbowed him to get his attention.

"Gods you have sharp elbows," he said, barely managing to contain the yelp of pain. "There are much gentler ways to get my attention."

"You were too far away for that to be effective," she said, handing him a plate. "What were you thinking about?"

"The final meeting I had with the rulers of the other four Faedoms," he said, digging in. "I still half expect one of them to come riding up to the house, demanding I take up the throne."

"You know that's not going to happen," she said, putting her plate aside to scoot closer to him. "Especially since the country has more peace and prosperity under the ruling council than it ever did with a monarch."

"I know that, darling, but I can't help but worry," he said, looping an arm around her waist.

"There's nothing to worry about, as far as the country knows, Tatiana never had an heir. Those that knew she did were either bought off or now work for one of the other four Faedoms, you know this. Finnian Ophir never existed."

"I know. We're just Mister and Missus Penndra, the eccentric reclusive couple that live on the lake."

"Do you regret it?" she asked, her hand reaching for his.

"Not a fucking chance in hell darling," he said, intertwining his fingers with hers. Matching gold bands glinted in the sun as he pulled her hand closer to kiss it. "What about you? Do you regret leaving the order?"

"Not at all. Twelve years of nothing but death and blood is far too much for one soul to take. I only regret not leaving it behind sooner."

"If you'd done that, I don't think we'd be sitting here now," he said as the wind blew some of the nearby cherry blossoms from the trees. A few landed on her golden hair, providing a dash of color to his golden light. "And I wouldn't get to do this." He put his own plate aside and pulled her into his lap and kissed her with everything he had. "I think you made me a promise at the start of winter. Something about peeling a dress off?"

"I think I found that specific dress a couple weeks ago," she whispered, smirking at him.

"That one, this one, I don't really care," he said huskily. "I want you darling."

"Take what's yours then," she said, pressing against him and kissing him again.

Their plates were long forgotten as he picked her up and carried her back inside where they spent the rest of the afternoon lost in each other.

Finn had drifted off sometime in the early evening, exhaustion winning out over his desire to stay awake and watch the sun drift below the horizon with her. Ari sat there, embracing the silence, stroking his hair as the light faded around her. She looked around the room, shaking her head slightly, thinking about the little girl in the orphanage boldly declaring that one day, she'd have a big house where all her friends would be welcome, and nobody would ever be hurt again. Her mind moved past that girl to the two friends she'd lost to the cruelty of the queen and the greed of the man who ran the orphanage, and she wondered what they'd say about her now. Eventually she turned her thoughts to the woman who'd trained as an assassin all those years ago, the one who found a brother in Danril, a father-like figure in Lord Simeon, and a lover, partner and forever with Finn. Did everything from the moment the queen had her ripped from her mother's arms lead right to where she was now? Was all this part of some greater plan? Her racing thoughts and heart stirred the sleeping Finn who blinked himself awake and looked at her.

"What's got you all worked up now?" he asked, rubbing his eyes as he sat up.

"Just thoughts of fate and destiny," she said. "I didn't mean to wake you."

"Your heart's beating ridiculously fast," he said, taking her hands. "Are you sure you're ok?"

"I'll be fine. I was just thinking about everything that's led up to this moment in time, people I lost, people I gained, the things I've done," she said, her fingers interlaced with his.

"Are you sure you don't regret any of it?" he asked. "If you're unhappy Ari..."

"No, I have no regrets. Not about what I did, not about who I had to be, and not about leaving it all behind for this," she said, squeezing his hands tightly. "I just wonder how much of it was fate that led me here."

"I don't question it," he said, leaning over to kiss her. "Whatever decisions, good or bad, that led us to this moment, it's worth it."

"I don't understand how you almost always know just what to say," she said, laying her head on his shoulder.

"Too many books, not enough human contact," he said, causing her to laugh. "Do you ever wish you could've met your family?"

"Only very rarely," she said, getting up to turn on the lamp to chase away the darkness. "If I had them, then we wouldn't be here. I wouldn't have Danril, or you, or Simeon, and thinking about life without all of you makes me sad."

"Then don't question destiny or fate, darling," he said as she sat back down, "no matter how dark the road was to get here, this is where we are now, and this is where we're meant to be. Family isn't always blood, it's those you find along the path you walk."

"Too many books again?" she asked, poking him in the side.

"Trust you to ruin a moment," he said with a groan as he watched the moonlight stream into the room.

"You know you love me," she replied with a laugh.

"For now, and for always," he said, pulling her against him.

Ari sighed and snuggled against him, just content to be in the moment. He was right about everything, from the dark path she'd walked, to the family she'd found to guide her to the light. She'd learned a few things on that path but the biggest lesson life had taught her was that as long as there was love, she would be able to weather any storm.

Afterword

THIS BOOK WAS WRITTEN as part of the Inkfort Publishing derby - check out the community and other entries at https://inkfortpress.com/

Made in United States
North Haven, CT
29 September 2024

58083920R00121